Freeman Wills Crofts was born in
died in 1957. He worked for a Northern ᴵ.....
company as an engineer until 1929, before turning to
detective fiction.

His plots reveal his mathematical training and he
specialised in the seemingly unbreakable alibi and the
intricacies of railway timetables. He also loved ships and
trains and they feature in many of his stories.

Crofts' best-known character is Inspector Joseph French.
French appears for the first time in *Inspector French's
Greatest Case*. He is a detective who achieves his results
through dogged persistence.

Raymond Chandler praised Crofts' plots, calling him 'the
soundest builder of them all'.

FREEMAN WILLS CROFTS

Sir John Magill's Last Journey

HOUSE OF
STRATUS

This edition published in 2000 by House of Stratus, an imprint of Stratus Holdings plc, 24c Old Burlington Street, London, W1X 1RL, UK.

www.houseofstratus.com

Typeset, printed and bound by House of Stratus.

A catalogue record for this book is available from the British Library.

ISBN 1-84232-413-6

This is the Story

SIR JOHN MAGILL, a well-known figure in the public life of Ulster, is coming to Ireland via the Stranraer – Larne route. He never reaches his destination. No trace of the missing man can be discovered. What strange fate has befallen Sir John Magill? Inspector French is called in, and admits that it is his most baffling case. With that admission we feel sure all admirers of Inspector French will agree. And they will follow eagerly the various stages in the unravelling of this, the greatest of Inspector French mysteries.

TO MY MANY GOOD FRIENDS IN
NORTHERN IRELAND

CONTENTS

THE SETTING OF THE STORY

SCOTLAND YARD

It was on Monday morning, the 7th of October, that Inspector French first heard the name of Sir John Magill. A commonplace name enough, certainly a name bearing no suggestion of exasperating mystery, still less of grim and hideous tragedy. All the same there came a time when French might well have said of it, as Queen Mary is supposed to have said of that of Calais, that when he died it would be found graven on his heart.

For the Sir John Magill Case proved perhaps the most terribly baffling of all the baffling cases French had tackled. Never had truth seemed so elusive, nor had he been put to such shifts to capture it, as during that long drawn-out inquiry. Never had his conviction been stronger that crime, ugly and sinister, lurked behind the activities he was investigating, yet seldom had the proof that all was well seemed more convincing. In short, many times before the case dragged on to its inevitable and dramatic close French found himself wishing nothing so much as that he had never heard of the unfortunate man who gave it its name.

French had had a busy year. Since the night, now thirteen months past, when he and Sergeant Carter had fought for their lives and the life of Molly Moran on the deck of that spectral launch in Southampton Water, he had handled no less than five major cases. Moreover, four months of the time had been spent with a score of associates in trying to trace the author of one of those terrible series of sex murders which every now and then recall the shuddering days of Jack the Ripper. By the time this unhappy madman had been laid by the heels, September was well advanced, and then had come the blissful break of French's annual holidays.

He had spent it among the old world towns and rocky hills of Provence. When he was tracing the movements of the Pykes in the Burry Port – Dartmoor tragedy he had worked along the French Riviera and up through the Rhône Valley to Lyons and Paris. He remembered that Jefferson Pyke had recommended a stay at Avignon, and the night he had spent there on that investigation had convinced him of the excellence of the advice. Accordingly this autumn he had made the old city of the popes his headquarters. From there he and Mrs French had explored the country by automobile excursion, had marvelled at the arenas of Arles and Nîmes, with bated breath had crossed the Pont du Gard, had seen medievalism in the walls and towers of Aigues Mortes, had climbed through the sinister ruins of Les Baux; in short, as far as fourteen brief days would allow, had steeped themselves in the enthralling atmosphere of Roman France. And now he had scarcely settled down to a winter's work when the name of Sir John Magill had flashed into his firmament as a portent of menace and evil.

It was then on Monday, the 7th of October, shortly after French had reached the Yard, that a telephone call summoned him to the room of his immediate superior, Chief Inspector Mitchell. With him he found a tall, well-built man with that in his carriage, even as he sat, which bespoke the drill ground. A strong, rugged face, a powerful jaw and a pair of light blue eyes sparkling with intelligence showed that this was a person to be reckoned with. But in spite of the suggestion of ruthless strength, there was a directness in the look and a good humour in the expression to which French felt immediately drawn. The man was quietly dressed in a suit of brown tweed, his grey Stetson hat and cloth overcoat lay on a chair, while on the ground beside him stood a brown paper parcel shaped like a cardboard hatbox.

"Ah, French," said Mitchell. "This is Detective Sergeant Adam M'Clung of the Royal Ulster Constabulary, stationed at Belfast. He thinks we've let one of our problems slip over to Ireland by mistake and he's come to see if he can't shove it back on us."

Sergeant M'Clung glanced quickly at the chief inspector and then smiled. "I don't know, sir, that that's just the way I'd have put it," he said in a pleasant voice, though with an intonation that was strange to French, half Irish, half Scotch it sounded. "Pleased to meet you, Mr French. I've known your name for many a year, but I've never had a chance of speaking to you before." He held out an enormous hand which closed like a vice on French's.

"The sergeant was just telling me he crossed over last night by Kingstown and Holyhead," went on Mitchell. "But I thought, sergeant, it was Kingstown no longer?"

"That's so, sir," Sergeant M'Clung agreed. "It's now officially Dun Laoghaire, but" – he shrugged, and French enjoyed the note of tolerant superiority of the northern speaking of Free State activities – "there's not many that bother their heads about that; not from the north anyway."

"I know Dublin well," Mitchell said reminiscently. "Used to be over there often before the troubles. I liked it. But I never got to Belfast. You've been there, French, haven't you?"

"Only once, sir, and it's a goodish while ago. I was in Belfast in '08, during the Royal visit."

M'Clung turned to him with evident interest.

"It's queer you should have mentioned that, Mr French, for I was just going to speak of it. I'm over here about what's happened to Sir John Magill, and it was through that same Royal visit that he got his knighthood."

"And what has happened to Sir John Magill?" Mitchell inquired.

"That's just it, sir. Barring that he's disappeared in circumstances pointing to foul play, that's just what we don't know. And that's just where we want your help."

"Well, sergeant, we'll do what we can. Suppose you tell us all about it."

The sergeant moved nervously, then leaning forward and thrusting out his face towards the others, he began to speak.

Though this was the ringing up of the curtain on as grim a tragedy as had taken place for many a long day, there was no suggestion of tragedy in the bearing of the three detectives. Rather they gave the impression of businessmen assembled to discuss some commonplace detail of their firm's operations. The room with its green-tinted walls and dark plainly finished furniture looked what it was, an office for the transaction of clerical business, and though the Englishmen listened to their companion with grave attention, for all the excitement they showed he might merely have been reciting the closing prices of British Government stocks.

"I'd better tell you who the Magills are first," said Sergeant M'Clung. "They're a wealthy Ulster family who made their money in linen. At the present moment old Sir John, if he's alive, is supposed to be worth not less than a million and there are pretty valuable mills as well.

"These mills are in Belfast – at the head of the Shankill Road – and the family lived at a place called Ligoniel, up in the hills overlooking the city. They had a big house there with fine grounds, though it's sold now and the place broken up for building.

"The family consists of five persons, Sir John, his son, his two daughters and his nephew. Lady Magill is dead these many years.

"Sir John was born in '57, that makes him seventy-two this year. The son, Major Malcolm Magill, is over forty, and the daughters, Miss Beatrice and Miss Caroline, can't be far short of it."

"Are these three married?"

"The son is married, sir, but neither of the daughters. Well, that's about the family, for the nephew has lived away from the others from a child. Now there's one other thing I must tell you so that you'll understand what's happened. While Sir John was in Belfast, living with his daughters near Ligoniel, he managed the mills himself. He also took a lot of interest in the city, in politics he was a prominent Unionist and he was also one of the leaders of the Orange Order. All that time up to the end of the War the mills were very prosperous, making any quantity of money. In 1922 Major Magill was demobilised and came back to Belfast and then Sir John, feeling he was tired of the work, handed over the whole concern to the son. He and the daughters left Belfast and settled down in London, at 71 Elland Gardens, Knightsbridge. From that day till last Thursday, so far as we know, Sir John has never been back in Ireland."

French had already begun the dossier of *L'Affaire Magill* by noting on a sheet of official paper all these names and dates. The details so far were somewhat dry, but there was that in M'Clung's manner which suggested that a crisis in the story was approaching. Mitchell sat with his arms crossed, but as French ceased writing he moved.

"That's five people you've mentioned, sergeant," he said. "Let's see that I've got 'em right. There's Sir John Magill, the head of the family, aged 72, who has disappeared; his son Malcolm, who became a major during the War, his two daughters, Beatrice and Caroline, and a nephew, name still unrevealed."

"That's right, sir. Well, to continue, Major Magill took over the running of the mills. He left the small villa he had at Ligoniel, not far from the big family house, and settled down beyond Larne, on the Coast Road to Portrush."

Mitchell interrupted again.

"You're mentioning a lot of places, sergeant. We'd better see where they are. Get hold of the atlas, will you, French?"

M'Clung moved round the table.

"There's Belfast," he explained, pointing with a huge finger of a rich dark brown shade. "And there's Larne, and this is where the Coast Road runs."

They bent over the map.

"I follow you," said Mitchell. "This big south-west cut into the land is Belfast Lough, with Belfast city at its head. Larne is on the coast just outside and above the entrance to the Lough. Looks about twenty miles away."

"Twenty-four, sir."

"Twenty-four, is it? Then this Coast Road that you speak of runs from Belfast through Larne and along the shore to the north?"

"That's right, sir. It's mostly a tourist road and there's plenty of traffic on it in summer, but not much in winter. It was on this road, about four miles beyond Larne, that Major Magill took the house. It was not a big house, but there was a nice place with it, sheltered by a wood and with a good view out over the sea.

"It was a good way to come into business every day, the most of thirty miles each way, but Major Magill travelled pretty quick in his Rolls Royce. He lived there with his wife and two daughters, both children. Well, gentlemen, that's pretty well the way things were when this business happened."

Sergeant M'Clung's hand stole absently to his pocket, then came hurriedly away. Chief Inspector Mitchell, recognising the action, pulled open a drawer.

"Won't you smoke, sergeant?" he invited, holding out a box of cigars. "A little tobacco helps a story."

The sergeant accepted with alacrity and the three men lit up. Mitchell was a strict enough disciplinarian, but he considered a little relaxation in minor matters made the wheels of life rotate more easily.

"Last Friday morning," resumed M'Clung, "we had a visit at Chichester Street – that's our headquarters in Belfast – from Major Magill. He told us he had an extraordinary story to report, but whether there was anything criminal in it he couldn't say for sure. Our Superintendent[1] Rainey saw him at once and he sent for me in case an investigation should be required.

"Major Magill said that on the previous Tuesday evening – that was three days earlier – he'd had a letter from Sir

[1] NOTE – There is no such rank as superintendent in the Royal Ulster Constabulary. I have used it in order to avoid referring to an existing officer. F W C

7

John. Fortunately he hadn't destroyed it and I brought it over to show you."

M'Clung paused while his hearers bent over the letter. It consisted of a single sheet of grey-tinted paper headed "71 Elland Gardens, Knightsbridge, SW1" in small black letters. It was written in a strong and masculine, but elderly hand and read:

DEAR MALCOLM,

I hope to go to Ireland next week about my linen – silk invention, which at last looks as it was going to come to something, though not quite in the way I had hoped. I expect to arrive in Belfast on Thursday and would make my way down to you that evening if you could put me up. Please reply to the Grand Central Hotel whether this would be convenient.

Your aff. father,

JOHN MAGILL.

"Did Major Magill know what the invention was?"

"He did, sir. He said that his father was a bit of a mechanic and that for years he had been trying to find an improved way of combining artificial silk with linen, in the hope of getting some valuable new product.

"Major Magill was pleased at the thought of his father coming over and he replied to the hotel that he would be glad to see him on the Thursday evening. On his way into work on that same Thursday morning he called at the hotel. He saw his letter waiting there, but Sir John hadn't turned up. So the major went on up to the mills. During the afternoon he rang up the hotel to make further inquiries, but still there had been no word of Sir John. The major, while a little surprised, assumed his father had been somehow delayed and that he would turn up on the following day."

Sergeant M'Clung paused to draw at his cigar, which he apparently found hard to keep alight during the processes of narration. In spite of his North of Ireland accent and occasional strange turns of phrase, the man was telling his story well. His hearers could picture the little drama as it slowly unfolded and with placid attention they waited for the denoument.

"Major Magill reached home in due course that evening and there he found that though Sir John's luggage had turned up, the man himself had not arrived nor had he sent any message. The luggage had come from Larne and the major therefore telephoned to the station. The station-master replied that Sir John had reached Larne that morning by the Stranraer boat and had gone on by the boat train to Belfast, and that he had asked that his luggage be sent to Major Magill's, mentioning that he was going down there himself that evening.

"Once again the major rang up the Grand Central Hotel, but still there was no news there of Sir John. The major was rather worried about him, but he supposed he would be down later and they went on with dinner. Then just about nine there was a phone from Sir John.

"He was ringing up, he said, from Whitehead. I should explain, gentlemen, that Whitehead is a little town on the northern shore of Belfast Lough, about thirteen miles from Belfast. It's on the way to Larne and Sir John would pass through it if he was going down there.

"Sir John said he'd had a busy day and hadn't been able either to call at the mill or to get down sooner to Larne. He was now in Whitehead, where he had gone to look up a man on business. But when he had inquired where his friend lived he had learned that he had moved to Bangor a couple of years earlier. Sir John was therefore stuck in Whitehead, for there wasn't a train to Larne for an hour. So he wanted the major to take out the car and come for him. If the major could do so he would walk out along the Larne road to meet him.

"Well, the major was puzzled about the whole business, but he supposed there was some good explanation. Anyway he wasn't long getting out the Rolls. It's about ten miles from Larne to Whitehead and his place is four miles on the other side of Larne, say a fourteen mile run altogether. He did it in about half an hour. For the last couple of miles he went slowly and kept a good lookout, but he didn't see a sign of Sir John. It was dark at the time, but his headlights were bright and he was sure that if the old man had been on the road he would have seen him. When he got to Whitehead he inquired at the two or three telephone places open at that hour. At the station he got what he wanted. The stationmaster told him that an elderly gentleman had come off the Belfast train arriving at 8.47. He had asked to be directed to a Mr Rimbolt's house, an engineer employed in one of the Belfast works. The stationmaster knew Mr Rimbolt. He had lived at Whitehead formerly, but a couple of years earlier had moved to Bangor. When the old man heard this he asked where there was a telephone and the stationmaster had shown him the booth on the up platform. The man had gone in and a few minutes later the stationmaster had seen him come out and cross the bridge towards the town.

"The major went back to the car and searched the roads and made inquiries at houses in Whitehead where his father might have called. But he couldn't get any trace of Sir John and at last he gave it up and went home. He wasn't exactly alarmed about the old man, though he thought the whole thing more than queer. Next day he called first thing at the Grand Central Hotel and there he got news that seemed queerer still and that made him think something really was wrong."

Again M'Clung paused, shifted his position, and drew his dying cigar up to a fervent heat. Neither Mitchell nor French spoke. So far the story did not seem to call for remark and in a moment the Ulsterman resumed.

"As Major Magill walked into the hotel the first person he saw was Sir John's private secretary, a man named Breene. Mr Breene, it seemed, was also looking for Sir John and he was more puzzled and upset than the major. He said that on the Monday previous Sir John had told him he was going over for three or four days to Belfast and that he wanted Breene to accompany him. It was about his linen – silk invention. He had an appointment with an engineer, with whom he was thinking of entering into an agreement. He wasn't sure whether this agreement would come off, but if it did he would want Breene to make a draft to send to the lawyers and also probably to get out details for a patent specification. One day would do the thing so far as Breene was concerned and he might have the other two or three days with his people. It seems that Breene is a Belfast man who had gone over to England with Sir John and his people live at Comber – that's a small town about eight miles from Belfast.

"The major immediately asked Breene when he had last seen Sir John. Breene told him in London, for they had travelled by different routes. Sir John had crossed by Larne and Stranraer, as he liked the short sea passage and didn't require to be in early. That service gets in at 9.10 a.m. Breene had gone by Liverpool, which gets in about 7.30, as it enabled him to go down and breakfast with his people at Comber before meeting Sir John. Sir John had asked him to be at the Grand Central Hotel at half past ten and he had been there promptly to time. That was on the previous morning. Sir John had not turned up and Breene had waited in the building for him ever since.

"This story made the major anxious. He feared something must have gone wrong. So he told Breene to wait on at the hotel in case the old man turned up and he himself came along to report at headquarters. He asked us to make some private inquiries. Well, we did so, but from that moment to this Sir John Magill has never been heard of."

"Disappeared without trace?"

"Not altogether, sir. I'm coming to that. Our people started a search at once. They got the local men on the job everywhere and I was sent to Whitehead to try and pick up a trail from there. I wasn't there an hour till I'd found something.

"About a mile or less from Whitehead along the road towards Larne there were signs of a struggle. It's a lonely, deserted place. The road runs on an easy curve between fairly high hedges. There is a grass border at each side with a sod mound and the hedges grow from the back of the mounds. The marks were on the grass, which was trampled and beaten down. Unfortunately none of the prints were clear. Twigs were broken from the hedge. Here and there were traces of blood, very little blood, not more than half a dozen drops. I searched round and I found a hat sticking in the roots of the hedge. It was trampled and there were two stains of blood on it. It was a good grey felt hat stamped with a London maker's name and the letters 'J M'. I have it there in the parcel to show you. I searched on round for the most of the morning, but there wasn't another trace of anything, neither of the body if the man was murdered, nor of a car stopping nor of anything at all. And not another thing has been heard of Sir John anywhere."

"That sounds a puzzle and no mistake, sergeant," Mitchell commented slowly. "I suppose you tried round the houses at Whitehead?"

"Yes, sir. When we found the hat we thought the thing must be serious, so we made public inquiries. We had a house-to-house call in all the town and surrounding country, but we couldn't hear of anything."

"Was the man in Bangor expecting Sir John?"

"No, sir. He was absolutely surprised at the whole thing. He had no business with Sir John and hardly knew him."

"I suppose your people checked up Major Magill's statement?"

"At once, sir. We started men at Larne Harbour to trace the old man's movements. They found two stewards on the boat, both of whom had been on that service for years. Both had known Sir John when he was living in Belfast and both recognised him again. He had booked a private cabin and went straight to it when he got aboard at Stranraer and stayed there all the time. He didn't have anything to eat though it was a calm morning and he was quite well. When they were coming into Larne one of the stewards went to call him and found him asleep.

"He'd gone ashore at Larne Harbour and spoken to the stationmaster about his luggage. 'I want this stuff sent to my son's. Major Malcolm Magill's,' he had said. 'I'm going on to Belfast and I'll be down again in the evening.' He asked the cost and paid. The stationmaster saw him into the Belfast train.

"Our men then saw the guard of the train, who happened to be at the harbour. He remembered seeing the man in question talking to the stationmaster and the stationmaster seeing him into the train. Before the train started he collected the tickets and he noticed Sir John alone in a first-class compartment. He noticed him again on the platform at Belfast. He was carrying a medium-sized despatch case."

Chief-Inspector Mitchell reached forward and carefully removed the ash from his cigar.

"Bit of luck getting all that evidence surely?" he remarked, while French nodded emphatically.

"It was, sir, and yet not so much as you might think. There aren't many cross by that morning service at that time of year and Sir John was striking-looking enough to have been noticed."

"Lucky for you, sergeant, all the same. Well, you've got him to Belfast."

"Yes, sir. At Belfast we lost him, but we made a cast round and we soon picked him up again. He had gone to the Station Hotel, that's at the Northern Counties station where he arrived. He must have gone straight there, for our men were able to check up the time and it was just after the boat train came in. He saw the reception clerk and said: 'I'm Sir John Magill. Is there a letter for me?' There wasn't, and he thanked the clerk and said it didn't matter. He sent the hall porter for a taxi and drove off."

"That might explain why he didn't call at the Grand Central, might it not?" French suggested. "He mixed up the hotels and went to the wrong one."

"That's what Superintendent Rainey thought," M'Clung returned. "Our people saw the hall porter and from him they got the taxi man. He said that Sir John had told him to drive to Sandy Row, where the Donegall Road crosses it.

14

That is in a more or less working-class part of the city. Well, they drove to the place and Sir John paid the taximan. As the man was starting he saw Sir John standing in an uncertain-looking way on the pavement. Except for the stationmaster at Whitehead that night when Sir John telephoned to Major Magill, that was the last time anyone saw him, at least, so far as we've been able to learn up to now. The superintendent said he'd 'phone if anything else came out."

"The stationmaster confirms the incident?"

"In every detail."

The sergeant had evidently reached the end of his story. He made a brief peroration to the effect that when Saturday night came and the affair had not been cleared up, Superintendent Rainey, in consultation with Major Magill, had decided to call in Scotland Yard in the hope of finding a solution of the mystery in London.

All three men shifted their positions as if turning over a fresh page in the proceedings.

"You certainly haven't lost much time," Mitchell declared. "I congratulate you on some good work. It's not easy to check up a trail so thoroughly as you have done."

Sergeant M'Clung grinned self-consciously, delighted at the compliment. "We would have liked to have done better," he protested. "We would have liked to find the murderer if it was murder."

"I dare say. All the same I don't think you've got much to reproach yourselves with. But so far we've been talking about Sir John. Now what about Major Magill himself? Did you check up his statement of his own movements?"

M'Clung gave the other a shrewd glance as if he fully appreciated what lay beneath the question, but he merely answered: "The superintendent put a couple of men on it,

15

but when I left they hadn't finished. They found out that the major left home and returned back there at the time he said and that he called at the station at Whitehead. But when I left they hadn't been able to get confirmation of the rest of his movements. It wasn't so easy as tracing Sir John for the major was mostly alone."

"Quite; I'm not criticising. I was merely wondering about the major himself. Motive and opportunity, you know. We don't know if he had notice, but he certainly seems to have had opportunity. You considered that of course?"

M'Clung smiled. "We did that, sir. But we thought he was all right. They're a well-thought-of family and of good position. Major Magill is well in with the Northern Ireland Government set, a friend of the Prime Minister's and all that. It's hardly likely he'd be guilty of murder. Of course we can't say for sure, but we don't think there's anything to be got that way."

"There was no bad feeling, I take it, between father and son?"

"Not that we ever heard of."

"But you said that Sir John had not been over for seven years. That doesn't look like friendly relations."

"It's not the whole story, sir. If Sir John didn't go over to Belfast the major came over here. He said he'd been in London with his father within the last month."

Once again Mitchell nodded slowly. He paused in thought, then resumed his questions.

"Well, sergeant, there's one thing clear at all events. Sir John Magill reached Ireland safely and it was in Ireland that this mysterious affair happened. Now you've come across to consult us. Just what do you want us to do?"

"Well, sir, it seemed to Superintendent Rainey that this wasn't a local crime at all. He thought it had likely arisen out of something that had happened over here. And if so, it would take you to go into it. He wasn't going to suggest what you might do, but he thought you might look up Sir John's history."

"If your superintendent is correct the matter would certainly have to be dealt with from here. I suppose he hadn't anything more definite in his mind?"

"No, sir. He said that of course the immediate thing was to get the hat identified. Then he suggested that we should check up the motive for Sir John's journey and get a list of the people who knew he was going to travel. He thought it would be worthwhile trying to find whether anyone had an interest in his death. Also he wondered if the old man had much money on him and if so, who would be likely to know about it."

Mitchell smiled. "I see that your superintendent's ideas are very like our own. Those are the lines we should go on, eh, French?"

"That's right, sir. It seems the kind of case you'd get to the bottom of from routine work. Who had an interest in his death? Who of these people were in Northern Ireland at the time of the crime? It seems to me we wouldn't have to go much farther than those two questions."

"I agree and I'm afraid it's you for it. You see, we pretty well must act, whether we want to or not. The Belfast authorities have put in a formal application for assistance through the Home Office. Everything is in order and you may take over as soon as you can. Will you go over to Belfast?"

"I don't really know, sir, as yet. I think I should get what I can here first at all events and then be guided by circumstances. What do you think, sergeant?"

The sergeant grinned. "We'll be very glad to see you in Belfast, Mr French, if you decide to come over. But I think what we want mostly lies in London. However, as you say, you'll know better later on."

For some time further they discussed the case, finally deciding that French should carry on as suggested. M'Clung not being required in London, he was to return that evening to Belfast, keeping French advised of developments there and undertaking to meet him should he decide to go over.

2

KNIGHTSBRIDGE

It was with mixed feelings that French settled down to consider his new case. As a rule he disliked working with a strange police force. In spite of the invariable fact of his having been invited to assist, jealousies arose. Those whose work he was doing felt that they had been weighed in the balance and found wanting. Hence he was frequently met by a veiled opposition, the overcoming of which took half his energies. Moreover with the best will in the world strangers could not give him the help he was accustomed to from his own trained staff.

On the other hand, if he had to go to Ireland, here was a new and by all accounts a very pleasant country to explore. It was true he had once before been in Belfast, but on that occasion his job had occupied all his time and he had been unable to see anything of the place. Now he promised himself at least a Sunday in Portrush and a trip round the far-famed Coast Road, should these delights prove at all possible.

Of course it was by no means certain that the case would take him to Ireland. Indeed he felt he would be surprised if the matter should not prove to be wholly Irish. Sir John had spent his life in Northern Ireland and his connections there must be of the closest. A successful businessman usually makes enemies. One who takes a strong lead in politics invariably does so. Who could tell what old enmity might not have flared up as a result of this last visit.

But with these possibilities French saw that he had nothing to do. Rightly or wrongly Scotland Yard had been asked to intervene and that intervention had crystallised into the making of certain inquiries by himself. He had his instructions and the sooner he carried them out, the better for all concerned. A visit to Sir John Magill's house seemed to be his first move, and he therefore put aside the routine work he had been engaged on and set off to Knightsbridge.

71 Elland Gardens proved to be a comparatively small double house in an old-fashioned but aristocratic-looking terrace. The door was opened by an elderly butler who might have stepped out of a play, so incredibly true was he to type; in fact the whole scene of French's arrival and announcement might well have been taken from the stage of a theatre. Sending in his official card, French asked for either or both of the ladies.

Inside the house the evidences of wealth were more apparent. Even the entrance hall contained costly objects of art, and the library, into which French was shown, was a veritable museum. Silver predominated, and tables and shelves bore almost priceless examples of the skill of the old craftsmen. Books lined the walls between the ornaments, and the light reflected from them and the walnut furniture was mellow and restful. In the centre was an old-fashioned desk, closed, a table bearing a half-completed model of some machine stood in a window, and deep armchairs were placed here and there on the thick carpet. In one corner was a built-in safe.

French had scarcely taken in these details when the door opened and a lady entered. Slightly below medium height, she was plain of feature and rather stern of expression. But her manner was gracious enough as she advanced towards French.

"Detective Inspector French?" she said, glancing at the card in her hand. "We were expecting a representative from Scotland Yard. My brother, Major Magill, wrote that the Belfast police were consulting you. Won't you sit down?"

She spoke calmly, but French could see that her nerves were on edge and that she was holding herself on a tight rein.

"We had a communication from Belfast this morning," he answered with the respectful courtesy which he found so much lightened his labours when dealing with this class of witness. "In consequence I have called to obtain some information about Sir John."

"I will gladly tell you anything I can," she replied, with evident sincerity. "What do you want to know?"

French bowed slightly. "You will understand, madam, that I know nothing about the case and must therefore begin at the beginning. But I shall be as brief as possible. Tell me first, please, a little about your family and household. Just a word about each member."

The lady paused, evidently to arrange her thoughts, then began: "Our family consists of only five members, my father, my brother Malcolm, my sister Beatrice, myself and our cousin Victor. My father, my sister and I have lived here since we moved from Belfast about seven years ago. At that time my father gave over the direction of the mills to Malcolm. I should have said that he owned large linen mills in the Shankill district of Belfast. Malcolm lives with his wife and two children in Ireland, near Larne. He is now the managing director, indeed the virtual owner, of the mills and he goes there to business every day.

"My father and sister and I have lived here very quietly. Beyond visiting a few friends we don't go into society. Though at one time my father took a good deal of interest in parliamentary and municipal affairs, he ceased to do so when we left Belfast. During these last seven years he has indulged his two hobbies, mechanical invention and the collection of silver, specially old silver. You see what he has in this room, and the collection in the music room is even finer."

"I was admiring it before you came in. I'm not an authority, but even to me a lot of it looks almost priceless. You mentioned a cousin, a Mr Victor; is it Mr Victor Magill?"

"Yes, he is the son of Arthur Magill, my father's younger brother."

"Tell me about him, please."

"My Uncle Arthur was in partnership with my father in the mill until he died in – I'm not quite sure of the year, but it was about 1901 or 1902. Victor was at school in Belfast then and it was intended that he also should go into the business. But after my uncle's death his wife moved back to Reading; she was the daughter of a manufacturer of that town. She took Victor from school in Belfast and he went to some English school. From there he went into the regular army. He was invalided out after the War had lasted a couple of years and is now agent for a firm of motorcar manufacturers. I believe he does very well out of it too."

"I follow you. Now, Miss Magill, I want to ask you a straight question. Do you know, or can you suggest anything, no matter how trifling, which might in any way throw light on Sir John's disappearance?"

Miss Magill made a despairing little gesture.

"Absolutely nothing!" she declared emphatically. "The whole thing is utterly puzzling. My father is the last person to be mixed up in anything abnormal."

"His health is good?"

"His health is excellent. For his age it is even remarkable. If you had seen him sawing or planing in his workshop you wouldn't ask. He is as hale and vigorous as a man of forty."

"I suppose I need scarcely ask this either, but still, what about his mind? Any signs of old age showing there?"

There were none. His mind was as clear as French's own. Even his memory, whose decay first announces the sere and yellow leaf, remained clear and strong. Nor was there any mental weakness in the family. Nor yet, so far as Miss Magill knew, had he any trouble or worry on his mind. French tried again.

"Can you tell me if Sir John has any enemies?"

He had none. Miss Magill was positive. Sir John was somewhat retiring in disposition, not given to making friends easily, but in a quiet way he was popular. No one, she felt sure, harboured ill feelings against him. Business rivals? No, she was certain there were none. Political? Nor political either. French would get no help that way. He turned to another point.

"Do you happen to know why Sir John went to Belfast?"

"Something about one of his inventions, he said. I'm afraid I can't tell you the details. He's always working at some invention. As I think I said, he has a workshop fitted up at the back of the house with a lathe and other quite big tools. He's certainly extraordinarily clever with his hands and makes the most beautiful things in both wood and metal. The work has been a splendid outlet for him and I'm sure has helped to keep him fit."

"Hobbies have kept many an elderly man alive," French declared oracularly, "and constructive hobbies are the best of all. Now, Miss Magill, I have heard that Sir John is a rich man. Is that so?"

"That's a comparative term, isn't it? I don't know exactly what his income is, but he must be pretty well off. The linen business in old times was very profitable and during and immediately after the War he made a lot of money. Of course it's different now. Linen has been passing through a bad time lately."

"So I've heard. But that wouldn't have affected Sir John, since he has given over the mills to Major Magill?"

"No. Poor Malcolm has the loss and the worry, I'm afraid. However, things are supposed to have turned the corner now."

"I hope they have. Could you tell me the terms of Sir John's will?"

Miss Magill glanced at him almost reproachfully. The question brought home to her the dread conclusion to which she was evidently so unwilling to open her mind. But she answered calmly enough.

"Only in a general way. My father has great pride of race and a strong desire to perpetuate the family name. After comparatively small legacies to myself, my sister and my cousin Victor, the remainder goes to my brother Malcolm for his lifetime. If Malcolm had a son it would go on to him. If Malcolm had no son it would go on Malcolm's death to Victor for his son."

"And has Major Magill a son?"

"No. My brother has two daughters, but no son. On the other hand Victor has two sons, but no daughter."

"I follow. Let me see if I've got that right. As things are, the bulk of Sir John's money goes to Major Magill. Owing

24

however, to its being entailed, the major will only have the life use of it. At his death it goes to Mr Victor Magill in trust for his eldest son."

"I believe that's correct, though I'm not absolutely sure. My father is reticent in disposition and we did not care to question him on such a matter."

"Naturally. Can you tell me who is Sir John's legal adviser?"

"Messrs Hepplewhite, Ingram & Ingram, of 71B Chancery Lane."

"Thank you. Now, Miss Magill, Sir John crossed to Belfast via Larne and Stranraer on the night of Wednesday, the second instant. Do you know who took his tickets and arranged his journey? Did he do things like that for himself?"

"I expect Mr Breene did that. Mr Breene is his secretary."

"Ah, then I should like to see Mr Breene. Who else is there in your household?"

"Just Myles, the butler, Nutting, the valet and chauffeur, and three women servants."

"All reliable?"

"So far as I know, absolutely."

"Thank you, Miss Magill. I'm sorry for having had to give you this trouble. I'm afraid I shall have to see your servants now and also to go through Sir John's papers."

She raised her hand. "Just a moment. Now, Mr Inspector, you've been asking me a lot of questions and I'm going to ask you one in return. Quite honestly, what do you think has happened to my poor father?"

French was accustomed in such circumstances to this demand. He always answered it as truthfully as he could.

"Honestly, Miss Magill, I don't know. I haven't enough information to say. Everything is being done to find out."

"Still," she persisted, "you must have some idea?"

French shrugged. He was sorry for this kindly lady who evidently felt her position so keenly, yet who had eased his task by so sternly controlling her feelings. There was real sympathy in his voice as he replied: "Well, we must admit things don't look too well. I don't want to buoy you up with false hopes; all the same I don't think you need necessarily accept the worst."

She nodded. "I suppose that's all you can say, and thank you for saying it." She rang the bell. "Do everything you can to assist Mr French," she told the butler. Then shaking hands with French, she left the room.

"Well, Myles," French began, "this is a sad business about Sir John."

The butler closed the door and came forward, standing respectfully before French.

"I have heard no details, sir, except that he has disappeared. I should like to know – Sir John has been a good master to me – I should like to know if anything further has been learned?"

"I'll tell you all I know myself, which isn't much," French said kindly. "But first, I wonder if you could give me a little information." He unpacked the hat and held it out. "Did you ever see that before?"

"Sir John's!" the man said instantly. Then he took the hat and examined it carefully. "Yes, sir," he declared firmly, "there is no doubt whatever about it. It is the hat Sir John was wearing when he left here. I brushed it for him and I am quite certain." He turned it over and stared at the blood stains. "This is terrible, sir," he went on in a lower tone. "Does this mean – an accident? That he is dead?"

French shrugged.

"It certainly doesn't look too well, does it?" he admitted. "It was found on a lonely road a mile from where Sir John was last seen."

"And there was no sign of the body? Excuse me, sir, but as I said, Sir John was a good master to me, indeed, if I might say it without presumption, a good friend. I should be sorry if anything were to happen to him."

There was genuine feeling in the man's tones and French at once told him all that was known.

Myles was a good deal upset by the recital. That Sir John was the victim of foul play he seemed to have no doubt. "I hope you'll get them, sir," he said earnestly. "I hope they'll hang, whoever did this. He was a good master." He shook his head sadly.

"Well, Myles, the best thing you can do to help that on is to answer my questions. And first of all, can you get me a photograph of Sir John? And, wait a minute, of Major Magill and Mr Victor as well?"

"Certainly, sir." He left the room and in a moment returned with three cabinet portraits. One showed the head of the house of Magill as a rather fine-looking old man with a large nose, jaws bordering on the nutcracker, a high forehead and very intelligent eyes. Between him and his son and nephew as well as Miss Magill there was a certain family resemblance, on which French commented.

"Yes, sir, all the family are somewhat alike in appearance. But it's coming out more strongly in the second generation. Mr Victor's son is Sir John over again."

"Wonderful thing, heredity," French remarked, and he went on to question the butler as to the family relations and to possible enemies of Sir John. But he did not get much information. According to Myles the missing man, while thoroughly good-hearted, had been somewhat distant in manner and a trifle secretive in disposition. Intercourse with his associates was therefore restrained in cordiality. But with no one was Sir John on bad terms, in fact, it was rather the other way about.

One point French noted as possibly important. When questioning Myles as to Sir John's recent letters, telegrams and visitors, the man stated that on two recent occasions a stranger had called. His card showed that he was a Mr Coates and that he came from Belfast. Unfortunately Myles could not remember the remainder of the address. The man was tall and well built, with very bright red hair. Quite a remarkable-looking man. On the occasion of each call he had stayed with Sir John for about half an hour.

"I suppose you'd know him if you saw him again?" Myles declared he couldn't be mistaken and French, having indicated that the interview was at an end, asked for Mr Breene.

The secretary was a somewhat striking-looking man of about five and thirty. Tall and spare without being actually thin, he gave the impression of extreme physical strength and fitness. His head was small, altogether out of proportion to his height. His face suggested a curious blend of the Red Indian and the Scandinavian; high cheekbones and ruggedly chiselled features combined with fair hair and the lightest of blue eyes. Energy, ambition and decision were written on every line of the man's features. In fact before he opened his lips French realised that here was one who would get what he wanted or know the reason why.

"I crossed over last night," he explained in answer to French's question. "There was nothing to keep me in Belfast and things were getting behind here."

"I should be glad, Mr Breene, if you would tell me all you can about this unhappy affair. And first: as to yourself. Have you been long with Sir John?"

"Eight years. He appointed me private secretary while he was still running his mills in Belfast. When he gave them up and moved over here he asked would I care to remain with him as general confidential secretary and assistant. He made me a liberal offer and I accepted."

"You're an Irishman yourself?"

"A Belfast man. My brother and sister still live near Belfast."

"There can't be much for a secretary to do here?"

"There isn't. It is simply that Sir John likes to amuse himself in his workshop and can't be bothered with correspondence."

French nodded and asked what sort of man Sir John was. He invariably repeated his questions to as many witnesses as possible in order to discount individual idiosyncrasies.

"Well," Breene returned, "he is not what Americans call a good mixer. He is dry in manner and retiring in disposition and doesn't make friends easily. And between ourselves, though I've no complaint to make, he is not particularly liberal about money. But when you've said that you've said everything. He is straight and honourable and in his own way kindly. He is the type of man that the better you know him, the better you like him."

"Is he on quite good terms with all the other members of his family?" French asked the question perfunctorily, but he watched keenly for Breene's reaction. He was considerably interested by the result. Though the man said, "Oh, quite," without perceptible hesitation, French could have sworn it was with less conviction. He thought quickly. If, as Miss Magill said, Malcolm had suffered losses during the linen

29

depression, if the old man was not liberal about money, if Malcolm was to a considerable extent his heir...Added to all that curious business at Whitehead...French decided to bluff.

"I rather gathered," he said, with a sidelong glance and bending forward confidentially, "that relations between Sir John and his son were just a trifle strained?"

"An exaggeration," Breene answered promptly. "Admittedly they didn't see eye to eye about money matters. But to say that relations were strained is untrue."

French chuckled inwardly as he bluffed again.

"Probably you are right. It was this money question that I had in mind all the same. I wish you'd explain just what took place about it."

"There's no mystery about that," Breene declared. "Major Magill, as you doubtless know, was in difficulties in connection with his business. Linen has been having a bad time in Ireland lately and more than one old and respected firm has gone down. As far as I understood it, the major was faced with having to close down, which of course he didn't want to do. He wrote asking Sir John to put some more capital into the concern, so that he might install some new and more efficient machinery. But Sir John wouldn't. He took the line that when he was in charge he had had to meet difficulties and that the major could do the same. It was not perhaps very reasonable, as the slump was due to conditions the major had very little control over; mostly it was the result of the War. But there it was. Sir John wouldn't move. The major came over to see him a couple of times, but it was no good. But they were perfectly friendly and all that, for I saw them together."

"Quite," French agreed. "I suppose you cannot tell me where I could find Sir John's will?"

"I don't even know if he made a will, though I suppose he must have."

"What does he keep in the safe? Can you open it for me?"

"No. Sorry I can't help you there either. Sir John keeps the key himself and only on one occasion did I see inside. It seemed to contain only papers, but there may have been objects of his collection too valuable to leave unprotected."

It suddenly occurred to French that here was rather a serious difficulty. Though he had not actually gone the length of formulating the words, "The Case Against Malcolm Magill," he realised that the formulation on such a phrase was by no means an impossibility. From the information gained in Ireland Malcolm was *a priori* the most likely person to have disposed of Sir John's body, and now here seemed the beginnings of a theory of motive. For to Malcolm's unprosperous condition must be added the fact that he stood to gain by his father's death.

French pulled himself up sharply. This would never do. Cases were not conducted in such a way, at least not successful cases. Let him get his facts before jumping to conclusions. At the same time…He turned to Breene.

"I understand that Sir John went to Ireland about some invention?"

Breene agreed. Sir John was always working out some idea. He was very ingenious and worked as if brought up to the trade.

French nodded.

"Do you happen to know the exact nature of this Belfast business?"

Breene took out a cigarette case and automatically selected a cigarette, as an afterthought handing the case to his companion.

"To a limited extent only," he answered. "Sir John warned me to say nothing about it, but I suppose I'm free from that now. Not that it seems of any importance." He twirled his flint and held out the lighter. "For some years Sir John has been working on one invention which would really be valuable if he could bring it off. He has been trying to find an improved way of combining artificial silk with the finest linen. He thinks it might be possible to produce a fabric which would be as light and smooth as silk, while strong and uncreasing and giving good wear. He believes such a fabric, if cheap enough, would supersede both real and artificial silk. A jolly fine idea, if he could only do it. There'd be an immense future for such a product. Incidentally it would set the Ulster linen trade on its feet again, make it boom, in fact."

"Incidentally also it would make the inventor a millionaire – if he handled his cards well."

"Quite. Well, Sir John had found a name for his new product; he was going to call it 'Sillin', a portmanteau of 'silk' and 'linen', you understand. But unfortunately that was all he had found. The product itself eluded him. His visit to Belfast was in connection with it."

"Just how, can you tell me?"

"I can't. He told me he was going to see an engineer in Belfast about it and as he might want to enter into an agreement with him he would like me to go over to take the necessary notes. Also he said something about a possible patent. It looked to me as if either he or the engineer thought they had solved the thing, though he did not say so."

In answer to French's questions Breene repeated the story M'Clung had already told. He, Breene, had crossed via Liverpool, gone out on arrival to his brother's at

Comber, breakfasted and returned to Belfast in time to be at the Grand Central Hotel at half past ten, the hour at which he was to meet Sir John. There all that day and night he had waited fruitlessly for the old man. Next morning he had determined to go up and see Major Magill at the mills, but just as he was about to leave the hotel the major had entered. Since then he had made a statement to the Belfast police, and after consulting the major, had returned to London.

"I suppose, Mr Breene, you have no idea who Sir John had the appointment with?"

Breene had no idea. He had at first supposed it might be a firm of engineers named M'Millan & Maxwell, as these people were constantly doing work for Sir John. This view had been supported by the fact that their works were in Sandy Row, to which Sir John had driven. But when the police had gone to this firm they were told that Sir John had not been to them. So far as Breene knew Sir John had not written to anyone in Ireland before leaving.

"You're wrong there," French pointed out. "He wrote to Major Magill asking if he could put him up."

Breene hadn't known about that. He certainly hadn't written such a letter. Nor, he said in answer to French's further questions, had he met or heard about a caller from Belfast named Coates, nor could he imagine who this might be.

"Who arranged Sir John's journey, Mr Breene?"

"He did it himself except for the actual taking of the tickets. In the ordinary course I should have done that and gone with him to Euston and seen him off. But as I told you I crossed that night by Liverpool, which meant my leaving Euston nearly two hours before him. Nutting therefore saw him off. Nutting is the chauffeur."

French nodded.

"There is just one other thing," he concluded. "I want you to tell me about the relations between Mr Victor Magill and the family here."

"There was nothing remarkable about their relations," Breene answered. "As a matter of fact I have not seen a great deal of Victor, though of course I know him quite well. He has visited Sir John occasionally since I have been here, but I don't know whether on business or as a friend."

French bluffed again.

"I understand relations were strained there too?"

"If so, I know nothing about it."

"Well, Mr Breene, I'm much obliged to you. That's all I want, except to look through Sir John's desk. I have Miss Magill's permission."

"So she told me," Breene returned dryly. "Here are the keys. I suppose you'll not want my help? I've an appointment down town shortly."

French reassured him with secret satisfaction. Solitude was the very thing he wanted. He would see the other servants and then get along with the search of the desk.

Nutting, the chauffeur, was the first comer. He was able to tell very little. He positively identified the hat as that Sir John was wearing on the night in question. He had driven him to Euston, taken his tickets for the journey and the sleeper, and seen him into the train. The berth had been engaged and the attendant was expecting him.

More as a matter of form than otherwise French saw the maids, though from them he learned nothing. Then locking the library door, he settled down to go through the desk.

It did not take French long to see that Sir John, or Breene, whichever of them used the desk, was a man of method. The top was clear, save for a tickler file open at the current date and a small pile of papers evidently awaiting attention. The three lower drawers on each side had been made into one, and contained a modern vertical correspondence file. Separate drawers held neatly docketed papers relating to various subjects, bills, receipts, investments. But nowhere could French find anything to help his quest.

His eye strayed longing to the safe. It was quite on the cards that inside lay Sir John's will, and a sight of Sir John's will, he felt, was vital to his investigation. However, at present at all events, he had no power to have the safe forced. He could only go to the solicitors in Chancery Lane and hope for the best. But he greatly feared that in spite of the persuasiveness of his tongue, of which he had a not inconsiderable opinion, they would be unwilling to let him see the document.

Wishing, as he so often did, that the men of the CID were as well favoured in such matters as their confrères in other countries, he rang for Myles, and having handed him the keys of the desk, was shown out.

3

BELFAST

French's researches at Elland Gardens had occupied him during the whole of that Monday afternoon, the first of his new inquiry. It was not, therefore, till the following morning that he was able to call on Messrs Hepplewhite, Ingram & Ingram, Sir John Magill's solicitors. From them, unfortunately, he learned little. Mr Ingram, senior, whom he interviewed, admitted that he had drawn up Sir John's will, but on its completion he had sent it to Elland Gardens, in accordance with the old man's request. For this reason he found himself unable to state its contents, though so far as his memory went its terms were as suggested by the inspector. This was the extreme limit to which Mr Ingram could be induced to go, and with this French had therefore to be content.

At his next visit, to the motor agency for which Victor Magill acted as representative, he drew almost as complete a blank. It was true that he did not expect to learn much. But as a matter of routine, it was necessary to see everyone who might in any way throw light on the case.

Messrs Hopwood & Merrythought were agents for a number of the most expensive makes of luxury cars on the market. Mr Hopwood, the senior partner, when assured of the gravity of the affair, proved willing to tell French all he knew about his travelling agent. But it did not amount to much. Victor Magill had joined the firm some five years previously and during this period had proved himself an excellent salesman. In private life he mixed with a smart crowd, belonging to at least three exclusive clubs. This gave him opportunities of doing unobtrusive business, which he utilised so tactfully that while selling an ever-increasing number of cars, he was accepted by his clients as their bene- factor rather than as the unmitigated nuisance such sales- men so often are. He was paid a retaining fee of £500 a year, with a large commission on results. This commission had grown every year until in the previous year it had amounted to over £1500. From Victor's mode of life Mr Hopwood imagined he must also have considerable private means.

As a result of French's routine, but probing questions, Mr Hopwood admitted that at one time Victor had seemed very short of cash. For the most of half a year stringency had obtained and there had been hints of gambling and serious debt. Mr Hopwood had been a good deal worried about the affair, though he had not had sufficiently definite information to justify him in taking the matter up officially with Victor. Then suddenly, some four months previously, things had come right. Whether Victor had made a lucky venture with the Goddess of Chance or whether he had come in for a legacy, the senior partner did not know, but Victor was again evidently flush and the ugly rumours of debt died down.

With regard to Victor's personality Mr Hopwood had little to say. In the senior partner's view Victor was a thorough man of the world, suave, polished and excellent company in any society. He was at present on holidays, a yachting cruise up the west coast of Scotland, and was not expected back for another two or three weeks.

As French returned to the Yard he felt rather up against it. Had he been acting alone he would unhesitatingly have gone to Ireland. Not only did he believe that the solution of the mystery lay there, but he felt that he had done all that was necessary in London. He smoked a couple of pipes over it and then went in and put his views before Chief Inspector Mitchell.

The chief inspector heard him without comment.

"If that's your view," he said at last, "better go over and say so. See their superintendent and have a chat with him. And see here, French. Do anything you can for them. If they want you to stay and lend a hand, do so. Better ring them up now and go over tonight."

From the tone of the Belfast superintendent rather than from his actual words, French sensed that he would be a welcome visitor. Evidently they were getting no farther with the case, and equally evidently they were worried about it. French would have expected a resentment at his appearance in Ireland, but nothing of the sort was suggested by the superintendent's reply. It was finally arranged that he should cross via Larne and Stranraer and that Sergeant M'Clung would meet him at the station in Belfast.

It did not seem possible that anything could have occurred during Sir John's journey which might have borne on his subsequent fate. At the same time French determined to travel as the old gentleman had done and to keep a careful note of his surroundings so as to visualise the other's experiences.

He began therefore by engaging a sleeping berth at Euston. On inquiry he was directed to a stationmaster's office on No. 6 platform. There a clerk made the reservation, handing him a voucher. This voucher he presented at the booking office when taking his tickets, a first-class return for the journey and a single for the sleeping berth.

The train left at 7.40 p.m. from No. 12 platform. There he found that all arrangements had been made for his reception. His name was on the list on the window of the sleeping coach and the attendant was expecting him and showed him to his stateroom. Immediately after starting the man came to him for his tickets. He was most civil, making a point of addressing French by his name and fixing up when he should call him next morning.

For a time French sat watching the lights flit by, then thinking he would be more comfortable in bed, he undressed, switched on his reading lamp and became immersed in a novel. At the end of a couple of hours this palled and he turned off the light and composed himself to sleep.

His efforts in this line were not particularly successful and he lay listening to the rhythmic beat of the wheels on the rail-joints and dreamily wondering whether Malcolm Magill had really killed his father. There were few stops. At only one had he the curiosity to look out: it was Carlisle. Presently he heard Dumfries called and then he fell into a really deep sleep, from which he seemed instantly to be aroused by the attendant with a tea tray and the words, " *'Alf* an hour to Stranraer, sir."

A gorgeous colour scheme in the eastern sky was ushering in the dawn as French stepped from the train at Stranraer Harbour. On the platform at the door of the sleeper was the ubiquitous attendant, who with a "Good morning, Mr French. Thank you, sir," saw him off the premises so far as his car was concerned. A few yards down the pier brought him to the steamer, at the gangway of which his ticket was checked. A short delay and there came the welcome sound of the breakfast bell, and when French came on deck again they were halfway down Loch Ryan.

In the early sunshine of that autumn morning the surroundings of the loch struck him as quite beautiful. The shores, particularly on the starboard side, rose gently into bare rounded hills, which grew wilder and rockier as they approached the open sea. Between were wooded valleys which French no sooner saw than he longed to explore. But it was the colouring that appealed most to him, the dark greens of grass and leaves, shaded here and there to greys and russets, the golden browns of heather and bracken, the darker tints of rock, turning almost to black at the base of the cliffs, the thin blue of the sky and the steel grey of the water, all these were presented with the soft rich tones of the western atmosphere. Then out into the open sea, with the sugar loaf of Ailsa Craig standing blue and sharp on the northern horizon and the Irish coast a faint line right ahead.

French enjoyed every minute of that crossing. The sea, he knew, could be as rough here as anywhere, but on this charming morning it was like the proverbial glass. For the hour or more of the passage he paced the deck, watching the Scotch coast fade and the Irish grow. And when at last they turned round the end of Islandmagee and entered Larne Lough, he saw that the Irish side was nearly, if not quite, as beautiful as the Scotch.

He took the broad gauge train on the left of the platform, and as he sat waiting for the mails to be transhipped, he could follow vividly Sir John Magill's movements six days earlier. There was a traveller talking to the stationmaster, no doubt just as had Sir John, and there it chanced was the guard passing and looking at both. Presently this same guard collected French's ticket, as doubtless he had collected Sir John's. History indeed seemed to be repeating itself for his, French's, benefit.

The run to Belfast occupied about half an hour. The line ran along the shores, first of Larne Lough, then of Belfast Lough. Just where they came down on the latter French noted the little town of Whitehead. Waiting for him on the platform at Belfast was Sergeant M'Clung.

"How're you, Mr French?" he exclaimed, pronouncing the "How're you?" with the rhythm of "bowery." "You must have had a good crossing this morning."

French described his journey, and as they passed to the entrance of the station M'Clung pointed out the hotel at which Sir John had called.

"I've a car waiting," he explained. "We'll go along to Chichester Street. The superintendent's expecting you."

Police headquarters was about a mile from the station and there in a comfortable little office sat Superintendent Rainey. He was a thick set man of medium height, with a rather stern face which, however, lit up and became attractive when he smiled. He did so as French was shown in.

"Very good of you coming over, inspector," he said pleasantly, rising and holding out his hand. "You had a good crossing, I expect?"

French wondered if this remark was made by every Belfast citizen to every traveller arriving in his city. He reassured the superintendent.

"What about a spot of breakfast?" went on Rainey. "That six o'clock affair on the boat's all right, but it hardly runs you to lunch."

French thought that in his case it might. But Rainey would not hear of proceeding to business until his visitor had had something to fortify his inner man, and French not caring for spirits, M'Clung was instructed to take him to an adjoining restaurant for coffee. There for a while the two men sat smoking, chatting principally of the beauty spots of Northern Ireland which M'Clung said French must see before he went back.

"You came over at the right time, inspector," Rainey began when they were once more seated in his office. "I have a visitor coming in whom you'll be interested to meet: Victor Magill."

"Victor Magill?" French repeated with a smile. "It's well I hadn't made my report. I'd have told you he was cruising somewhere up the west coast of Scotland."

"You would have been right in a way," Rainey admitted. "When you got your information he was there. His launch touched at Oban and there he got wires which Major Magill and the sisters had sent. He had just time to catch a train to Glasgow and get the Belfast boat. He got in this morning and went up to see the major at the mill. It was from there he 'phoned me he was coming down. I told him to call at twelve so that we could have our discussion before he came. And now, inspector, I hope you've some good news for us?"

"Not very much, I'm afraid," French answered, and he launched into a detailed account of his activities in London. The two Belfast men listened attentively and when he had finished Rainey summarised the position.

"That is to say, inspector, you have learnt that Malcolm Magill was in low water and that he stood to gain a large sum at his father's death. Secondly, you have not been able to find anyone else with an adequate motive. Victor Magill and the daughters were legatees also, but as far as you know to nothing like a sufficient extent to account for murder. In any case these legacies supply no real motive at all, as all three were well enough off. All three besides have alibis. On our present information, therefore, these three may be at least temporarily eliminated. There are no other suspects."

"That's right, sir."

"On the grounds of motive, therefore, Malcolm Magill is so far our only suspect. And when we look into the circumstances of the actual disappearance we again find him our only suspect. On the other hand all we know of the history and character of Malcolm Magill is in his favour. That's about it, I take it?"

"That's about it," French repeated, while M'Clung nodded appreciatively. "All the same, superintendent, I shouldn't put too much dependence on a man's previous character in a case of this kind. I've seen too many cases of the most unlikely people going wrong, and I'm sure so have you."

"I agree and I don't attach too much weight to it. All the same it counts. Now, inspector, the only other point you learned was that someone named Coates, with a Belfast address, who was otherwise unknown to his household, had recently called on Sir John?"

French agreed.

"Now I'll tell you what we've done. We've gone over for the second time the whole story as M'Clung told it to you. We've learnt nothing to add to it but we've got a fairly complete corroboration as to its truth. First, with regard to Sir John himself. We find that he was practically under observation during his whole journey right from London up to the point at which he left the taxi in Sandy Row. You learn that he drove from his house to Euston and started in a sleeping berth on the 7.40 to Stranraer. We checked his arrival at Stranraer and his going on board the boat: we found the man who carried his luggage. At Larne he was seen leaving the boat and entering the train. Again at Belfast he was in sight of one or more people from the moment he left the train until he reached Sandy Row. So far as Sir John is concerned the story is absolutely confirmed."

"Jolly good to get all that independent evidence," French commented tactfully.

"Principally a series of lucky flukes," Rainey corrected. "Now with regard to Major Malcolm Magill. Here also we've got practically complete confirmation as to his movements. M'Clung didn't tell you that?"

"Gilmore hadn't finished, sir, when I left," the sergeant pointed out.

"Neither he had," Rainey admitted. "Well, I'll tell you now. Malcolm Magill's statement was, if you remember, that he got a telephone from his father asking him to come to Whitehead to pick him up and that he, Sir John, would walk out along the Larne road to meet him. That call came, according to Malcolm, at a minute or two before nine. We have checked it up both at Whitehead Station, where it was made, and at the exchanges, and it was actually put through at 8.53."

"Good enough," said French,

"Good enough, yes," Rainey repeated. "The major went at once and got the car. He estimates that he left his house, Lurigan, at about five minutes past nine, and this is confirmed both by his wife and the housemaid. Under the circumstances it was natural for Mrs Magill to look at the clock, and the housemaid states she heard the car leaving about five minutes after the clock had struck. So that also is good enough."

French again signified his agreement.

"The major states that he drove at a fair speed until he was within a couple of miles of Whitehead, the extreme point to which he thought his father might have walked. Then he slowed down to ten or fifteen miles an hour, keeping a sharp lookout for foot passengers. He met no one and therefore went on into the town to make inquiries. He found that the post office was closed and he was directed to the station where there was a booth on the up platform. He saw the stationmaster, who told him about the elderly gentleman who had come off the Belfast train at 8.47 and who had made a call from the booth. That, the major states, was about 9.45, and this hour is confirmed both by the stationmaster and by an estimate of the time it ought to have taken Malcolm to come from Lurigan. So that was that."

Superintendent Rainey glanced at French as if to invoke his commendation. French hastened to bestow it.

"Major Magill imagined his father must have got a lift to Larne and he started home again. But he states he was unhappy about the whole affair, and when he had gone seven or eight miles it suddenly occurred to him that he might have missed the old man through the latter making a call in Whitehead. He therefore turned round and went back again. There were two families in Whitehead with whom the Magills were on fairly intimate terms and he drove first to one and then to the other. But neither knew anything of Sir John, and though they telephoned to other possible houses, no one had seen the old man. The major states that some considerable time was occupied with this telephoning, so that it was almost eleven when he left Whitehead. This again is not only confirmed by an estimate of the time these movements should have taken, but also by the exchange and the local residents. At the last house the daughter declared that she looked at the clock as the car started and that it was exactly ten-fifty-five.

"The major states that he drove slowly back looking out again for foot passengers, and that again he saw no one. This time, however, he drove home, arriving about eleven-thirty, which once again checks in with distance and probable speed. When he had garaged the car and had a whisky and soda he rang up his friends in Whitehead to report progress, as they had asked him to do. This call has also been traced and it was put through at exactly eleven-forty-three. Incidentally the hour of his arrival home is confirmed both by Mrs Magill, who had waited up to meet Sir John, and by the servants, who slept over the garage and heard the car being put in."

French made a gesture of astonishment.

"I don't think, sir," he declared, "I ever heard such complete confirmation of any story. Major Magill's movements have been confirmed as absolutely as Sir John's."

M'Clung looked delighted by what he evidently took to be a compliment to the Belfast force. But Rainey shrugged.

"More lucky flukes," he declared. "Next with regard to the secretary. Breene's story seems also to have been true. He certainly travelled over by Liverpool on that night and went down to his brother's at Comber. He left Comber, so his sister thinks, about half past nine, and as the only suitable train leaves at exactly 9.30, I think we may take it that he travelled by it as he says. That train arrives at 9.50 and he reached the Grand Central Hotel, ten minutes away, at 10.30. About half an hour of this time is therefore unaccounted for. He says he took a walk through the streets, and as that would have been an eminently likely thing for him to have done, I think we may accept that also. The staff at the hotel absolutely confirm his further statement. He arrived about 10.30, asked for Sir John and said he would be in the lounge if wanted. We have seen his bill and found waiters who served him at lunch, tea and dinner that day and at breakfast the next morning. We have also seen the chambermaid who called him."

"Nothing there, sir," said French.

"No," agreed Rainey, "there's nothing there. But French, I'm far from satisfied about Malcolm Magill. Things are very black against him."

Of this French was by no means convinced.

"I don't know, sir," he answered. "Looks to me mighty like an alibi."

"You think so," said Rainey, thoughtfully lighting a cigarette. "I'm not so sure. Assuming Sir John has been murdered – for remember we don't even know that yet – why could Malcolm not have done it?"

"Well, there's all this that you've been telling me. Besides that there's the disposal of the body. I don't see how he could have disposed of the body. Suppose he met Sir John, murdered him, staged the struggle and hid the hat. What would he do with the body? He couldn't leave it on the road. He couldn't take it in the car to those people in Whitehead, any of whom might have offered to accompany him on his search. Nor could he hide it, at least not without leaving some trace of beaten-down grass or something of that sort, and no trace was found."

Rainey moved uneasily.

"But hang it all, French, Sir John has disappeared. Malcolm Magill had the motive and the opportunity and so far as we know no one else had either. These difficulties that you raise..." He held up his hand as French would have spoken. "Let's go back to fundamentals. If he didn't murder Sir John, where is Sir John? What's happened to him?"

French shook his head.

"I realise that all right, sir," he admitted, "but you've just pointed out yourself that the murder theory is still only an assumption. What if Sir John disappeared voluntarily?"

Rainey made a gesture of agreement.

"That's quite true, French. Better still, it leads us to something we do know, and that is that we're theorising too soon. I've something more to tell you – two things in fact.

"The first is a small matter. Among our other lines of inquiry we made a house-to-house visitation in Sandy Row and the adjoining streets in the hope of finding someone who expected or actually met Sir John. That, I regret to say, brought us nothing.

"The second is that we issued a description of Sir John and circulated it to the police throughout the whole of Northern Ireland. And to this we got a reply which I confess surprised me."

Rainey paused to emphasise his climax. French was impressed by all he had heard. If there was any more efficient way of handling a case than that these men had adopted, he felt he would like to know of it.

"Sir John had been seen once again after he left Sandy Row," went on Rainey. "You noticed that big hill with the flat top and the precipitous front to the north of the city as you came in?"

"I was admiring it, sir," French declared. "It reminded me of pictures I had seen of Table Mountain."

"I never saw Table Mountain," said Rainey, "and whether it's like it or not I don't know. It's called the Cave Hill and it's about twelve hundred feet high, with a splendid view from the top. Along its lower slopes runs the main road to Antrim, and from this Antrim Road a steep path leads to the top, the Sheeps' Path. Now half an hour after Sir John

Magill reached Sandy Row, a constable saw him get out of a tram at the foot of this path, and after looking round in a surreptitious sort of way, hurry up it. The path disappears immediately into trees, so that the constable lost sight of him at once. Of course he was some distance away, but he is positive he made no mistake about it's being Sir John."

"By Jove, sir, very strange that! Have you any idea what he might have gone up there for?"

"Well, a possible suggestion is that it was to meet someone about his invention. But there doesn't seem to be any reason for such a theatrical kind of secrecy."

"That path doesn't lead near any houses?" French asked.

"It leads up through the grounds of Belfast Castle. But there are many private houses along the inland side of the Antrim Road and no doubt you could get to these from the path. You could go along parallel to the road on the side of the hill and drop down at the back of any of the houses. But why?"

"Somebody in one of those houses working at the same idea?"

The superintendent glanced at Sergeant M'Clung.

"That's what M'Clung suggested," he answered, "and we have made a list of the occupiers of the houses for investigation. But I'm not hopeful of it myself."

"Have you any other theory, sir?"

Rainey shook his head.

"I confess I haven't. Sometimes I wonder if the old man hadn't gone dotty, but there's little to support that."

"Mightn't he have just been out for a walk?"

"We considered that also," the superintendent admitted, "but I think it's unlikely. Sir John was too old and didn't seem keen on that sort of thing. Then there was his secretive manner when he disappeared up the path. No, it's certainly a puzzle – unless the constable made a mistake after all."

Rainey paused and there was silence for some moments. Presently he went on: "Now there are one or two inquiries suggested by your statement, inspector. M'Clung, you get away to M'Millan & Maxwell's and ask them if they know anything of a Coates who might have called on Sir John, or who is interested in inventions or silk or linen. At the same time I'll get a systematic search made among all of the names in the city. With any luck we should get something there."

French agreed that both these avenues should be explored. Once again he felt impressed by the efficiency with which the case was being handled. These North of Ireland men had nothing to learn from London. He had to admit that even he himself could not have done much more in the time.

In half an hour M'Clung re-entered. A glance at his face gave his news.

"No good, sir," he reported. "I saw M'Millan himself. They don't know anybody called Coates that would suit."

"Had they been working on this silk – linen invention?"

"Never even heard of it, sir."

"I thought that would be the way," Rainey declared, "so I'm hardly disappointed. Better luck next time, sergeant."

Before either man could reply a knock came to the door. "Gentleman to see you, sir," a constable said, handing Rainey a card.

" 'Mr Victor Magill.' Yes, this is the time I asked him to call. We'd better see him, inspector."

He glanced at French, and the latter having signified his agreement, he told the constable to send Mr Magill in.

– 4 –

BELFAST

Victor Magill was a small man, thin and wiry, and walking with a considerable limp. His features were strongly marked, the bones standing forward. His eyes were surmounted by a heavy frontal projection, his cheekbones were high and his chin and jaw well developed. A mobile expression and a nervous, eager manner gave him an appearance of energy and force, but this was countered by a weak mouth.

"Good morning, Mr Magill," Rainey greeted him. "I am Superintendent Rainey and this is Detective Sergeant M'Clung of our service. You have come at an opportune moment, Mr Magill, for we have with us here Detective Inspector French from Scotland Yard, who has come over to consult with us about Sir John's disappearance."

"This is a terrible and most mysterious affair," Victor said as he shook hands. "I came directly I heard of it. My cousin, Malcolm, has just been giving me the details. He would have come down with me, but he had a directors' meeting. I should like to know if you have learned anything fresh?"

"I'm sorry to say we have not," Rainey answered. "We were just checking over how we stood with Inspector French, and we certainly haven't much to go on. When I got your phone this morning I began to hope that you were going to give us some information."

"I?" Victor Magill shook his head. "I should be only too thankful were I able. But I'm afraid I know nothing that could help you. In fact the thing staggers me altogether. My poor uncle was the last man to be mixed up in anything abnormal. He was so conventional and – respectable is scarcely the word – I might perhaps say that he was a pillar of ordered society. I suppose" – he hesitated – "you have no doubt that he is dead?"

"We don't know," Rainey returned, "but I must admit it doesn't look very hopeful."

Victor shook his head. "I'm afraid not. If he were alive we would have heard of him before this. I can see that Malcolm has lost hope too. Very sad and puzzling beyond belief."

"How did you hear of it, Mr Magill?"

"Malcolm and my cousin Caroline – Miss Magill, you know – both sent me wires. I have been on a yachting cruise, or rather a motor launch cruise up the west coast of Scotland. I left a list of places where we'd call. It was at one of these, at Oban, that the wires were waiting. That was yesterday morning. I just managed to catch the twelve o'clock train for Glasgow, which brought me in time for last night's steamer to Belfast. This morning I went up to see Malcolm at the mill and then came straight down to you."

"Very glad to have the benefit of your views," said Rainey. "May I ask if you have formed any opinion yourself as to what might have happened?"

Victor made a gesture of impotence.

"Not the faintest," he declared. "The whole thing is utterly inexplicable to me. My uncle seemed so well the last time I saw him. He was in fine spirits and even cracked jokes, not his usual way at all."

"When was that, Mr Magill?"

"On Sunday; Sunday week, that is; the Sunday before he left town."

"Four days before he disappeared?"

Victor agreed.

"And nothing passed at that interview which would tend to explain the disappearance?"

There was nothing – absolutely nothing. Victor would have been only too thankful if he could have made some suggestion, but he could not.

"He was in unusually good spirits on that Sunday, you say. Do you know of any special cause for that?"

"Well, I do. He had just pulled off an invention that he had been working at for years and he was frightfully bucked. He was like a child with a new toy."

"We had heard that he made a hobby of mechanical work. Do you know the nature of this invention?"

"Oh, yes, he told me all about it. It was in the park that I met him that Sunday afternoon. I said: 'Well, uncle, how's the magnum opus?' for he had shown me his trial models and I knew he thought he was near a solution. His face broke out into smiles and he caught me by the arm in his eagerness – a thing that normally he would never have thought of doing. 'Got it, my boy,' he almost shouted. 'I've got it at last.' He tapped his breast pocket and repeated: 'Got it here. I'm not telling the others, for between you and me they've always been a bit superior about my efforts. But you've always believed in me,' he said, 'and I'll tell you.' "

"And he did?"

"Yes, he showed me his sketch plans. His idea was an improved combination of artificial silk and linen. He said that at last he had found a way of running a very fine linen thread through a solution of the silk so that it came out coated with silk, same as very fine electric wires are coated with a liquid insulator. He'd got this silk-covered thread all right in his workshop, but he didn't know how it would weave up and he was going to Belfast to get a special loom fitted up to try it."

"That's important news, Mr Magill. We knew that it was about this invention that Sir John had come to Belfast. Do you know who he was going to meet here?"

Victor had no idea.

Rainey nodded, then leaning forward, he spoke more earnestly.

"I hope you can tell us something more than this, Mr Magill. Do please think carefully. Was there any reason why Sir John might want to disappear? Had he no enemies? Was there no one who wanted his money? We are speaking in confidence. Tell us even your slightest suspicion, no matter how unsupported by evidence. Even if you're wrong no harm will be done. A hint at this stage might prove invaluable."

It was no use. Victor would have been only too glad to help, but he knew no more than Rainey.

"I confess I'm disappointed," returned the super-intendent, "but of course it can't be helped. You can't manufacture evidence any more than we can."

For some minutes they continued discussing the affair. To French, Victor seemed not only shocked by what he evidently believed would prove a tragedy, but he appeared also personally distressed about his uncle's fate. In fact he presently put his feelings into words. "I didn't see a great deal of my uncle," he said, in answer to one of Rainey's questions, "but I had a great respect and indeed admiration for him. And I think he liked me. He was always very decent to me anyway and I should be distressed on personal grounds to think of anything happening to him."

Presently the conversation swung round to Victor's cruise, and French, speaking for the first time, began to press for information. It was not likely to be needed, but there was no harm in knowing where Victor had been at the time of the tragedy.

"That's a matter, Mr Magill," he said, "in which I happen to be a good deal interested. A friend of mine has a motor launch and he wants me and a couple of other men to join him in just such a trip. It fell through this summer, but we hope to do it next spring. Would you mind dropping business for a moment and telling me something of your itinerary?"

Victor Magill looked at French with a slight surprise. His manner conveyed delicately that he had expected a more serious consideration for his family tragedy from a representative of Scotland Yard. But he replied politely enough.

"Certainly. The trip was suggested by a friend of mine named Mallace, who is keen on that sort of thing and has done a lot of it. Mallace has business relations with Barrow and knows the town intimately. He knew of a motor launch there for hire, a fifty-foot boat with good cabin accommodation and he asked me and two other men to join him on a cruise up the west coast as far as Skye."

"My friend's boat is not so large," French interjected.

"Fifty foot is a convenient enough size," Victor went on. "You want to keep your boat as small as possible for ease of handling as well as economy. On the other hand she must be big enough to stand a fair sea. Among those islands it sometimes blows up so quickly that you can't run for shelter. This boat suited us well. Normally one person could handle her and she was dry in a sea – full decked and plenty of freeboard. But she was slow. Old and rather clumsy and slow."

"Petrol fuel?"

"No, she had a petrol paraffin set. She was economical in oil, but a bit smelly. That's the worst of paraffin."

"It creeps, doesn't it? Ends by getting in the beer and the butter."

Before answering Victor gave a derogatory little cough and his manner made it clear that he intensely disapproved of the line the conversation was taking. But French did not seem to mind, continuing in his pleasant way to extract information as to the other's movement.

He and his friend Mallace, Victor explained, had travelled up from London to Barrow on the day express on the Wednesday, three days after he had seen Sir John in the park. They had reached Barrow about eight and had left almost at once for Portpatrick. There next day they had picked up the other two members of their quartet. One of these had been motoring in Scotland and had driven to Stranraer, garaging his car there till the end of the cruise. The other had unexpectedly been detained in London and had been unable to travel to Barrow. He had therefore travelled to Stranraer by the night train on Wednesday, going to Portpatrick on the Thursday.

"Then," said French, "he must have travelled in the same train as Sir John."

Victor stared at him.

"I suppose he must," he agreed. "I hadn't thought of that. In fact, I didn't know till this morning how my uncle had travelled. That's certainly a coincidence. Well, Joss, that's my friend's name, can't have seen him or known he was there, or he would have said something about it.

Though on second thoughts, I don't believe they knew each other."

"Then you really didn't make up your party till you reached Portpatrick?"

"No. Mallace and I weren't in more than a few minutes when the others joined us. Mallace had business in Stranraer, so we lay in port all day and that night left for Campbeltown. From Campbeltown we went to Port Ellen in Islay, then to Jura by Oronsay and Colonsay and through the Firth of Lorne to Oban. We were to go on, and the others have gone on, through the Sound of Mull to Skye, round Skye and home by the Sound of Sleat, Staffa and Iona and down the Sound of Jura. Quite a decent round."

"By Jove, yes! A jolly trip," French declared. "I'm afraid we'll not manage anything so elaborate, but it's been very interesting to hear what you did."

There was a pause, then Victor turned to Rainey.

"Well, Superintendent, I thought of staying over here for a day or two. I don't suppose you'll want me, but if there is anything I can do you'll find me with Major Magill. I'm going down to Larne now. I take it you're pushing the investigation all you can."

"You may rely on us, Mr Magill. Directly we get news we'll pass it on."

"None of that very illuminating," said Rainey, when Magill had taken his departure. "If we find this thing out, we're going to have to do it for ourselves. Now, inspector, we've talked enough about it. Let's decide on what we're going to do and get on with it. Any proposals?"

With the change in the superintendent's manner French also became more official.

"If you ask me, sir, I think we should concentrate on finding the body."

Rainey jerked himself round in his seat.

"There's not much doubt about that," he agreed. "Certainly we should find the body. There's nothing we'd all like so much as to find the body. But how do you suggest we should do it?"

French also moved uneasily.

"Well, sir, of course that's the trouble. I've been trying putting myself in the murderer's place. There he was with the body; fatal evidence which he'd got to get rid of. Now it seems to me that one or two things must have been done. Either the body must have been put into the sea or it must have been buried. And on the face of it the latter is the more likely."

Rainey looked up sharply.

"Why do you say that?" he asked.

"Only from my general experience," French answered. "I've had a number of cases in which bodies were got rid of in the sea and I've never known one successful. The bodies were always washed ashore or seen from a ship or hooked by a fisherman or got hold of in some other way. Of course I know this is not conclusive."

"No, it's not conclusive," Rainey agreed, "but it's my own opinion also and I've already gone into it. As it happens it's supported by a further consideration, not conclusive either, but still carrying a certain weight. It is this. There are only two places where such a scheme might be attempted. There is the sea on the Belfast Lough side of Islandmagee, that is here" – he pointed to the map – "and there is the sea along the Coast Road beyond Larne. These two places are on the open sea, for I think we may dismiss Lough Larne from our consideration – no one would be mad enough to try to hide a body in that shallow, land-locked area. Now take these others in turn. With regard to the coast near Whitehead there is nowhere, except in

Whitehead town itself, where you could get a car, especially a Rolls-Royce, anywhere near the actual shore. To get the body down would involve carrying it a long way. Further, most of the paths lead past houses and nearly all these houses have watchdogs. Now we have made inquiries, and no dogs were heard to bark that night. So the chances are against Whitehead."

French nodded without speaking.

"Now with regard to the Coast Road shore," Rainey went on. "Here the actual difficulties would be less – the road runs beside the beach and is lonely and deserted. But here with a flowing tide a strong current sets along the coast which would tend to wash the body into the path of shipping approaching Belfast. If Malcolm knew that, and he can scarcely have failed to do so, he would think twice before running such a risk. So that, quite tentatively, your second theory, burial, looks the more likely."

"That's just the way I should put it, sir," said French.

"Well then, it seems to me a matter of eliminating unlikely places and searching the remainder for signs of digging."

Rainey smiled ruefully.

"Some job, inspector," he protested.

"I don't think it would be such a very big job," French returned. "From what the sergeant here tells me, I should say that the areas that need be considered are very small indeed. There are no old mines or disused quarries or uncultivated lands in the neighbourhood. In fact, sir, I was going to suggest that somewhere about the major's own estate would be the most likely. The sergeant said it was sheltered by a wood. Where else could he guarantee the necessary privacy?"

Rainey paused.

"It's an idea and you may be right," he said dubiously. "M'Clung, you have been out at the place. What do you think of the inspector's idea?"

M'Clung moved uneasily.

"It might be right enough, sir," he answered without enthusiasm. "There's certainly a planting between the Coast Road and the avenue that wouldn't likely be disturbed. You couldn't tell what might have been done there."

"We'll have a look at it," Rainey decided. "Now, inspector, that's your theory, and very good it seems as far as it goes. But it does not go far enough. Sir John's coming to Ireland, his going first to Sandy Row, then to the Cave Hill and then to Whitehead, all seem to me to require some agent besides Malcolm. In short, I don't see how Malcolm could have arranged these."

French admitted that no more could he.

"Very well," Rainey went on, "that brings us back to my original theory – that the full solution is to be found in London."

French shook his head. He did not see what more could be learned in London. He was very willing to go back and try again, but he had little hope of the result.

"I think you'll have to try," Rainey insisted, "but wait till we see what this search of Lurigan produces. You might go down there with M'Clung and have a look round. To work properly in London you should know all that's known here. Of course call in and see me before you go."

"We'll have a bite of lunch, Mr French," M'Clung suggested as they left the room, "and then get away on down."

But the start was destined to be delayed. On returning to headquarters for the necessary search warrant they were told that Superintendent Rainey had that moment telephoned that they were to be stopped and sent in to him. They found him leaning back in his chair with a letter in his hand, at which he gazed with an expression of the keenest interest. He glanced up as they entered.

"Sit down again," he directed. "Here's something that'll surprise you. Look at this."

5

LURIGAN

Superintendent Rainey passed over a short, typewritten letter. The paper was of medium quality, a sheet torn off one of those multitudinous blocks or pads which are sold in every stationer's, and which unless through some accident, are so impossible to trace. The typing suggested that the writer was a novice in the art, there being seven mistakes in the lettering and three in the spacing. With some satisfaction French saw that the machine used had worn type. There should be no difficulty in identifying it, were he only lucky enough to come across it. The letter read:

Belfast, 7th October

The Chief of Police, Belfast.

SIR,

In view of certain rumours which, as you know, are current, I feel it my duty to inform you of the following facts:

While driving alone in my car along the Coast Road towards Larne at about 2.30 on the morning of Friday, 4th inst., I felt cramped from long sitting and decided to stop for a moment to stretch my legs. I did so just after passing Ballygalley Head and close to the gates of

Lurigan, Major Magill's residence. Among the trees of the small plantation between the road and the avenue I saw that some operations were in process. At least one figure was moving about and there were occasional gleams of a light. I do not know who was there or what he was doing, nor did I go to investigate.

This fact may have no significance – I trust it has not. But for the reason mentioned I think it my duty to report it to you. I do not wish to be brought into the affair, and as I can see that – whether there is anything wrong or not – my evidence is not essential, I am suppressing my name and address.

Yours, etc.,

XYZ

French gave vent to a low whistle as he read this communication.

"Bless my soul!" he said, "that's a bit of a coincidence, that is! Here were we talking about possible operations on that night at Lurigan, namely, the burial of Sir John Magill's body, and here not an hour later comes in a letter to say that such operations were actually seen! Here, sergeant," he went on, obeying a gesture from Rainey, "have a look over that. I suppose, sir," he turned back to the superintendent, "it's not likely to be a hoax?"

"A hoax? I should say it is, extremely likely. But we'll take it seriously for all that. I always do so in such cases as a matter of principle."

"So do we, sir. And many a vital hint we've got in just such a way. Two-thirty a.m.!" He paused, then added: "What's to prevent Malcolm committing the murder, arriving home at eleven-thirty, as he says, garaging the car with the body inside, and when his wife was asleep stealing out of the house, getting the body out of the car, and burying it?"

"Sounds all right, inspector," Rainey agreed. "That'll be something more for you to look into when you're down there this afternoon."

"We'll certainly look into it. I suppose, sir," French went on, "we couldn't get anything from the letter? The paper is ordinary, but the typewriter's old and distinctive."

"Not much good, that, to find our man," Rainey returned. "Useful to identify him if we had him, of course."

"What about fingerprints?"

"I'll have the paper tested, but the same remarks apply."

"The envelope?"

Rainey tossed it across.

"No help there either, I'm afraid. You see, it's simply addressed with the same machine to 'The Chief of Police, Belfast.' I'll try the inside of the flap for prints, but there's not much chance of getting any."

There was a pause, then Rainey continued: "Well, is that all? If so, I think you and M'Clung should get away. I'll see you when you get back."

The day was one of the finest French remembered for the time of year, as he and the sergeant set off in a police car for Larne. The road led along the shore of Belfast Lough, with high above them on the left the dominating outline of the Cave Hill. "There," said M'Clung, pointing to a couple of black dots at the bottom of the precipitous cliffs near the summit, "are the caves it gets its name from. They say they're prehistoric dwellings, but I don't suppose anyone knows that for sure." Some nine miles out came Carrickfergus with the fragments of its old walls and its splendidly preserved church and castle, built, tradition has it, when the second Henry sat on the English throne. Then on again, rising to a high windy cutting in the rock, aptly called the Blow Hole, where they called a momentary halt to see the view. From the shore far below them Belfast Lough stretched away to the city itself, with the range of the Antrim hills dominating it to the west and the County Down coast and its islands and lighthouse opposite. To the north were Lough Larne and Islandmagee, while farther east the Scotch coast showed dimly with, very faint and spectral in the far distance, the rocky cone of Ailsa Craig. M'Clung swung down into Whitehead and pointed out the telephone booth at the station, then returning to the main road, drew up at the place at which the hat had been found. After a look round they ran on through the picturesque country to Larne and out along the Coast Road.

About four miles beyond Larne, a few hundred yards before the turn round Ballygelley Head, lay Lurigan, the only house in sight. From the road, indeed only the chimneys were visible, for it stood back on a little plateau some fifty or sixty feet above the sea. M'Clung parked the car and they got out and looked about them.

Curiously enough, the point at which they had stopped formed the junction between two varieties of scenery. In front all was bleak and rugged. To the left was the series of cliffs which terminated in Ballygelley Head, not very high, but rocky and precipitous and strikingly massed, with the road at its base and the sea at the further edge of the road. All harsh and forbidding, without trees, and softened only by patches of rough grass clinging here and there on the stone. But the view looking back towards Larne might have been in another country. Here in the foreground the rocky cliffs gave place to grass slopes, which a little further along were covered by a thick matting of alders. These softer outlines ran back in a wide sweep to the headlands at

Larne, with the spiky memorial tower showing in the gap at the mouth of the harbour. Beyond, the line of Islandmagee continued on, with Muck Island looking as if some giant had chopped a bit off the end of the promontory.

The sea was a gorgeous blue right out to the horizon. Straight opposite, some five or six miles out, were the islands and lighthouses of the Maidens. Behind them, faintly in the distance, was Ailsa Craig, with far away on the left the hummock of Kintyre and on the right, to balance the picture, the long line of the Wigtownshire coast. Everywhere were birds, mostly gulls, poised or slowly wheeling on their graceful wings and uttering mournful cries as they went about their lawful occasions.

But interesting and delightful as were these sights, it was not upon them that French concentrated. The car had stopped at a quarry near a slight bend of the road, and not a hundred yards behind them was the Lurigan entrance. The drive, facing towards Ballygelley, swung round quickly through nearly two right angles and ascended the grassy slopes until it dived into a thicket of alders. There it turned inland, leaving a wide belt of trees between it and the road. To this belt M'Clung pointed.

"There's what we want, Mr French," he declared. "That'll be where our friend XYZ saw the moving light." There could be no doubt on the matter. The plantation was the only part of the Lurigan estate which could be overlooked from the road. If XYZ were telling the truth it was among these trees that they might expect to make their find.

Having noted the area inside which they must search, the two men climbed to the wood and began walking backwards and forwards, examining every inch of the surface. Here and there there were stunted firs and beneath them the ground was more or less clear, but the alders made a dense undergrowth. Search through these thickets was slow, but the men worked steadily on, not passing a single foot until they were sure the ground had not been disturbed. And then as they had reached the centre of the little wood, French's nerves gave a thrill and he came to a sudden stop. Yes, XYZ had not misled them nor had their deductions been faulty. Here was what they had been looking for.

Screened by alders before and behind was a clump of branches which at once attracted French's attention, for their leaves were drooping and they stood at awkward and unnatural angles. He gave one a sharp tug. As he expected, it came up without difficulty and proved to have no roots. Softly he called to M'Clung and the two men began to clear away the clump. The branches covered a freshly sodded mound some six feet long by two feet wide. Moreover on all the surrounding ground were traces of yellow clay.

"Boys, Mr French!" whispered M'Clung, his excitement causing him to revert to the speech of his fathers. "Did ever you see the like o' that? It's a grave!"

"It's a grave sure enough," French agreed, "and if it was made on that Friday morning as XYZ's story suggests, it's not hard to imagine whose body's in it."

M'Clung shook his head.

"It looks like the major," he declared. "It's hard to see who else could have done it."

"We'll consider that later," said French, glancing at his watch. "It's now after five o'clock and it'll be dark in no time. Suppose you run back to Larne and ring up your chief and arrange with him about opening this up. I'll stay here till you come back. I'm sure Superintendent Rainey will agree that Major Magill should be present at the opening. And if you ask me, mum's the word. This should be sprung on the major."

When M'Clung had gone French began slowly to pace to and fro. Certainly he agreed with the sergeant, this discovery did look bad for Major Magill. So far as he could see, no one but the major could have carried out the crime. No one else had the opportunity and the means. If the body of Sir John Magill lay here in this lonely plantation, it could only have been brought from Whitehead in a car, and who beside the major had on that night at once the necessary car, the motive and the knowledge?

In about an hour M'Clung returned and with him two constables from the Larne barracks. French joined them on the road.

"I rang up the superintendent," said M'Clung. "He says we can't open this up without an order from the Ministry of Home Affairs and he'll get one tomorrow. He'll come down first thing the day after. Meantime, Mr French, we're to clear out now and these two men will watch the place."

"Right, sergeant. What do we do then? Go back to Belfast?"

"A matter for yourself, sir. You'd likely be more comfortable in Belfast, but if you stay over in Larne it will save you an early start. The superintendent is starting at six-thirty to get the major in before he leaves for town."

"You're going back, are you?"

"I am, sir."

"Then I'll go too."

At thirty-three minutes past six two mornings later a large car left the city. In it were French, Rainey, M'Clung, two constables and Dr Finley, the police doctor. They retraced the road along which French had driven a couple of days earlier. The morning was exquisitely fresh and the colouring warm and vivid in the light of the rising sun. At a good speed they ran to Carrickfergus, then after a slack through the town, they pressed on again, until in just an hour and four minutes after starting they pulled up outside the gates of Lurigan.

For some minutes Rainey moved about, examining the grave and the lie of the surrounding land. Then with French he walked to the door and knocked.

"Is Major Magill about yet?" he asked the somewhat surprised-looking servant.

"He's in at breakfast, sir."

"Then give him my card and say that I should like to see him as soon as he has finished."

They were shown into a drawing-room on the right of the hall, from the bow window of which there was a fine view out over the sea. But they had not long to enjoy it. A thin, dark energetic looking man soon bustled into the room.

"Good morning, superintendent," he said doubtfully, holding out his hand. "Nothing wrong, I hope?"

"Let me introduce Detective Inspector French of the CID," said Rainey gravely. "We want to see you, Major Magill, on rather serious business, but we can wait till you've finished your meal."

Malcolm Magill's face changed.

"What?" he exclaimed. "Is there any news. Anything about my father?"

"There is some news," Rainey returned, "but, as I say, we can wait till you've breakfasted."

"Let's get on right ahead with it now," said Malcolm briskly. "I was just finishing and I've had all I want. Will you smoke?" He held out a gold cigarette case.

"No, sir, thank you. We want you, if you'll be good enough, to come out with us."

"Good Lord, but you're darned mysterious," said Malcolm with a smile, though there was no laughter in his eyes. "Is it close by?"

"Not five minutes away."

As they left the house the superintendent said in formal tones: "I have to tell you, Major Magill, that acting on information received, a search was made two days ago on this property." As he spoke his watch on the other was very keen. "A discovery was made, a very suggestive discovery, which may or may not prove important. Investigation of it was put off until this morning in order to have the benefit of your presence. This is the explanation of this early call. Here is the warrant under which we are acting."

French, also watching keenly, saw the bewilderment in the major's eyes change subtly to apprehension.

"As I said, you're darned mysterious," he repeated, but there was less assurance in his tone. "What is the nature of this discovery?"

"You will see in a moment."

By this time they had reached the point at which it was necessary to turn aside from the drive into the plantation. A moment more and they passed through the screen of trees and came in sight of the grave.

French found himself wondering whether anyone could show such signs of amazement as Major Magill did without really feeling it. Either the man did not know the grave was there or he was one of the best actors French had met. In somewhat shaky tones he gave vent to an oath and demanded of the superintendent what this thing meant.

"That's what we're here to find out," Rainey answered. "We wondered if you would care to make any statement about it. You needn't, of course, unless you like."

"Statement?" Magill cried. "I? Good heavens, super-intendent, you don't imagine I know anything about it, do you? I can assure you the thing's an absolute mystery to me. What it means or who made it I haven't the slightest idea."

"I'm glad to hear you say so," said Rainey. "The suggestion made is that this is a grave and it looks like a grave, so we're going to open it. It was necessary for you to be present while we did so."

The hint underlying the superintendent's words was not lost on Malcolm Magill. He paled somewhat and was evidently acutely uneasy. Both French and Rainey continued to watch him keenly. Two or three times he made as if to speak, but finally relapsed into silence, while a troubled look settled down on his features.

"Now, men," said Rainey, after a short pause, "start in and open this up."

Two constables armed with pickaxes and shovels stepped forward and began to remove the loose sods from the mound. But they had not got far before the group was hailed by a fresh voice. French, swinging round, saw Victor Magill approaching through the bushes.

"Hullo, everybody!" he called cheerily. "What's all this about? Morning, superintendent. I saw you from my window as I was finishing dressing. What on earth are you up to, Malcolm?"

At that moment he caught sight of the grave. He stopped dead and stood staring as if his eyes would leap out of their sockets.

"Good Lord!" he exclaimed in changed tones. For a moment he stood motionless, then moved slowly forward.

"What's the idea?" he went on. "Is this a treasure hunt? If so, don't let me interrupt." But his attempt at facetiousness did not ring true.

71

It was Rainey who replied.

"We don't know what may be here, Mr Magill," he said gravely, "but we are just about to find out. We were hoping that Major Magill or perhaps yourself could give us some information."

"I shouldn't think that was likely," Victor returned. "If either my cousin or myself knew anything that you should hear, you may be satisfied you would have heard it long ago."

Victor spoke coolly, but French could see that he was deeply moved. He stood looking at the mound with a frown on his features as if he was unable to credit the evidence of his senses. Twice French was thrilled to see him shoot little questioning glances at Malcolm's pale, troubled face. But he was not showing the same evidence of emotion as Malcolm. A real dread appeared in the latter's eyes and he was evidently unconscious of the fact that his hands were working convulsively.

A sense of impending disaster seemed to have fallen on all present. All remained silent, watching impatiently while the excavation slowly deepened. French was irresistibly reminded of a similar scene in which he had taken part – on the lonely Yorkshire moors near the ruins of the sinister old house of Starvel. There he had been searching for treasure – and had found a body. Here…?

But he had not so long to wait as he had expected. The excavation had scarcely reached a depth of two feet when one of the constables gave an exclamation.

"There's something here, sir," in evident excitement, and probing with his shovel. "See!"

"Open it up," Rainey directed curtly.

The atmosphere grew more tense as the little group moved instinctively closer and stared more fixedly into the hole. The constables worked more energetically, carefully removing the earth. As they did so a form gradually became revealed. It was wrapped in rough canvas and it was that of a human body.

"A stretcher, major," Rainey said in a low tone. "Can we have an old door or something?"

Major Magill nodded and with French and one of the constables moved towards the house. In the yard there was a small ramshackle wooden shed, and from this they tore the door. By the time they returned the remains had been cleared of earth, and they were reverently lifted on to the door. The canvas was rolled back, and there, unmistakable even to French, lay the smallish body and strongly marked features of Sir John Magill.

6

LURIGAN: LONDON: BELFAST

Except for a hoarse cry from Malcolm as the shroud was lifted aside, everyone stood as if turned to stone, staring silently at all that was left of the late magnate. The remains were a ghastly spectacle, for Time had already begun his terrible work. But of their identity there was no question. Apart from the formal identification given presently by both Malcolm and Victor, it was plain that here lay the original of the photograph.

Slowly the door with its grim burden was carried to the house and the preliminary examination began. French and M'Clung, setting their teeth, stripped off the clothes and took them to another room, while the doctor busied himself with the body. Rainey, evidently troubled by the problem with which he was faced in connection with Malcolm, hovered, frowning, between the two.

The clothes gave little of interest. The garments themselves bore no marks of any kind. Not even were they stained with mud or dust, as might have been expected from the condition in which the hat was found. The pockets contained just those articles which a man in Sir John's position might be expected to carry. There an old-fashioned but valuable gold watch, a knife, keys, a cigar case and loose coins to the value of 27s. 4d. In the pocket book were a number of cards bearing the words "Sir John Magill, 71 Elland Gardens, Knightsbridge, SW1," the return half of a first-class ticket from Euston to Belfast, via Larne, one or two unimportant letters, and notes amounting to £54 10s. On the little finger of the left hand was a ring bearing a large, blood-red ruby, worth in itself a considerable sum.

"There's only one thing here that may help us," French declared to Rainey.

"The keys?"

"Yes, sir. With luck we'll find the key of Sir John's safe and with luck we'll find his will in the safe. The will should be useful."

"Too late to matter. Now that we've found the body we could get powers to open the safe."

"No doubt, sir, but the key will save trouble, seeing we've permission to use it. Incidentally the money and ring prove that the motive was not robbery."

"Well, we never thought it was." Rainey spoke irritably. He was looking worried and French had no doubt as to the cause. Clearly the man couldn't make up his mind whether or not to arrest Major Magill. French could sympathise with his dilemma; it was one on whose horns he himself had often been impaled. If Malcolm vanished or committed suicide and were afterwards proved to be guilty, Rainey would be held to have shown unpardonable laxity and his very position might become precarious. On the other hand to arrest an influential man, a friend of the Ulster Prime Minister and intimate with the ruling classes, would, if he were found innocent, be an almost greater blunder. French said something of what was in his mind. "Yes, confound it," Rainey returned, "that's just the trouble. If the man's guilty and gives me the slip there'll be the very devil to pay. If I

75

charge him needlessly it'll be worse. I'm considering holding my hand and waiting developments."

"I think you'd be wise, sir, if I may say so. In cases of doubt I've usually found it the best policy. It's what we do at the Yard."

"I daresay you're right," Rainey answered. "Hullo, here's the doctor looking as if he wanted us."

Dr Finley, the police doctor, was tall and thin and efficient-looking. As he joined the others he glanced round to see that they were alone.

"You told me something about this case on the way down, superintendent," he said, "from which I understood, rightly or wrongly, that Sir John had been the victim of a crime of violence. His blood-stained hat, for example, had been found?"

"That's right, Dr Finley. The hat was found and there were traces of blood and marks of a struggle on the ground at the place."

"Then you'd expect some signs of bleeding from the body?"

"I certainly would."

"Well, there aren't any."

"What?" Rainey exclaimed. "No signs at all?"

"None."

"Then what was the cause of death?"

"I'm not absolutely certain. Before I give an opinion I must make an autopsy."

"Good heavens, doctor, this is very surprising! You evidently have a suspicion of what took place. You won't tell us?"

"I hardly like to put forward suspicions," Dr Finley returned. "If I make an autopsy I can tell you at once."

Rainey shrugged, but made no further comment.

"Right, doctor. I'll get you the authority. You'll want some help. Get whoever you think best and I'd be obliged if you'd push on with it as quickly as possible." Then as the doctor disappeared into the next room he turned to French. "What do you make of this, inspector? It gives our theories a jar, what?"

"It may settle your problem about Major Magill, sir."

Rainey looked at him sharply. "Meaning?"

"If that blood didn't come from Sir John it must have come from the murderer. If it came from the murderer some trace would remain for twelve hours, a cut hand, a swollen lip or nose. Major Magill was at headquarters within twelve hours of the crime. The question is – Were there any signs of injury on him?"

"Good, French, very good! I'll swear there were no marks of any kind, but we'll ask M'Clung." They strolled over to where the sergeant was at work. "You saw Major Magill when he called at headquarters on the morning after the murder. Any signs of injury or bleeding about him?"

For a moment M'Clung looked doubtful, then his expression cleared. He was positive there had been no such indications. Of course a man's nose might bleed without leaving marks, but he was sure Major Magill's had not bled from injury.

" 'Pon my soul, French, that's very puzzling. If those drops of blood came from neither Sir John nor Malcolm Magill, who did they come from? Who else was there?"

He paused, whistling tunelessly between his teeth. "However," he went on, "there is something to be thankful for. This settles the hash about the major. Under the circumstances I wouldn't be justified in arresting him."

"It would be wiser not, sir, if I might say so. Particularly if it turned out that death was from natural causes."

Rainey swung round.

"From natural causes? Oh, come now, French. What about the struggle?"

"I think, sir, there might be an explanation of that, but it's admittedly a bit far fetched. Suppose the major, in going back towards Whitehead, found Sir John lying dead on the road. Or suppose that he found him in good health and that Sir John got a heart attack and died after they met. Sir John might have fallen and the major might have thought his head had struck the ground and would show a bruise. The major would see that he was in an awkward hole. He was alone with his father. It would be known that he was hard up and that he would stand to get a large sum at the old man's death. He might get panicky that his story wouldn't be believed and fake the struggle and bury the body."

"Your own argument: the blood?"

French grinned.

"He could have cut his arm above sleeve level."

Rainey smiled reproachfully and shook his head as he thought over this.

"I suppose it's possible," he admitted, "but to my mind it's darned unlikely. However, we'll keep it in view. Now, French, is there anything else? I must get in touch with the coroner and fix up about the inquest."

The first question to be settled was whether the inquiry should be concluded immediately or adjourned for further investigation after the taking of formal evidence of identity. After considerable thought Rainey decided – rather against French's advice – to recommend the former. He explained to the coroner, first, that the attention of the police had been called to the affair, not by the discovery of the body, but by Sir John's disappearance, and that the time which had elapsed since that disappearance had enabled all the obvious inquiries to be made, and second, that such further investigation as might be desirable could best be made secretly, the publicity resulting from its being discussed at the inquest tending to defeat its aim.

All this seemed to French to be special pleading of a rather blatant kind and with some amusement he recognised in it Rainey's endeavour to shift the responsibility of the arrest or otherwise of Malcolm Magill from his own shoulders to those of the coroner's jury. If that august body should bring in a verdict of guilty against Malcolm his hand would be forced and he could not be blamed if Malcolm was afterwards proved to be innocent; whereas if in the face of the evidence the jury plumped for a person or persons unknown it would give him moral support in a policy of apparent inaction.

Eventually it was decided that unless some unforeseen point arose during the hearing, adjournment would be made, and the inquest was fixed for the afternoon of the third day. This was Friday and the hour of 1.30 p.m. on the Monday following was agreed on. It was believed that this would give ample time for the post mortem as well as the search for the will in London, while so far as the remains were concerned, it was felt that another three days' delay would make little difference. The coroner decided that the inquiry should take place at Lurigan, as he thought that the jury should view not only the body but the grave also.

Armed with Sir John's keys, French that night crossed back to London and next morning opened the safe in the deceased's study. He had asked the senior partner of Messrs Hepplewhite, Ingram & Ingram, Sir John's lawyers, to be present, as well as the secretary, Breene. Immediately he found the missing will. After a glance he put it aside and spent a couple of hours going through the remaining papers. But there was nothing else bearing even remotely on the old gentleman's fate. Nor was there a trace of any plans, either of the linen – silk invention or of anything else. Then, having asked Sir John's stockbroker to join them, he and Mr Ingram read the will and worked out what its provisions meant at the current date.

The summary given French by Miss Magill proved substantially correct. £50,000 was left to each of the sisters, Beatrice and Caroline, the Knightsbridge house going in addition to the elder sister. Another £50,000 was consumed by small legacies to servants and others as well as in gifts to charities. Of these Breene's name was down for £5,000. A sum of £400,000 was left in trust. Malcolm was to have the life use of it and at his death it was to go to his son. If Malcolm had no male issue it was to go to Sir John's only other male relative, Victor Magill. He also was to have the life use of it and similarly at his death it was to go to his son. Of this arrangement Malcolm and Victor were appointed trustees. If Victor had no son the money at his death was to be divided equally among any surviving members of the family. All these bequests were to be free of legacy duty, the residuary legatee being Malcolm.

The whole of these provisions seemed clear enough except the last, but to ascertain the amount coming to Malcolm as residuary legatee meant a spell of exceedingly hard work lasting for the entire afternoon. Even then a good many of the figures arrived at were estimates rather than actually calculated amounts. But at last a sum was reached which it was agreed could not be much in error. By this Malcolm as residuary legatee received £124,000.

It followed therefore that as a result of his father's death Malcolm would receive £174,000 absolutely, as well as a life interest in £400,000 more. And French believed that if

Malcolm were unscrupulous enough to commit a murder for gain, he would have little difficulty in converting at least a portion of this trust to his own use.

Here then was all that the most exacting jury could require in the way of motive. Malcolm was in financial difficulties, Malcolm stood to gain by his father's death, Malcolm...As French sat in the 8.30 Stranraer boat train on Sunday night he ran over the familiar steps of the argument. And the more he did so, the more adequate they sounded.

He went through to Belfast and by half past nine was seated once more in Rainey's office. The superintendent did not seem over-pleased with his report.

"That's life," he grumbled. "And it's drama too," he added as an afterthought. "Here you turn up with a bit of evidence that a couple of days ago we'd have given our ears for, and while you're getting it we're learning that it's no use to us. I'll tell you," he went on in answer to French's look. "We've learned a good deal since you left. We've pretty well got proof of Malcolm's innocence, or rather we never could get a conviction against the evidence that's turned up." He shook his head disgustedly.

French still looked his question and Rainey went on in the manner of a professional demonstrating a mathematical proposition.

"First look at it from the point of view of time. Sir John was alive in Whitehead at nine o'clock on Thursday night. He was murdered – for it was murder – either that night or shortly after. It was just a week till we found the body and both doctors agree that death must have taken place about a week earlier. They couldn't tell that to the day, but they're both prepared to swear death took place before Sunday."

French nodded.

"Now, will you admit one other point? The man who buried the body was the murderer?"

This also seemed unquestionable. It was the obviously likely thing; besides there was no suggestion in the evidence of a second person being involved.

"Very good, sir," French agreed.

"We know already that Malcolm Magill must have left his home by the usual time on the next morning, Friday, because of the time he called at the Grand Central Hotel and here. But we've since learned that he went from here to the mill and remained there till the afternoon. Then he motored to Derry and spent Friday night, Saturday and Saturday night with some friends at a little place called Culmore. He returned on Sunday, reaching home in time for tea. All that we have checked up and it has been established beyond question. It therefore follows that if Malcolm did not bury the body on that Thursday night or Friday morning he did not bury it at all."

Once again Rainey paused for French's agreement.

"The question then left is: Did Malcolm bury the body on Thursday night or Friday morning? If he did, he is guilty, if not, he is innocent."

French nodded as he changed his position.

"That's what I like, sir," he declared; "getting things cut and dry like that. There's no doubt you're right so far."

"I think it's right enough," Rainey agreed. "Now that night is divided into two parts, up till Malcolm's arrival home, and after it. Let us consider the first part.

"Malcolm's movements with the car have been absolutely demonstrated. He could not by any possibility have run to Lurigan with the body before his final return at 11.25 – there would not have been time. Therefore if he brought the body to Lurigan it could only have been on that last journey. Further, on that occasion he left Whitehead at 10.55 and reached Lurigan at 11.25 – fourteen miles – an average of twenty-eight miles an hour, good enough for night travelling. It would therefore have been utterly impossible for him to have stopped on this trip to bury the body. Therefore he could not have done it till after his arrival home."

French readily agreed.

"Now from 11.43 at night, when Malcolm rang up his friends at Whitehead, until 7.0 next morning, when both the servants heard him going to his bath, we have Mrs Magill's positive statement that he never left the house. Of course such a statement doesn't amount to much if unsupported, though I think if you knew the lady you'd give it a good deal of weight. But it so happens there is confirmation. For two or three days before this, Malcolm had been slightly unwell, some small internal upset. Whether due to worry about his father or from some other cause, this developed on his return home into a sharp bilious attack. Mrs Magill was up with him most of the night and the servants were wakened, first to look for a bottle of medicine which had been lent to the cook and which she had not returned, and secondly, to heat water for hot water bottles. About five in the morning the attack passed over and Malcolm fell asleep. When seven o'clock came Malcolm insisted on getting up, though he was by no means well. The Magills' statement is amply confirmed by the servants and we have questioned everyone so carefully as to preclude the possibility of a concerted story. The house was disturbed practically all night and in my opinion it would have been utterly impossible for Malcolm to have slipped out secretly and remained out for the time required for burying the body."

French was puzzled. This seemed conclusive enough, and yet…

"Suppose the major deliberately took something to upset himself," he said doubtfully.

Rainey twisted impatiently.

"Suppose he did, French, suppose he did. How would that affect things? If Malcolm had given his household mild sleeping draughts, that would be another matter. But surely to goodness he wouldn't do anything to keep them awake. Besides there's another – "

There was a knock at the door and a constable entered and saluted smartly.

"Beg pardon, sir," he said. "The Commissioner's compliments and he'd be obliged if you could step up and see him now," adding as a sort of personal aside, "he's got some gentleman from the Home Office with him."

Rainey swore impatiently. "That'll take me the rest of the morning till it's time to start for that infernal inquest. And there was more I had to tell you, also confirming Malcolm's innocence."

French sighed. If all this new evidence were true it meant that they hadn't begun to solve their case.

"But there's no suspicion against anyone but Malcolm," he lamented.

"No," said Rainey as he rapidly collected papers from his desk, "and I'll tell you why. The murderer is an Englishman and the secret lies in England."

French shrugged. If the superintendent was going to take that line there was nothing more to be said. But Rainey gave him no time to say anything, even if he had wished to.

"Don't misunderstand me or think I am criticising what you have done, French," he said kindly. "It's not that at all. Simply I believe there's more in this case than we've yet tumbled to. We may never get it. But I think we should try. Sorry I've to go. We'll get a bite of lunch and make your own way down to Larne. I'll see you at the inquest."

– 7 –

LURIGAN

As the appointed hour drew near a formidable fleet of cars blocked up the approaches to Malcolm Magill's house. Besides the coroner, the police, the jury and the witnesses, a goodly number of the general public had attended in the hope of gaining admission. The details of the finding of the body had got into the papers, and apart from Malcolm's prominent position, the sensational nature of the case had aroused intense interest all over the province.

The dining-room, a long low room with bow window at both side and end, had been cleared for the occasion. At the head of the table sat Dr Wylie, the coroner, a medical practitioner with a reputation for extreme shrewdness as well as kindliness and professional skill. Near him were Rainey, French and M'Clung. Beside M'Clung was a small, dark, vivacious-looking man whom French did not know. At the foot of the table on a couple of rows of chairs sat the jury. Representatives of the press were accommodated at a side table, while the remainder of the room was filled by two or three constables, a long row of witnesses and as many members of the general public as could squeeze themselves in.

After the preliminaries and the viewing of the body and grave had been completed, the coroner briefly addressed the jury. He was afraid, he said, the case was a complicated one and would occupy a good deal of their time. He knew, however, that they would give this ungrudgingly in the interests of justice. But before going on to the evidence he thought he would only be interpreting their wishes if he were to express to Major Magill and Mr Victor Magill, who, he understood, was also present, as well as the other members of the late Sir John Magill's family, their sympathy with them in their tragic loss. And now, sergeant, who was the first witness?

At this the vivacious man jumped up and said that he appeared for Major Magill. In answer to French's look Rainey whispered that he was a Mr Dinsmore, one of the best-known and most skilful criminal lawyers in Northern Ireland.

Sergeant M'Clung, instructed by Superintendent Rainey, was in charge of the case for the police, and very nervous he looked. It was his first really big case and he found the presence of so many "high up" people embarrassing. However he rose to his feet and in a firm voice called "Malcolm Howard Magill!" indicating immediately that this mode of address was not of his own choosing by adding in a more deprecating tone, "Come forward, if you please, sir."

Malcolm looked pale and ill at ease as he stepped to the table and was sworn. The ceremony over, M'Clung solicitously pulled forward a chair, and when Malcolm had seated himself his examination began.

Under the coroner's not unskilful lead Malcolm first deposed that the body on which the inquest was being held was that of his father, John Porter Magill. He next told of his father's career in Belfast and retirement to London, and of the handing over of the mills to himself. He described the relations which had obtained between himself and his father, including his recent request for financial assistance and its refusal. He denied absolutely that this refusal had led to any estrangement or bitter feelings on the part of either concerned. Then he recounted the receipt of Sir John's letter saying he was crossing to Belfast and asking to be put up, his own call at and subsequent telephone to the Grand Central Hotel, and his surprise at not seeing Sir John at the mill. He told of the telephone from Whitehead and of his taking out his car to search for his father. In detail he described his movements with the hours of his arrival and departure at the various places, followed next morning by his call at police headquarters in Belfast. Finally he spoke of the discovery of Sir John's body in the plantation and his own horror and mystification thereat.

During Malcolm's evidence there was more than one passage at arms – skilfully veiled under the guise of a respectful request for information – between his solicitor, the vivacious Mr Dinsmore, and the coroner. It was surprising to both French and Rainey to notice how little attempt Dinsmore made to hide the fact that he considered his client's position precarious. To every question which might bring out a fact prejudicial to Malcolm he strenuously objected. Some of these objections the coroner finally admitted and some he did not.

These activities of Dinsmore's revealed to an otherwise unsuspecting jury the significance of a good deal of the evidence. French observed more than one juror looking at Malcolm with a surprised, questioning air. And the further Malcolm's evidence went, the more self-conscious and uneasy Malcolm himself appeared. He evidently realised what was indeed the fact, that he was making a painfully bad impression on his audience.

However, his evidence came to an end at last and he stepped back from the table. When he had signed his deposition Herbert Breene came forward and took the oath. He stated that he was an ex-army man and that he had acted as secretary to Sir John for the previous eight years. He told about Sir John's statement that he was crossing to Belfast to see an engineer about his linen – silk invention and his instruction that he, Breene, should be at the Grand Central Hotel at 10.30 the following morning to take details of any agreement that might be come to between them. He described his fruitless wait in the hotel all that day and night. He had seen the body and he identified it as Sir John's. The deceased was a wealthy man, blessed with good health and a cheerful disposition. He, Breene, did not believe he had an enemy in the world.

Here the coroner asked some searching questions as to the alleged disagreement on financial matters between Sir John and Malcolm. But he did not get much from Breene, who merely said that so far as he knew there had been a difference of opinion, but neither serious nor heated and not in any sense a quarrel.

Breene gave his evidence quietly, but with a convincing force. "I'll take you next yourself, sergeant," the coroner decreed and M'Clung in his turn took the oath.

Asked to recount in his own words the steps taken by the police as a result of Malcolm's call, the sergeant described the checking of the movements first of Sir John and then of Malcolm and Breene, as recounted in Malcolm's statement. Then he told of the discovery of the marks of the struggle and of the hat. He mentioned Malcolm's second visit to police headquarters to suggest that the co-operation of Scotland Yard should be sought, following this with an account of his own visit to London and French's taking over of the English end of the inquiry. Next he read the XYZ letter and described the search of the Lurigan plantation and the discovery and opening of the grave.

While all this evidence was being given, popular interest, which had been keen enough at the start, had grown to fever heat. The reason for Malcolm's uneasiness seemed now to be realised on all sides, and while no one would meet his eye, he became the object of covert stares from all parts of the room.

Myles, the butler, was next called. He identified the clothes in which the body was found as those Sir John was wearing on the night he left London. He also identified the hat, produced, as that worn by Sir John on the same occasion. He confirmed Breene's evidence as to his master's character and temperament, bearing testimony to the kindness he himself had received at his hands.

The stationmaster at Larne was the next witness. He had seen the remains and they were those of a gentleman who had come off the Stranraer boat on the morning of Thursday, 3rd October. This gentleman had given his name as Sir John Magill. The stationmaster then went on to tell of Sir John's request that his luggage should be sent to Major Magill's, and how he had seen him leave in the train for Belfast.

Superintendent Rainey then got up and said that evidence had been obtained from various witnesses which led to the presumption that Sir John had spent the day in Belfast, travelling to Whitehead by the eight o'clock that night. None of this information, however, had seemed material to the police and they had not therefore called these witnesses. Should, however, the coroner desire, they would be produced.

To this the coroner replied that he noted the superintendent's statement, and should he think it necessary when he had heard the remainder of the evidence, he would say so.

The stationmaster at Whitehead was next called. He deposed that a man, whom he afterwards identified as deceased, had come off the 8.0 p.m. train ex Belfast, arriving at Whitehead at 8.47. He told of deceased's inquiry for Mr Rimbolt and his annoyance when he was informed that Mr Rimbolt was then living at Bangor. Finally he described deceased's inquiry about a telephone, his use of the booth on the up platform, and his subsequent departure from the station in the direction of the Larne road.

A good deal of this evidence had seemed to the audience tame and dull after the sensational suggestions as to Malcolm's possible part in the affair. But when the next witness proved to be Detective Inspector Joseph French of the Criminal Investigation Department of New Scotland Yard, interest revived sharply. No one present except the police officers had ever seen a real live CID man and he was immediately accepted as the *pièce de résistance* of the entertainment. There was a little buzz through the room as people settled themselves to listen more intently.

French, however, proved a disappointing star turn. His quiet businesslike manner did nothing to quicken the pulse or touch the emotions, nor did the matter of his testimony arouse any excitement. His evidence, in fact, was practically confined to the discovery of the will, of which he handed in a certified copy. But the doctors stimulated the flagging interest.

Dr Finley was the first to be called. He began quietly enough by stating that he had examined the remains and had found that while there was a bruise above the right temple, the skin was not anywhere broken. But when after being reminded of the bloodstains on the road he repeated his statement to Rainey and French that this blood could not have come from the deceased, the proverbial pin could have been heard to drop. Everyone sat staring at Finley with an air of tense expectancy.

"Were you able from your examination of the remains to state the cause of death?" the coroner went on imperturbably.

"No, sir," Finley answered, "not with certainty."

"You therefore held a post mortem?"

"I did, with the help of my colleague, Dr Simpson."

"And did this reveal the cause of death?"

"It did."

"Just tell the jury what that was."

Interest still further tensed as those present instinctively leaned forward the better to hear the reply.

"Death was due to shock following a severe blow on the head above the right temple. The skull was fractured though the skin remained unbroken."

"How in your opinion might such an injury have been inflicted, Dr Finley?"

"It seemed to me that some soft and yielding though heavy weapon had been used, such as a sandbag."

There was a little movement among the audience. Things at last were going as they should. The coroner went on: "In your opinion, doctor, could this blow have been self-inflicted?"

"Quite impossible, I should say."

The coroner wrote for some seconds, then looked up.

"There is also the consideration that no such weapon nor indeed any kind of weapon was found," he remarked, continuing: "Now, Dr Finley, another thing. Does the position of this bruise suggest anything to you as to the positions which deceased and his murderer must have occupied when the fatal blow was struck?"

Dr Finley answered without hesitation.

"If the murderer were right-handed I should suggest that he was standing behind and rather to the right of deceased. If he were left-handed the reverse would be the case; they would be standing face to face."

Again the coroner wrote.

"Was that all that you learned from your examination of the remains?"

"It was all that my colleague and I learnt directly. But to make the examination complete we sent the stomach and certain other organs to the police analyst for chemical analysis."

"And did you get a reply from him?"

Dr Finley assented. "I believe he is in court," he added.

After a few more questions Dr Simpson was called. He corroborated Dr Finley's evidence in every particular. Then M'Clung called "Professor M'Grath!" and a fresh-faced man looking more like a successful businessman than a professor of science, entered the box.

"You are Professor Henry M'Grath, gold medallist at the London University and the holder of many other scientific distinctions, and now act as police analyst of Belfast?"

"That is so."

"Did you receive from Drs Finley and Simpson certain organs taken from the body on which this inquest is being held?"

"I received certain organs. I understand they were taken from the body you mention."

"Did you submit these organs to analytical tests?"

"I did."

"Please tell the jury what you found."

At this question interest, if possible, intensified. The audience once again instinctively bent forward, the better to hear the reply.

"I found in the stomach and intestines a trace of trional."

"Trional? That is a sedative, isn't it?"

"Yes, it's used for sleeping draughts."

"And what quantity did you find present?"

"About twenty-five grains."

"Is that enough to cause serious injury?"

"Oh, no. It represents a single fairly large sleeping draught only. It should not have had any permanent ill effects."

The audience, cheated of their sensation, relaxed. But not a few faces showed bewilderment. The coroner wrote industriously.

"Then your evidence is that at some time previous to his death the deceased had taken a sleeping draught?"

"That he had taken a quantity of trional such as might be found in a sleeping draught," Professor M'Grath amended.

"How soon would such a draught take effect?"

"It is not possible to say with any degree of accuracy, as the time is modified by so many unknown factors. Different people react differently to drugs, and the same person will react differently according to his condition. For instance, if a man has just eaten a heavy meal, reaction will be slower than if his stomach were empty."

"I can understand that, professor, but can you not give us some idea?"

"From half an hour to two hours, I should say. I couldn't go closer."

"Half to two hours," the coroner repeated. "Now, professor, can you say how long this draught was taken before death?"

Professor M'Grath shook his head.

"That is even more difficult to answer. The most I could say is, probably within eight to ten hours, but I could not state that with certainty."

"Might it have taken place within four or five hours?"

"Undoubtedly it might."

French was a good deal impressed by this evidence, which was clearly what Rainey had been going to tell him when interrupted. It certainly tended to confirm Rainey's theory of Malcolm's innocence. If the sleeping draught might take effect within half an hour, it could have been taken before, say, nine o'clock. And though the professor would not commit himself as to the time between the taking of the draught and the murder, from his reply it would seem at least several hours. If therefore Malcolm really had been ill that night, he was innocent.

The evidence also explained a point which had given French a good deal of worry. The murderer, whether Malcolm or some other person – for French was still not convinced of Malcolm's innocence – had conveyed Sir John, alive or dead, from Whitehead to Lurigan in a car. French concluded that it was in a car because he could see no other way in which the journey could have been made. Now, would anyone risk carrying a dead body in that way, when at any moment some accident or unforeseen circumstance might lead to the stoppage of the car and an investigation of its contents? French had always doubted it. But if the criminal drugged his victim with a harmless sleeping draught before starting the run, and murdered him only when he was about to destroy the evidence of his crime by hiding the remains, that would be an entirely different proposition. French was interested also in the choice of the sedative, one which could be purchased without a doctor's prescription.

It was now beginning to look as if Sir John had been met and drugged shortly after he left Whitehead, probably on the pretext that a nip of brandy on a cold night would do him no harm. There would then have been no danger in driving him to Lurigan. If his presence were discovered he would no doubt be asleep, but he would wake well and unharmed and no suspicions would arise.

The more French thought over this theory, the more convinced he became that it was the truth. Moreover the hours worked in. If Sir John had been drugged about nine or half past, four to six hours later would bring it to half past two when XYZ saw the operations in progress in the plantation. This would –

French suddenly awoke to the fact that he was daydreaming and missing what was going on. At once he switched his mind back to the proceedings, to find that Professor M'Grath was just returning to his seat. He was the last witness and when the coroner had adjusted his papers he addressed the jury. After some preliminary remarks on the serious and tragic nature of the evidence, he proceeded to recapitulate it in detail. Then putting aside his notes, he went on in serious tones: "Your duty is threefold. First, you have to say whose in your opinion is the body on which this inquest has been held, provided you are satisfied as to the identity in your own minds. Here I do not think you will have much difficulty. Secondly, you have to state the cause of death, again provided the evidence has left no reasonable doubt in your minds. Here again I think you will find your task easy. The medical evidence to my mind is clear, and I am sure you will agree that the deceased met his death as the result of a blow delivered by some heavy but yielding weapon such as a sandbag. Unfortunately that does not end the matter so far as you are concerned. You are to say, if you feel that you can do so from the evidence, how this injury came to be sustained. And here I need scarcely remind you that such an injury might conceivably have been caused in one of three ways: as the result of accident, suicide or murder. Should you think that the evidence justifies you in so doing, you will say to which of these three categories the present instance in your opinion belongs. Unfortunately again, even this may not end the matter so far as you are concerned. Should you find that this death falls into the last of the three categories, that it is in fact a case of murder, then you must consider who may be guilty of that murder. If in your opinion the evidence on this point is inconclusive, you will bring in a verdict of wilful murder against some person or persons unknown. On the other hand, if you feel reasonably certain from the evidence of the identity of the murderer or murderers, you will bring in your verdict against that person or those persons." With a peroration about the importance of their office, the coroner dismissed the jury to consider their verdict.

And a lot of consideration it evidently took! For upwards of two interminable hours the remainder of the little gathering waited, afraid to go away and unable to settle down even to talk connectedly, while the shadows lengthened across the lawn and the light faded from the western sky. Rainey, French and M'Clung were frankly bored and anxious to get away, Malcolm Magill was pale and apprehensive, even Victor and the solicitor, Dinsmore, were anxious-looking, while the spectators still hoped for their sensation. Not one of them but would have given something he valued to have that period of waiting at an end.

At last, just after seven o'clock, there was a movement, and the jury filed back into their places. Everyone straightened up and the atmosphere once more became tense as the coroner asked the momentous question, "Gentlemen, are you agreed on your finding?"

The jury, the foreman assured him, were agreed on their finding, but it was not the finding which most of those present expected to hear. A scarcely veiled disappointment could even be seen on more than one face as the foreman read out the verdict, disappointment at being baulked of a major sensation. For no mention was made of Major Magill. The verdict was the familiar one of wilful murder against some person or persons unknown.

8

BELFAST

"Well," said French, when next morning he had reached Superintendent Rainey's room at police headquarters, "that verdict was a surprise and no mistake. I'd have bet long odds they'd have found against the major. They didn't know all that we know about his illness."

"A case of the benefit of the doubt," Rainey returned. "A local man of well-known family; employer of labour and popular at that. It all counts. They didn't want to commit themselves unless they were forced."

"But they believed him guilty all the same."

"I daresay they did. Still I question if they weren't wise. They did their duty. They found the cause of death and left it at that."

French smiled as he thought of Rainey's effort to shunt the problem of arrest.

"You, sir, and I have more responsibility than if we were one of twelve on a coroner's jury. What they think or the verdict they bring in makes no matter to anyone except themselves, but what you think may make a very serious difference to quite a number of people."

Rainey nodded, though there was something suspicious in the glance he shot at French.

"I should like my friend the coroner to hear you," he declared. "He has a pathetic belief in the value of – "

The door opened and M'Clung looked in.

"Excuse me, sir," he said, "but there's a man here says he's got some evidence on this Magill case. If it's true it seems important. I thought maybe you'd like to see him yourself."

"By all means, M'Clung. Bring him in."

The sergeant disappeared and in a few seconds returned with a stalwart young fellow of about three and twenty. He had the unmistakable appearance of a working man in his Sunday clothes and he was no less obviously nervous and self-conscious.

"Good morning," Rainey said pleasantly. "You have some information for us? Come and sit down and tell us about it. Put out a chair for him, M'Clung."

The young giant sat down awkwardly and began twisting his cap in his huge bony hands. Rainey saw that some help would be necessary.

"You were right to come to us with anything you know," he went on encouragingly. "Now perhaps I'd better ask you some questions. To begin with, what is your name?"

"William M'Atamney." He put the accent on the "tam."

"Yes, and your business?"

"I'm a cleaner on the Northern Counties Railway."

"A cleaner? Oh, yes, an engine cleaner, you mean?"

"That's right, mister."

"And where do you live?"

"In Belfast, at 12 Monkton Street, off the Shore Road."

"And your work is in Belfast too?"

"Yes, I work mostly in Belfast, but whiles I'm sent away relieving at other stations."

"I follow you. Engine cleaners usually work at night, don't they?"

"They do that."

"I see. Now I think we know who you are. Just start now and tell us your news."

M'Atamney shuffled on his chair and gave his cap a special flourish.

"Well – ah – " he began, "it was Thursday was a week, Thursday night. Cleaner M'Givern he was off duty at Larne, an' they sent me down for to relieve him. Well, I had Number Fifty to clean; she's broad gauge, ye understand, an' I was workin' in the broad gauge shed." He paused to collect his thoughts, then went on again. "Well – ah – Number Fifty was wanted out early an' I'd wrought hard for to be sure she'd be ready. I had her all done only the wheels an' motion an' then I thought I was well enough on with her an' I might quit for a wee while an' have a fag. So I went out just for a wee walk to myself, don't you see?"

"I follow you," Rainey nodded.

"Well – ah – " resumed the cleaner, "it was a fine night, warm for the time o' year, but dark. I went across the yard and sat on the edge o' the passenger platform facin' the sea an' lit up my fag."

Rainey turned to French.

"I know the place, inspector. The railway runs immediately along the edge of Larne Lough. Between this platform and the Lough there are just two sets of metals, the platform line and a run round siding. That right, M'Atamney?"

"That's right, mister. Well – ah – I'd only sat there about three or four minutes when I heard steps comin' along the line from the Belfast direction. I thought to myself, 'Here's Billy M'Neill,' I thought – that's another cleaner who'd slipped home a bit before that for his meat – 'I'll give him a bit of a start.' So I sat there an' never let on till he was just opposite me, an' then I jumped out and shoved my electric torch in his face. Man, but I gave him the queer ould scare! He let a screech an' for a minute he couldn't move, an' then he just slipped past me an' away as hard as he could lick for the Harbour."

"And was it your friend?"

"It was not," M'Atamney returned darkly.

Rainey curbed his impatience, though his foot swung irritably.

"Yes? Then who was it?" he asked sweetly.

"It was him," the cleaner answered with dramatic emphasis and a backward jerk of the head.

"Him? Who?"

"Why him that was buried out at Major Magill's."

"What!" cried Rainey. "Sir John Magill? How do you know?"

"I know rightly," M'Atamney declared. "I saw him as well as I see you with the torch shone fair in his face. I'd seen his likeness in the Telly" – ("The *Belfast Telegraph*," interjected Rainey) – "An' then before I went home this morning I went round to Johnnie Gough, him 'at writes for the Telly, an' sez he, 'That was him right enough,' he sez, 'an' away you to the polis in Chi-chester Street an' tell them what you've seen. If you don't go, I will,' he sez, an' so I came on up."

"You did well. And what was the man like?"

"He was a weeish man, not very wee nor very big neither, an' thin an' with a bit of a stoop. His face was like the picture an' he had a bald head an' white hair. He hadn't any hat, but he had an overcoat on."

"You're positive of this, M'Atamney?"

"I'm certain sure."

"Was he walking quickly?"

"No, he wasn't. He was walking as if he'd gone a long way an' was queer an' tired."

"Did you speak to him?"

"No, I was that surprised I never said a word."

"Now, M'Atamney, here's an important question. At what time did all this happen?"

"Just half twelve. I know for I looked at my watch before I started so as I wouldn't stay too long."

"Well," said Rainey, "you've done well to come to us and tell us this. We're much obliged to you, I'm sure," and he went on with consummate skill to obtain further details which would enable corroborative inquiries to be made.

All the same, half an hour's question and answer convinced all three police officers. There could be no doubt that at half past twelve on the fatal Friday morning Sir John Magill had walked through the station at Larne in the direction of the harbour.

"By Jove, French!" Rainey exclaimed when M'Atamney had taken his departure. "That's a bit unexpected, isn't it? If that tale is true it about clears Malcolm Magill. If Sir John hadn't been drugged at 12.30, Malcolm's out of it, illness or no illness."

French gave a guarded assent. It certainly seemed likely that the old gentleman must have been alive up till at least five or six o'clock next morning, in which case Malcolm's participation in the affair was undoubtedly nil.

Rainey felt absently in his pocket, withdrew his pipe and slowly began to light it.

"Darned nuisance, the whole business," he grumbled. "And it's a case we particularly wanted to get squared up. Why our Minister of Home Affairs himself was on to the

Commissioner about it. Hang it all, French, we'll have to start at the beginning again and do a deal better this time."

French moved uneasily.

"Is it possible, sir, that we've started wrong?" he suggested deprecatingly. "We've so far been assuming Malcolm killed his father for the inheritance. Now that has broken down. But isn't there another theory, entirely different, but quite likely?"

Rainey swung round and stared at French.

"What's this you're going to spring on us now?" he demanded. "Good Lord! If you've got an idea, for any sake trot it out."

"I mean that Sir John may have had something with him that night worth more than his fortune: the plans of his invention."

"Oh, that?" said Rainey, twisting back to his former position. "I hadn't forgotten it, but it didn't seem to help. Just what is in your mind?"

"Simply that Sir John was murdered for the plans."

"Of course; but how? Put up your theory."

French was scarcely prepared for anything so definite, but he did his best.

"I suggest, sir, that though Sir John was not brought to Ireland by physical force, he was tricked into coming. I suggest he was tricked into going up the Cave Hill with the idea of robbing him there, but that this scheme went adrift; perhaps because he had not brought the plans with him. I suggest that his going to Whitehead and ringing up Malcolm was a subterfuge to escape his enemies, but that they got wise to it and followed him. I suggest that at Whitehead he again escaped them – with the loss of his hat. But in doing so he missed Malcolm and when he passed the cleaner at Larne I suggest he was making his way to Lurigan as to a sanctuary. I suggest his enemies followed him and caught him up before he reached Lurigan, murdered him and buried him in the plantation in order to throw suspicion on Malcolm should the body ever be found."

Rainey, who had got his pipe going, smoked steadily as he considered this.

" 'Pon my soul, French, that's not so bad. There are a lot of holes in it of course, but it's worth going into. And what" – he fixed French with an accusing forefinger – "what's the first thing that arises out of it?"

French grinned.

"I think so," Rainey answered the grin. "An English crime, arranged in England, by an English gang! What did I tell you? You get away back to England, French, and solve this mystery and then come over and tell us about it. Come now, let's get down to tacks. Who knew Sir John might have had the plans with him?"

French turned over the leaves of his notebook.

"I've got that here, sir. There were the two Miss Magills, Victor and Breene. Possibly Myles and Nutting, the butler and chauffeur, might have heard something also. And any of these may have mentioned it to still other persons. Lastly, sir, the man Coates, who called on Sir John, may have been told of it."

"Agreed. And that, I take it, eliminates all but two – Breene and Coates?"

"It eliminates the sisters and the other members of the household except Breene, for they were all in London on the night of the crime. But it doesn't absolutely eliminate Victor. He says he was on this launch trip and I'm sure he was. But we haven't proved it."

"Yes, you're right there. But it can easily be proved. Breene's case we've already gone into and we find he's out of it. And that brings us to Coates. French, we'll have to find Coates."

"Not so easy, sir. Your people have put in some time on that already."

"I know, and that very difficulty is the most suspicious thing about him. You'll have to try in London. You might be able to trace him from the house."

French agreed, but without enthusiasm. The task, he felt sure, would prove extraordinarily difficult, if not impossible.

Rainey moved as if anxious to bring the conference to an end.

"Well, we can't go on talking about it for the rest of our lives. Let's make a programme. We over here will push on with all the local inquiries. We'll try to establish in even more detail the movements of everyone connected with the affair. We'll try to trace Coates. We'll try to check the hour at which M'Atamney saw Sir John and learn the truth of Malcolm's bilious attack. We'll try to find the author of the XYZ letter. We'll try every mortal thing we can think of. In the meantime you go back and set to work at the London end. Try to trace Coates; try to find out if others knew of the invention; check up Victor's movements and make sure he is out of it. And while we're working one or other of us may get a brain wave. That OK?"

French, who felt that under any circumstances the criminal had done enough on Irish soil to enable the truth to be learned in Ireland, demurred at first. But he had to admit that the superintendent's division of labour was reasonable, and after some further discussion, the plan was agreed to. Eventually it was arranged that French should cross that evening and that M'Clung should accompany him, remaining to assist for a few days.

9

STRANRAER

At 7.30 next morning the two travellers arrived at Euston. M'Clung went to an hotel for breakfast while French hurried home for a glimpse of Mrs French. A couple of hours later they met at the Yard.

After an interview with Chief Inspector Mitchell, to whom French described his adventures in Ireland, a start was made on the new programme. French and M'Clung set off for Elland Gardens. Myles opened the door.

"Good morning, Myles," French said genially. "You're the very man I was looking for. This is my colleague, Detective Sergeant M'Clung."

"Will you come in, gentlemen?"

Myles showed them into a small room and waited expectantly.

French began by redeeming his promise to tell the old man what had taken place in the affair since his last visit. He gave away nothing which could not have been learned from the papers, but he made a friend. Myles expressed his appreciation in no uncertain manner.

"I'd like to see the man hang who lifted up his hand against the master," he added picturesquely.

"Well, you may help towards it," French returned. He leaned forward and spoke impressively. "What I want,

Myles, is this: the address of that man Coates who called on Sir John before he went to Ireland."

Myles was at once distressed. Greatly he regretted that he could not remember it. Since the inspector's first call he had tried again and again, but without success.

"I know," said French kindly. "I'm not blaming you for there was nothing to call your attention to it. But you may be able to get it for us all the same. You said that Coates called twice?"

Myles, whose manner had suddenly become eager, agreed.

"And on each occasion he left a card?"

"Yes, sir. He handed me the cards at the door. I put him into the waiting-room and took the cards up to Sir John."

"And what became of them?"

Myles did not know. Sir John might have put them into a drawer of his desk or into his pocket or the waste-paper basket or the fire. There was no means of finding out.

"They weren't in his pockets, because they were searched in Larne. And they're not in his desk because I looked through that when I was here before. Now what about the waste-paper basket? I presume that its contents are burnt periodically, but there is no chance that something may have escaped?"

Myles was sorry, but there wasn't the slightest. He himself invariably emptied the basket into the slow combustion stove by which the water was heated and he was certain that he had overlooked nothing.

"There must be some receptacle for cards," French persisted.

It appeared that there was, a drawer in the hall table. Cards that were not required for their addresses or other purposes were thrown into the drawer and burnt at intervals.

"Let's see it," French demanded, and they trooped down.

But though they went through some hundreds of cards, those of Coates were not among them.

"I'll try the desk again," French declared. "By the way, what about Sir John's other suits? Have you been through the pockets of them?"

Myles had not thought of that and a couple of minutes later they were in the deceased gentleman's dressing-room. Myles handed down suit after suit to French, who went through the pockets exhaustively. Four suits had thus been examined, when French gave a cry of triumph.

"More than we could hope for!" he exclaimed delightedly, holding up a bit of pasteboard. "Some luck that, eh, M'Clung? Read that."

The card was of small size, a social rather than a business one. It bore the name: "Mr Arthur Coates, 7 Talbot Terrace, Sandy Row, Belfast."

"Know the place?"

M'Clung looked perplexed.

"I do not, Mr French. Talbot Terrace? Never heard of it. But I don't know that district extra well."

"Your people will soon find it. I say, M'Clung, that's a great lift to us. Let's get the information across to Belfast. May I use your telephone, Myles?"

French was in high delight as they left the house.

"A wonderful bit of luck, M'Clung," he declared enthusiastically. "Extraordinary! When we get hold of Coates our job will be half done."

M'Clung was less exuberant. He seemed to have something on his mind and presently it came out.

"There's another thing I was thinking, Mr French," he remarked, "and that is that we never found out who engaged the old man's berth that night. No one in the house did it, and it's not the sort of thing he'd likely do for himself."

French stopped and favoured his companion with a slow stare.

"Upon my word, M'Clung, that's an idea! It's long odds but there's something in it. We'll go right along to Euston now."

Half an hour later they walked into the stationmaster's office on No. 6 platform. French produced his official card.

"I want," he said, "to see the gentleman who deals with berth reservations to Ireland via Larne and Stranraer," and when a clerk, languidly curious, had come forward: "On the train leaving Euston on Wednesday, the second instant, a berth was reserved in the first sleeper for Sir John Magill. I want to find out, if possible, when that berth was reserved and by whom."

The clerk's interest suddenly became real.

"That was the old gentleman who disappeared, wasn't it?" he answered. "It's lucky I saw about the disappearance in the papers or I shouldn't have been able to give you any information."

He explained that under ordinary circumstances it would have been impossible for him to answer French's question. He had a record of the reservations, but not of how they were applied for. In this case, when he had read about Sir John, he had looked up his notes and had then been able to remember the application.

"Here it is," he said, when French had praised him judiciously. He brought over a book containing the lists of the berth-holders. "See, 'Wednesday, 2nd October. No. 6 – Sir John Magill.' "

"That's the man," French agreed. "Now can you tell me whether he made the reservation himself or if not, who did?"

"Yes, I can tell you. It was made by a Mr Coates. You see, here it is. 'No. 5 – Mr Coates.' He came here and made the reservation in person. I remember him quite well." The detectives allowed themselves to exchange glances.

"What was he like?"

"A tall, broad shouldered man with red hair of a very bright shade. A rather remarkable-looking man."

Myles' very phrase!

"Then you'd know him if you saw him again?"

The clerk was comfortably reassuring.

"Mr Coates gave no address?"

"No, we don't require that; only the name."

"And he reserved both for himself and Sir John?"

"Yes, he said he and his friend, Sir John Magill, were travelling together and would like a pair of communicating berths. There is a door between Nos. 5 and 6, so I gave him those."

French felt instinctively that this was a suggestive fact, though he could not see exactly where it tended. But it made him even keener on following up the clue.

"There was no other conversation?" he queried.

It appeared that there was. Coates had stated that he lived some miles down the line and that he was anxious to please his little son by exchanging a flashlight signal with him as the train passed. He therefore would prefer a sleeper in which berths were on the right side of the coach, as he could open his berth window easier than that in the corridor. The clerk had replied that he had no plan of the coaches and could not therefore tell on which side the berths would be. To this Coates had replied that the thing

111

didn't really matter and the interview had terminated. The reservation had been made two or three days before the date of the journey and the clerk had not seen Coates again.

"I'm afraid," said French, "I'll have to follow up the journey in detail. What would you advise? Could I see the car attendant?"

"Oh, yes," the clerk returned, "but I can't give you the necessary information here. You should see the stationmaster next door and he will get the returns looked up and find out who was on duty that night and where you can see him. If you come this way I'll arrange it for you."

They went into an adjoining office where one of the stationmaster's assistants promised immediate research.

"All the same it will take a little time to look up," the assistant explained. "Will you come in and wait or will you call back?"

"Wait," said French promptly.

They were not however kept very long.

"You're in luck," the official told them presently. "Instead of your attendant being in Stranraer or Aberdeen or Holyhead or off the map altogether, he's here in town. He's on the 7.40 to Stranraer tonight."

"Fine," French exclaimed. "How can we see him?"

"The man's name is Henry Pugg and his address is 78 Linfield Street, that's close by, down by the departure side of the station. Would you like me to send someone with you?"

"Detection," French declared, as having declined the offer, he and M'Clung turned out of the station in search of Linfield Street, "is a great job when things go as they are now. It doesn't often happen though, does it?"

"It does not, Mr French, and that's a fact," M'Clung agreed wholeheartedly. "It's mostly going to places and getting no kind of an answer at all."

They discussed the cussedness of their craft till they reached the residence of Mr Henry Pugg. The door was opened by Mrs Pugg. She was sorry, but her husband was in bed. He was on night duty, the gentlemen would understand.

French explained that he was from Scotland Yard.

"I'd hate to disturb your husband," he declared, "but my business is really important. I'm afraid I'll have to ask him to see me."

The name of the great Yard had a magical effect, for she answered quickly, "Certainly, sir. I'll call him. Won't you come in?"

In a few minutes Pugg entered the room.

"Yes, sir? Sorry to keep you waiting, sir."

"Sorry to disturb you, Mr Pugg," French returned on the same lofty plane. "I'll tell you what I want. Do you remember a gentleman travelling with you from Euston to Stranraer on the night of Wednesday, the second instant? His name was Sir John Magill."

Interest flashed in the man's eyes.

"That's the gent wot afterwards disappeared, isn't it?" he asked.

"That's right."

"Yes, sir, I remember 'im well. I saw about the disappearance in the paper and I remembered 'im well. A small old gentleman with white 'air?"

"That's right," said French again. "He was in berth No. 6."

"Excuse me till I get my book." He vanished and returned with a black-covered notebook. "Yes, sir, that's right; No. 6."

"And in No. 5 was a Mr Coates?"

"Yes, sir."

"Numbers 5 and 6 communicate, don't they?"

"Yes, sir. There's a door between them, but they're usually used as separate berths."

"By the door being kept locked?"

"That's right, sir."

"Now can you remember on this particular night was the communicating door open or locked?"

"Locked, sir."

"Locked?" French repeated. "Are you quite sure of that?"

"Positive," Pugg returned. "I mightn't be able to tell you if it 'adn't been for that there account in the noospaper. But when I read it I thought about the run and I remembered about Sir John and about Mr Coates too."

"What you tell me is a bit surprising," French declared. "Do you know that Mr Coates specially applied for communicating berths for himself and Sir John?"

"I don't know nothing about that," Pugg said firmly, "but I know the communicating door was locked all night."

"Mr Coates might have opened it?"

"I don't think so, sir. Those are special keys and he wouldn't 'ave one."

"Did you see them speaking together at all?"

"No, sir. Never met or spoke a word, not so far as I know."

"They didn't arrive together?"

"No, sir, and they didn't leave together. I saw them both go at Stranraer. Sir John went first and Mr Coates followed after two or three minutes."

If the attendant were correct this was certainly a significant fact. It was difficult to believe that communicating berths should have been applied for if they were not wanted. And if they were wanted and Pugg was not asked to open the door, it meant that they were wanted for some secret and therefore presumably improper purpose. French considered.

"You say you examined the tickets of both men?"

"Yes, sir. The ticket collector doesn't come through the sleepers. I do the collecting."

"And both gentlemen were going through to Belfast?"

"No, sir," he answered, glancing once again at the book. "Sir John Magill had a through ticket to Belfast, but Mr Coates had booked to Stranraer only."

"Oh. Stranraer only?" This was a welcome fact. If Coates had stopped at Stranraer it should be possible to get on to his trail. Once again in the course of a very few hours French experienced a thrill of satisfaction, and from the look on M'Clung's features it was evident that his reaction was similar.

French continued his questions, but Pugg had no more to tell and presently the two detectives bade him good day and returned to the Yard.

Here further news awaited them. There had just been a reply from Belfast. There was no such address in the city as 7 Talbot Terrace, Sandy Row.

French was immensely pleased.

"We're on to it at last, M'Clung," he said in a low eager tone. "If we had this man Coates I believe we'd begin to see daylight. We should be able to get on to him at Stranraer. Another night in the train, curse it! Pity we didn't know yesterday."

M'Clung agreed that it was a pity, though half-heartedly. As a matter of fact he was enjoying himself profoundly. Here he was on one of the most important cases that had taken place in Northern Ireland for many a long day, in company with a famous officer of New Scotland Yard, a man moreover whom he found pleasant, friendly and approachable. And apart from the case and the chances of promotion which it might bring, he was having a delightful change from the monotony of his ordinary work, he was visiting new scenes under conditions of unwonted luxury, and he was laying up a store of experience which could not but be valuable to him in his career. Under these conditions, the longer the case went on, the better.

"Well," said French, "that's all we can do in the meantime. Will you engage berths on the 7.40 tonight. I have some things to attend to here, but I'll meet you at the station at 7.35."

They had a good journey and at 5.25 to the minute the train drew up at Stranraer harbour. French at once began work.

"We'd better see these steamer people before the boat sails," he said, and waiting till the passengers had gone on board, he tackled the officers who were checking tickets at the gangway. From them he went to the stewards, and indeed everyone who came in contact with passengers, but without result. When half an hour later he and M'Clung left the steamer, French felt fairly satisfied that Coates had not crossed.

At the harbour station a short inquiry sufficed. No train left until the boat came back from Larne between nine and ten at night. Coates could not therefore have left from there, nor had he been seen anywhere about.

"We'd better go and get some breakfast," French decided. "After that we can try the town station."

With the first of these proposals at all events M'Clung was in profound agreement. Accordingly they walked up to the town and turned into the King's Arms Hotel. French decided that he might improve the shining hour.

"I wonder," he said to the young lady in the office, when they had ordered their meal, "if you saw a friend of mine who passed through Stranraer this day fortnight? A tall, well-built man with bright red hair? He came off the night train from London."

The girl wrinkled her pretty eyebrows.

"What was his name?" she asked.

French leaned across the little counter. "As a matter of fact," he said confidentially, "he was travelling incog. He might have given the name Coates, or he might have given something else." He gave her a keen glance; then, as if satisfied with her appearance, went on: "I'd better tell you, but don't give me away." He bent still lower and spoke still more confidentially. "I'm an officer from Scotland Yard. See, here's my card. I'm after this man. I don't say he has committed a crime, but he has some information I want. If you can give me any help I'll be grateful."

She seemed thrilled. For a few moments she remained motionless, evidently thinking, then she slowly shook her head.

"I don't think so," she declared. "Red hair? Wait now a minute, there was a man – " Again she stopped, then she made a little gesture. "Yes," she exclaimed, "I believe I remember that man. Wait till I think." She pressed a bell. "Look here, Andy," she said to the waiter who appeared, "do you remember this day fortnight a man coming in for breakfast off the London train, a tall man with red hair? Didn't he meet another man coming in off a car?"

"Aye," the waiter returned concisely. "I mind them fine. They had their breakfasts about half seven."

"I thought so," said the girl, turning to French. "This – friend of yours came in as you say shortly after the London train arrived. He asked for breakfast, just as you've done, but before he had it a friend came in from a car. They had the fine greetings and in the end they breakfasted together. I remember the whole thing now as if it was yesterday. The friend was Mr – Mr – " She wrung her fingers slightly as if to aid her memory, then rapidly turned over the pages of a book. "Teer," she exclaimed triumphantly. "Mr Teer."

"Good," said French heartily, "that's fine. That'll save me a lot of trouble." As so often before he was feeling the happy thrill of the hunter who comes on a fresh spoor of the animal he is after.

"There was something about him too," the young lady went on eagerly. "That'll do, Andy," to the waiter, who had hung indeterminately in the background, but who now vanished. "I remember it all." She turned over the pages of her book. "On the Tuesday, that was two days before, we got a letter from Mr Teer, ordering a room for Wednesday night. I haven't got it, it's been destroyed, but it said he was motoring from Carlisle and he expected to get here late on the night. He wanted the room to be ready for him and the garage open for his car. Well, I arranged this, but he didn't turn up. Then next morning, that was Thursday, he arrived. He said he had been unexpectedly detained and that he would not now want the room as he was going on after breakfast. But I had to charge him for the room as we had lost another letting because of his reservation."

"Of course," French agreed smoothly. "I suppose from what you say he arrived about seven?"

The girl thought again.

"Yes, about seven," she said presently. "He had breakfast with the red-haired man soon after, then they sat and smoked in the lounge an hour or so. He went off in his car about half past nine, he and your friend."

"The red-haired man went with him?" French exclaimed. "Do you know where they went to?"

The girl had no idea.

"They didn't leave an address for letters?"

No, they had left no clue as to their movements. They had simply got into Mr Teer's car and driven off. She hadn't seen what direction they took, but maybe Angus, the porter, had. She would send for Angus.

But Angus was unable to throw much light on the situation. He remembered the men and their leaving in Teer's car. He also remembered that they had started along the street towards the right, but as this was the way in which the car was pointing after being brought from the garage, and as at the next corner they could have turned in any direction, the information was not helpful.

In accordance with his usual practice, French, before leaving the hotel, interrogated every member of the staff who had come in contact with either of the strangers. But he learned very little. No one had observed details which might help in a search for the men, nor had anyone overheard illuminating remarks.

The one useful fact was gleaned from Angus, the porter. He was an old chauffeur and he had noticed Teer's car. It was a Morris six of the familiar buff-brown colour and almost new. Unfortunately he had forgotten the number.

"Better than nothing," said French, as they distributed largesse and sallied forth on the next stage of their quest.

10

PORTPATRICK

"An outsider would say," French remarked as they strolled through the streets of the little town, "that with our excellent police organisation the first place for us to go would be the police station. But as a matter of fact I go there last." He glanced across at M'Clung to see if that worthy followed his argument.

"How's that, sir?" the sergeant said tactfully.

"It's hard to put it in words," French answered. "It's not that local men are officious exactly, but application to them involves a lot of wearisome explanations, and you lose your free hand. Of course often one can't do without the local force, but when one can, one does, or at least I do. Now there are two ways, so far as I can see, that we can get to work. We can go to the police here and ask them if they saw a new Morris six on that Wednesday morning. That's one way."

"That's the way I should have adopted," M'Clung declared.

"You may be right and we may have to come back to it. But there is another way that I'm going to try first. When it works it's the best way. It's to sit down and think where those men are likely to have gone and then to check up if they did so. Now just start in, M'Clung, and do a bit of guessing. Where do you say we should look?"

M'Clung hesitated and French went on.

"Begin by going over what we know about them." He counted on his fingers. "One, Coates had travelled from London. Two, the train that he came by stops at Dumfries, Castle Douglas and Newton Stewart. Three, Teer came by motor from Carlisle, or said he did. Four, they left in Teer's car about nine-thirty. Now, what do you make of it?"

Once again M'Clung hesitated and once again French went on.

"What direction did they go in?"

"Well," the sergeant suggested, "they didn't go towards Carlisle, because that's where they both came from."

"Right," French approved. "I see you have the root of the matter in you. That's the method. Always eliminate. Now you've eliminated the Carlisle direction. And note, of course, that that includes intermediate places except those close to Stranraer. They would have stopped at Castle Douglas or Newton Stewart if their destination had been easier got at from these places so we may say that they did not go east. Very well?"

"And they didn't go west, because that's where the sea lies."

"Right again. Roughly speaking, therefore, they went north or south. Now which was it?"

"I would think south, sir."

"Why?"

"Well, if they had been going north, they would hardly have come to Stranraer at all, unless of course it was to somewhere fairly close. But if it was any distance, say to Girvan or beyond, they would have gone by the line from Dumfries towards Glasgow."

"I agree, though, mind you, that's not so probable as your first two guesses."

"I know that, Mr French. Well then if they went south there's a likely place you'd think of at once, and that's Portpatrick. It's a tourist place where people do go and through Stranraer is the natural way. I would guess Portpatrick, sir."

"And so should I," French approved. "That's quite good, M'Clung. We may both be wrong, but we'll try it out. Let's get up to that town station and look up trains. Or there may be a bus."

Their visit to the station was opportune and half an hour later they were walking down the hill into Portpatrick. The little town looked very attractive on this pleasant October day. French, who had never been there before, was agreeably surprised. "The next time I want a quiet holiday," he told M'Clung, "this is the place for me."

"It used to be a more important place than it is now," M'Clung observed. "In old times it was the port for the north of Ireland. I remember my grandfather telling me about his seeing the mail packet sailing from here to Donaghadee. See the money that's been spent on this harbour and it's the same at Donaghadee. Only there the place is half silted up."

"Not very far across, is it?"

"I think about twenty-three miles, but I'm not just certain."

They continued discussing the changes time had brought about in travel until presently French returned to the subject of their quest.

"Going to that hotel turned out lucky in Stranraer. Suppose we try the hotels here to begin with."

Climbing the hill to the large building above the harbour, they soon were stating their business to the manager. French made no secret of his profession, showing his official card and explaining that he was on a murder case. Unfortunately the manager could only say that the persons described had not visited his hotel. On French's suggestion he called in several members of his staff, but these merely confirmed his own statement.

From the Portpatrick Hotel, the detectives visited the smaller hotels in the town and then the garages and petrol supply stations, in every case with the same result.

"Looks like the police station after all," French declared. "We passed it on the way down from the train. Let's go back."

The local sergeant was visibly impressed by a visit from so important a man as Inspector French. But unfortunately he had seen no one resembling either of the strangers, and though he questioned his entire force, nothing that could help French came out.

"That's all right," French said, as the man expressed his regret. "It's evident they didn't come to Portpatrick and to have learned that is progress. We can't expect to get them first shot. We'll try north up towards Girvan."

Having to wait nearly an hour for their train, the two detectives strolled down once more to the front and had another look at the harbour. Though French imagined the latter might be hard to enter during bad weather, there could be no doubt that when inside even the smallest boat would be supremely safe. The inner basin indeed looked less like a harbour than a great square stone tank. In the middle, moored by a bow anchor and warps which swung up in easy curves from the stem to the wall of the basin, lay a small steam yacht, and here and there without seeming arrangement were a few row boats and a couple of smacks. Whatever greatness the place might have formerly had certainly passed away. As a port it was dead. But there was the usual group of jersey-clad longshoremen leaning against a low wall and smoking stolidly.

"One of the mysteries I can never get to the bottom of is how those fellows live," French observed. "You see them at every watering place, a group of them just like that. You never see them move about or do any work. They seem to stand there smoking all day. How do they do it?"

M'Clung chuckled.

"Some of them are fishermen, Mr French. They're out at night mostly. And it's no joke, their job, I can tell you. I've been out and I know."

"Well, if the ones I've watched are out all night they never sleep, unless you'd call that standing there sleeping."

Again M'Clung chuckled.

"That's all right, sir, but they're not asleep, whatever they may look. I bet you they know all about us already, when we came and where we've been and maybe our business as well. There's not much they miss, I can tell you."

"That so?" said French. "Well, if they're so wide awake as all that, slip over and ask them if they've seen Teer's car."

M'Clung crossed what had once been a busy wharf and mingled with the group. None of the men moved except to fix him with their cold, fish-like eyes. He spoke and one shrugged his shoulder slightly and murmured some reply. M'Clung spoke again and the man nodded slowly. Finally M'Clung beckoned across the road. French went over.

"These men saw the car, Mr French," M'Clung said, and French silently commended the total lack of interest or eagerness in his manner. "It stopped and parked just here and the two men went aboard a motor launch which had just come in."

In spite of himself French started. A motor launch! Victor Magill's story of his holiday leaped into his mind. Could it be that this was Victor's launch and that Coates was Victor's friend – what was the name he mentioned? Oh, yes, Joss. Could Coates be Joss? As French rapidly recalled what Victor had said, the idea began to grow more and more likely. The launch had arrived at Portpatrick at about ten in the morning in question and had there picked up the remaining two members of the party. That tallied. One of these members, Joss, had travelled by the night train from Euston, the train by which Coates travelled, for French remembered pointing out to Victor that his friend must have used the same train as Sir John. The other friend, whose name Victor had not mentioned, had come by motor, as Teer had done. If these two men were not members of Victor's party, there was here a very remarkable coincidence.

And if they were?...French suddenly found a vista opening before him, a vista both suggestive and sinister...

But there was no time to consider it now. He must collect all the information he could. Later he could try piecing it together.

French gave the men an offhand greeting. Obviously he also was neither eager nor particularly interested in the affair. But if the men had really anything to tell him, well, talking was dry work and was there no place where they could get a drop of something to help the tale? It seemed there was, and not far away. The group adjourned in a body.

It would not be correct to say that the whisky which each man asked for loosened his tongue, but it did produce occasional monosyllabic replies to French's questions.

However, by dint of a laborious interrogation, mostly veiled, and a second treat all round, a considerable amount of information was obtained. Whether it was all that was available, French did not know, but it was all he could get.

It seemed that between 9.30 and 10.00 o'clock on Thursday, 3rd October, a motor launch had come into the harbour. Portpatrick is one of those blest places which have neither a harbour master nor dues, each visiting mariner anchoring where it seems right in his own eyes. The spot which had seemed right in the eyes of the master of this launch was just inside the inner basin, and there he had dropped his anchor.

The master – the longshoremen did not know whether or not he was the owner – was a short, pleasant-looking man of middle age. There was another man on board whom, however, they had not seen, as he kept below. But they had heard his replies to the short man.

A few minutes after the launch had anchored a motor had appeared, a new brownish-yellow Morris six. From this car had descended two men, both tall and well built, in fact one was almost a Hercules. He was dark, but his companion's hair was of a particularly bright shade of red. The two men had walked across to the basin, and seeing the launch, had hailed it. The short man had pointed to a boat which was tied to the steps and they had called for a volunteer to put them aboard. The boat was the property of one of the longshoremen and he had rowed them across.

French asked if they had said anything while in the boat.

It had seemed hard enough to extract mere facts from the circle, but this proved child's play compared to the difficulty of getting a report of the conversation. However M'Clung managed it at last.

While being rowed the few yards to the launch the two newcomers had discussed the question of which of them should take the car back – they didn't say to where. Then the short man had greeted them, saying that they were in good time as that he himself had only just arrived. One of the others had next asked where old Viccy was and the short man had said, "Casualty. Fell down the companion steps and crocked up his knee." Hercules had asked if the victim of this disaster was aboard, to which the other had replied that he was, and that he couldn't get out of his bunk. Hercules had then gone below and the boatman had heard greetings and the beginning of a conversation, until the short man had told him he was going ashore in half an hour and to come back for him.

When the half-hour was up he, the boatman, had returned and he then rowed both Hercules and the short man ashore. The two had immediately driven off. A couple of hours later Hercules had returned alone and had gone aboard. But it was not till dark – between seven and eight – that the short man had turned up. He also had immediately gone aboard. That was the last occasion on which there had been any communication between launch and shore.

"Did the launch go out that night?" French asked.

About midnight, the men said. It was a calm night and all had heard her, while a couple of them had seen her creeping out past the lighthouse.

"Did you happen to notice her name?" French asked.

They had. She was the *Sea Hawk* and was registered in Barrow. She was about fifty feet long, well decked over, with plenty of freeboard, and looked a good sea boat. But she was old and from the sound of her motor it was old too.

"I think that about does us in Portpatrick," French observed as they left the little harbour. He swung round suddenly on his companion.

"I say, M'Clung, what in the blessed earth were you and I thinking about not to spot that Coates belonged to Victor Magill's party? Bar myself, I think you're the biggest fool in Scotland!"

M'Clung could only murmur helplessly. He should have thought of it, but – he just didn't.

"There's not much excuse for either of us. When do we get a train out of this darned place?"

"In fifteen minutes." M'Clung had spent the few moments of their wait at Stranraer in studying the timetable.

"Good. That'll just give us time to go to the post office. I want to send a wire."

His message ran:

To Victor Magill, Lurigan, Larne, Co. Antrim.
Please wire your present address. Am anxious to see you. Reply King's Arms Hotel, Stranraer. French.

Conversation waned between the two men as they travelled to Stranraer and again as they strolled about the town or sat in the lounge of the hotel. French's mind was full of the suggestive information he had obtained and M'Clung, seeing his companion's preoccupation, tactfully kept his own counsel.

The double connection between Sir John Magill and the launch party puzzled French completely. That Victor Magill happened to be on a trip along the Scottish coast at the time of his uncle's death had, if stated alone, no significance whatever. That Joss should be on his way to join a yachting party when he travelled with Sir John also had no significance, even considering the peculiar episode of the adjacent sleeping berths and the false name. But when it turned out that Victor and Joss were members of the same party, that is, that there was a connection between Sir John and the cruise, firstly, through Victor and secondly, through Joss, the relative significance of these facts was profoundly altered.

Was it possible, French wondered, that there could really be any connection between the linen magnate's death and the yachting trip? It seemed an utterly far-fetched idea, and yet...

French considered once again Sir John's extraordinary actions on the day of his death and the more he did so, the more he felt that any explanation which covered the facts must be extraordinary too. He need not therefore refrain from accepting theories because they were either far-fetched or peculiar. He need not rule out a connection between the murder and Victor's cruise simply because such a connection seemed absurd.

So far, so good. Assuming that there might have been a connection, what could it consist of?

Not that Sir John could have been murdered by the launch party; they were at Portpatrick at the time of the crime. Of alibis French was usually sceptical, but this was one which admitted of no doubt whatever. It was true that one member of the party, Victor, had not actually been seen at Portpatrick, though he had been heard. While French had no doubt that Victor was there, he took a mental note to make further inquiries into the matter.

But if Sir John had not been actually murdered by the party, were its members not out of the picture? Could any of them be even remotely involved? French thought and thought and thought, and at length found himself forced to the conclusion that they could not. None of the four could have helped to bring about the old man's death. Except that Joss had acted in a somewhat mysterious way, there was nothing sinister about the cruise. French turned to his companion.

"What do you make of it, M'Clung?"

The sergeant took his pipe out of his mouth and gave it a little wave.

"Nothing, Mr French," he answered decisively. "I think I see what's been in your mind that there may be a connection between this launch trip and Sir John's death. Is that not it, sir?"

French nodded.

"Well, I thought maybe there was at first, but I don't think so now. Joss was up to something right enough, but Joss was at Portpatrick when the murder was committed so he couldn't have done it. And there was nothing to connect Victor with it at all. Besides he was at Portpatrick too. I don't believe we'll get anything out of the cruise."

"If," said French slowly, "you see a man coming out of a bar, you have no evidence that he has been drinking. If a man wipes his mouth when passing you on the road, it means nothing." M'Clung grinned, but French continued unmoved. "But if you see a man coming out of a bar and wiping his mouth; you see? It's not exactly an original example, but it's a good one for all that. Now there's what's bothering me. It's the cumulative effect of both Victor and Joss being connected with Sir John and with the cruise, added to Joss' little games on the journey down. I agree with you that I can't get a connection between the trip and the murder, but I just don't feel altogether happy about it. Do you?"

M'Clung felt happy enough. He was sure they would get nothing out of the cruise. But he thought they should have an explanation from Joss before dropping the matter.

"Well naturally," said French. "What do you think I wired to Victor for?"

"Here's the answer anyway," M'Clung returned, as a telegraph boy opportunely appeared at the door.

There were two wires, both for French. The first read:

Victor returned to 116B St John's Wood Road. Malcolm Magill.

The second:

Glad if you could let M'Clung return as soon as possible. Rainey.

French grunted.

"Ring up and get a couple of berths reserved for us tonight," he directed, "mine on the train to town and yours on the steamer for Larne. Then we'll go and amuse ourselves at this Earl of Stair's place. No reason why we shouldn't improve what's left of our minds. Goodness knows they need it."

LONDON

That night French travelled to London and next morning made his way out to St John's Wood Road. Victor was just about to start for his office, but he turned back with his visitor.

"Sorry to give you all this trouble," French apologised, "but I'll only keep you a moment. In fact I really only want to ask one question. You remember telling me of the friend who travelled by rail from London to Stranraer to join your launch party at Portpatrick. We agreed he must have travelled in the same train as Sir John and I should like to see him about the journey. There's just a chance that he may have seen or heard something of the old gentleman which might help me. I want you please to give me his address. His name you mentioned. It was Joss, I think?"

"Joss, yes," Victor returned, "Charles Joss. He's in the same line of business as myself. He's one of the travelling representatives of Sirius Motors, Ltd, you know, their London office is in the Haymarket. You'll find him there. He's a good fellow, Joss, but up till now he's had rather rough luck."

"How was that?" French asked sympathetically.

Victor shrugged.

"A bad bringing up, I'm afraid. His father wasn't all that might have been desired, and Joss himself had some trouble and left his job and went to the States. There I believe he made good and in 1914 he came home and enlisted. He was invalided out, I'm not sure exactly when, in '17, I think. Then he put in his bad time. He couldn't get a job, not for ages, and until actual want was staring him in the face. At last he met a man whom he had served with in France, and this chap was able to put in a word for him which got him his present job. He's doing all right now."

"I'll go and have a word with him."

"Well, you'll get him at that address, or if he isn't there they'll put you on his track. But you won't get much from him, I'm afraid."

"Possibly not, but why do you say so?"

"Because he didn't know my uncle."

"It doesn't sound promising," French admitted. "However in our business we have to make a lot of long shots that don't get anywhere. Just once in a while one of them does, and that makes it worth it."

"I suppose so," Victor agreed. "Anything else I can do for you, inspector?"

"Why, no," said French. "I don't think there is." He paused, then turned the conversation to the motor launch cruise.

"You went to Stranraer while your launch was lying at Portpatrick, I think you told me?" he said presently. "It's not a bad little town."

Victor glanced at him curiously.

"I don't think I could have told you that, inspector," he returned. "If I did, I unwittingly misled you. It was Mallace who went to Stranraer. Mallace is agent for the Lowe oil engines and on this trip he was combining business and pleasure. As a matter of fact," Victor smiled slightly, "I not only didn't go to Stranraer, but I didn't even see Portpatrick, though we lay there all that day."

French was suitably interested.

"It was my knee," Victor explained. "I fell down the companion steps. It was early on that Thursday morning when we were about halfway between Barrow and Portpatrick. I was carrying some cocoa up to Mallace when the launch gave a lurch and in trying to save the cocoa I lost my balance. The sharp edge of a step caught my knee just on the inside, you know." He rubbed the stricken member. "It hurt to put it under me, so I stayed in my bunk. Mallace wanted me to get a doctor at Portpatrick, but like a fool I wouldn't agree. I thought it was nothing, you understand. But when we got to Campbeltown next morning it was a good deal swollen, and I had a doctor there, a Dr MacGregor, a very decent chap as it turned out. Teer went up the town for him and brought him aboard. He said there was no real harm done and, that if I lay up as much as possible, there was no reason why I shouldn't go on with the cruise. But I was lame for several days, in fact it catches me sometimes still."

"Hard lines that, Mr Magill. It must have pretty well spoilt your holiday. I noticed you were lame when I saw you in Belfast."

"I got off well," Victor declared. "I've known a hurt like that lasting for three months."

For some time they continued talking cruises. Victor was responsive, even friendly, and chatted about the party's adventures without reserve. His manner was that of a truthful man, and French felt he might safely accept his statement. At the same time he took a note to get early in touch with Dr MacGregor, so that Victor's disablement might be established beyond question.

French made a move to go, but Victor seemed to enjoy talking and he therefore sank back in his chair and took another cigarette from the box Magill held out.

"I suppose," said Victor presently, "you don't know of a job that would suit either Myles or Nutting? My cousin is going to sell the house in Knightsbridge and those two will have to go. Nutting, of course, is a young man, but it's hard lines on Myles."

French was sorry. He knew of nothing, but he thought in these days any kind of domestic servant should be able to command his own figure. "Mr Breene would have more trouble than Myles in getting fixed up, I should have thought," he added.

"Breene!" Victor returned, to French's amazement, in accents of scorn and dislike. "Breene out of a job! You don't know the man, inspector, or you wouldn't have said that. Didn't you know? He's going – " He stopped suddenly, then shrugged his shoulders. "Perhaps I shouldn't have mentioned it, but it'll be common property before long and till then you can keep quiet about it. He's going to marry my cousin, my elder cousin that's selling the house. How the old man would turn in his grave if he knew!"

"But I thought Sir John liked Mr Breene?"

"As a secretary, yes. As a son-in-law – he would have thrown him out of his house if such a thing had been suggested. But there, I shouldn't have talked. Forget it, inspector, but remember those other two men if you hear of any vacancies."

French absently promised and excused himself. He was interested in the little revelation of character which had been made. Breene, he would have sworn, was a clever, forceful, determined man who would see that he got his own way in the minor affairs of life. But at the time he had not seen any indications of a desire to do so at the expense of others. Now as a result of Victor's story he believed he had been mistaken. There seemed to be a sort of ruthlessness in the man's strength.

As he sat in a No. 53 bus French took himself very seriously to task over missing this trait. He had always prided himself on his character reading. Here was a case where he believed he had made a slip. He took a mental note in future to pay even more careful attention to this side of his business.

In a dream he watched the kaleidoscope of the streets. And then another side of Victor's statement occurred to him. It did not seem very important at first, but the more he thought of it, the more impressed with it he became. Indeed he grew positively excited as he considered the vistas which appeared to be opening out in front of him. Was it possible that at last he had reached his solution?

If it were true that Breene had wished to marry Miss Magill and that Sir John would have opposed the match, were there not here all the elements that he required to complete his case? On many previous occasions French had wondered whether Breene might not know more than he had said. But French had always dismissed the idea on two grounds, absence of motive and Breene's alibi for the evening. Now here was a motive strong enough to account for any crime. Alibis, moreover, were notoriously misleading…

He returned to the Yard, sat down at his desk and proceeded to put his ideas on paper. "Herbert Breene," he wrote at the top of a clean sheet, then under that "Character."

Carefully he analysed the man's character, so far as he knew it, ending at "Conclusion" with the words: "This man has the qualities necessary for undertaking and carrying through a daring crime."

His next heading was "Motive," and under this he summarised what he had just been considering. Breene, the confidential secretary, might well have seen Sir John's will. Under this will Miss Magill was an heiress to the extent of £50,000, plus the house in Knightsbridge, worth more than a few thousands more. Therefore marriage with her would be extraordinarily profitable. Unfortunately her father's objection would be a fatal bar to such connubial happiness. Not that parental opposition as such would have mattered two straws. Its importance lay in the fact that it might have a cash basis. If Sir John had really objected to Breene as a son-in-law, he could have cut his daughter out of his will. His lamented decease therefore would have meant (a) that Breene could pay his court without the threat of a disastrous change in the will, and (b) that the will would become operative, the future Mrs Breene actually obtaining the cash. Under "Conclusion" in this heading French therefore wrote: "This man has an adequate motive for the crime."

"Opportunity" was his third heading. The details of this he had already thought out. Breene could have arranged for Sir John's visit to Belfast, if necessary by forged letter: he could have met him in Sandy Row and no doubt could have devised some scheme for sending the old man to the Cave Hill. He had dined at 7.00 and perhaps could have gone to Whitehead by the 8.00 p.m. train. Perhaps he could have spent the night between there and Lurigan, slipping into the hotel unseen in the early morning.

These last two items French queried, and under his fourth heading "Objections," proceeded to consider them in detail. Alibis consisting of evidence as to the presence of a visitor in an hotel were notoriously unreliable. In this case the man might have been present at dinner and might have been in his room when called next morning, but what evidence was there that he had remained in the building between these two hours?

There didn't seem to be any. From Rainey's report, Breene might have been there or he might not. It was a matter for investigation on the ground. French felt a sudden urge to go straight to Belfast and look into it himself. He recognised, however, that this would scarcely be the game. So he did the next best thing. Calling a stenographer he drafted a summary of his ideas to Rainey, suggesting that he should do the needful.

Half an hour later he passed through the great swing doors of Sirius Motors, Ltd's palatial showrooms in the Haymarket. By a stroke of luck Joss was in the building.

The moment French laid eyes on the man he experienced one of his thrills of delightful satisfaction. For there could be no doubt that before him stood the mysterious Coates! This was certainly the man who had called on Sir John Magill before the latter paid his fatal visit to his native country. This was the man who had engaged the communicating sleeping berths, who had travelled to Stranraer, breakfasted at the King's Arms and joined the launch at Portpatrick. He answered the description too closely for any doubt to be possible.

"Good morning, Mr Joss," said French, handing over his official card. "As you see, I'm a police officer. I'm investigating the death of Sir John Magill and I want to ask you one or two questions. I got your name from Mr Victor Magill."

Joss looked slightly perturbed, but he spoke pleasantly enough.

"Sit down, inspector." He pulled forward a chair. "I shall be pleased to tell you anything I can, but I'm afraid that will amount to just nothing at all. You see, I didn't know the late Sir John."

French gave an inward sigh of satisfaction. At last he was on to something definite. In his very first reply Joss had lied. French feared that the man might have had some plausible explanation for his conduct. Now this seemed unlikely.

"I think," he went on smoothly, "that you can probably tell me all I want to know. You understand, of course, that you are not bound to answer my questions unless you like?"

Joss shrugged.

"Oh, yes, I understand that all right," he said dryly. "I also understand that if I don't you'll use your position to compel me."

"Not necessarily," French rejoined; "but of course something of the kind might occur."

"I thought so." The man's pleasant smile had faded and his face had grown grim and his eyes waxy.

"Well," said French, "don't let us meet trouble halfway. Now, Mr Joss, there are one or two things about Sir John Magill's death which are puzzling us. One is, what he went to Ireland for. Can you throw any light on that?"

Joss' face expressed genuine amazement as well, French thought, as dismay.

"I?" he exclaimed. "I should think not! Didn't I tell you I didn't even know the man."

"You did," French admitted quietly, "but then, you know, that wasn't true." He bent forward and looked at Joss keenly. "You see, we know of your interviews with him under the name of Arthur Coates, of 7 Talbot Terrace, Sandy Row."

It was a blow. Joss almost visibly staggered back. Admission showed complete in his look, but in words he still tried to prevaricate.

"It's a lie!" he cried. "A darned lie! You don't know anything of the sort. I tell you I wasn't there!" He spoke confidently, but his face grew white and little drops of sweat appeared on his forehead.

French still spoke quietly, but his voice took on a certain hardness.

"Nonsense, Mr Joss: think again. You're too intelligent a man to take up that line. You may believe me that we know all about your visits. We can prove them in any court of law, if necessary."

Joss remained silent, staring sullenly at the other. He seemed to be deliberating what his answer should be, as if weighing the consequences. Presently he made up his mind.

"Well, and what if I did," he demanded truculently. "I haven't broken any law and therefore it's none of your business."

"That's all I wish to be convinced of," French said smoothly. "At present, however, I am up against these facts: You called on Sir John, giving a false name and a false Belfast address. A few days later Sir John went to Belfast, to that very area in the city, and the suggestion is that he was looking for that address. That same day he was murdered. You will see that wants some explanation. But if you can convince me that your action was innocent, the matter so far as you are concerned is at an end."

French paused. Joss was evidently thinking rapidly. He kept shooting little glances at French as if weighing his gullibility. At last he appeared to have thought of an answer.

"I guess, inspector, you've got it wrong," he declared. "I don't need to justify my action to you or anyone else. It's you that'll have to do the justifying. You've practically accused me of complicity in a murder and that's actionable. You can arrest me and prove your accusation or you can meet an action for defamation of character and wrongful arrest, whichever you like. But you have no third course." As he spoke his manner grew more confident and he went on tauntingly: "Well, what are you going to do about it?"

French called his bluff.

"Arrest you, of course, Mr Joss," he replied without hesitation. "If you don't satisfy me what else can I do? And in view of this I'd better repeat my warning. You are not bound to answer my questions and anything you say may be used in evidence against you. At the same time I offer you an opportunity of explaining your conduct, should you care to do so."

Joss' jaw dropped.

"You can't prove I ever spoke to Sir John Magill in my life," he said, but with less assurance.

French made a gesture of impatience.

"That, Mr Joss, is simply silly. Do you imagine I should take up the line I have if I wasn't sure? Of course I can prove it. The butler will swear you called on Sir John and gave in Coates' card, which card is now at Scotland Yard. He will swear that you did this twice. I assure you there is proof of your interviews that would convince any jury in the world."

"But that won't prove that I had anything to do with Sir John's Belfast visit."

"Won't it?" French returned grimly. "All right, Mr Joss, if that is your attitude I'm sorry, but there is no help for it. You must come with – "

With an involuntary gesture Joss threw up his hand.

"Stop," he cried. "I'll tell you. In a way there's no reason why I shouldn't, for I've done nothing illegal and you can't get anything on me. All the same I'm not proud of the thing and I'd rather not have said anything."

"Very good, Mr Joss. Just as you please."

Joss looked profoundly uncomfortable. French, outwardly indifferent, but inwardly seething with a delicious excitement, watched him, trying to fathom whether the man was going to lie or tell the truth. From his manner so far he couldn't tell. Joss certainly looked as if his tale involved something discreditable, which he was ashamed of bringing into the light of day.

"Well, Mr Joss. I'm waiting."

The man started as if from a reverie and with a little hopeless gesture he began: "It's a long story, for I must go back six years for its beginning. Six years ago I was in a bad way. I'd been invalided out of the army, and as I had recovered my health, my disability allowance had ceased. But I couldn't get a job, my little savings were gone, and I was face to face with destitution. I needn't labour the thing. I had my bad time. Not worse, of course, than hundreds of other poor devils who had chucked a good billet to join up. I had been an actor in the States – nothing very much, travelling shows mostly – but I couldn't get back there; hadn't the money for the journey.

"When things were about their worst I happened to meet a man I knew in Piccadilly – I'll give you his name if you

142

want it. We had served together in the Salient and down at Loos. He played the good Samaritan. He said he knew of a job – this job it was, and he lent me clothes – it was as bad as that. He brought me here and had a pow-wow with the manager, with the result that I got a start on commission. I did my best and made good in a small way. I got my name on the pay-roll and with good percentages I've not been doing so badly."

Joss paused and buried his face in his hands. For a moment he remained with head bowed, then raising it, he resumed: "That was all very well for a while, but like the darned fool I've always been, I've lately got off the rails again. I got in with a betting set and began going to race meetings and backing horses. Well, you can guess where that led to. I lost my savings and I got into debt. Then the time came when I had to pay a bet or be ruined, for as you know, Mr French, if there was any scandal of that kind I would have lost my social position and my job. I hadn't the money and I couldn't raise it, I had touched my friends too often. There was only one thing I could do and I did it. I went to the moneylenders."

Once again French nodded. It was an old and oft repeated tale, this he was listening to. The thought crossed his mind that if he were to get a ten pound note for every time he had heard it, he should by now be in a position to retire.

"That was out of the frying pan into the fire for me," Joss went on. "I had been bad before, but now I was ten times worse. I needn't weary you with the details. It is enough to say that about a month ago I found myself with a fortnight to find between six and seven hundred pounds. It was that or ruin.

"It's easy to talk about being faced with ruin, Mr French, but the reality's a different proposition. It's a darned terrible thing – awful! I had been down and out before and I knew what it was like, and I think there was nothing I wouldn't have done to save myself. And then I thought I saw a way out.

"It was something I'd like to forget, but there isn't much chance of that. I met Victor Magill and he had told me his uncle had succeeded with an invention he'd been working at for years – a new way of combining artificial silk with linen to give a smooth, strong fabric. We had talked about it and I was satisfied that the thing would be worth thousands. Well, here was I threatened with the loss of everything worth having in this world for the sake of a few hundreds, while old Sir John had wealth overflowing, ten times, a hundred times more than he could ever use. And here were thousands more going to pour into his pockets. I thought over it and I don't deny I was bitter. And then I saw how I might get a few of those thousands out of him and not really do either him or anyone else a bit of harm."

French, it must be confessed, was listening to this story with a good deal of disappointment. So far it rang true, and if it were it might explain Joss' puzzling actions in connection with Sir John, without throwing any light on the latter's death. It was therefore with more than a little anxiety that he bent forward to listen as Joss went on.

"I began by getting a few cards printed in the name of Coates, and I called on Sir John, saying I was from Belfast. I chose Belfast because the old boy had come from it and I knew it for I'd lived there before I went to the States. Also because it was the centre of the Irish linen trade. Well, I told Sir John that I'd heard he was interested in developments in the uses of linen. He said that was so, and I went on to

144

explain that a friend of mine and I had been working for years trying to find a scheme for combining artificial silk with linen, so as to get a smooth glossy fabric that would yet be strong. I saw I'd got him interested and I went on to say that at last my friend had succeeded and that we had made the stuff. As far as we could see from rough tests, it was a swell fabric, as smooth as silk, uncreasing and with any amount of wear in it. He was quite upset at that, and when I told him that we had no money to develop the thing and wanted to let someone with capital in with us, I saw I'd got him on the hook.

"What I really wanted, as you may guess, was to get hold of his plans and I fixed it, or tried to fix it, like this. I told him our apparatus was at our house in Sandy Row in Belfast and asked would he come over and see it. He jumped at the idea. He was to see our plant and get a copy of our plans and in return, if he was satisfied, he was to join us in the venture, putting up the necessary cash. He was also to take over the plans of his own invention, which by this time he'd told me about, with the idea of combining his scheme with ours to get improved results. When this was settled we fixed the date and route. For reasons I'll explain later I wanted him to travel by Stranraer, and as I found he was a bad sailor, I had no difficulty in getting him to agree to the short sea route. To clinch the matter I said I would engage the berth for him and to this he also agreed.

"It happened that I was joining Victor Magill and a couple of other men in a motor launch cruise up the west coast of Scotland. We were to start from Barrow on the Wednesday evening and work along the coast to Campbeltown and from there north. We were to call at Portpatrick on the Thursday. I told my friends I could not start with them from Barrow, but that I would join them at Portpatrick.

"Now I come to the part I like least to think about. Unknown to Sir John I engaged sleeping berths with a communicating door. For my scheme it was necessary to get into his berth without being seen in the corridor. I also bought a single dose of a harmless sleeping draught."

Once again Joss showed hesitation. His last two statements had given French a nasty jar. If he were going to admit drugging and theft – burglary, French supposed it would really be – it would go far towards proving the truth of his story. A man does not falsely plead guilty to serious crime. French had been reserving this matter of the communicating berths for Joss' confounding, but now the man had taken the wind out of his sails. French swore silently as the other resumed.

"I got down to Euston in good time for the 7.40 on that Wednesday evening and shut myself into my berth. I heard Sir John arriving, and when his man had cleared out I watched my opportunity, showed myself at his door unseen by anyone else, and said I'd some news for him and that I'd come in for a chat after the train started.

"When the attendant had gone his rounds I bolted my corridor door and set to work with a bunch of skeleton keys on the communicating door. I'm a bit of a mechanic in a small way, but it took me all I knew to get that door unlocked. At last, however, I did it. These doors, as you probably know, are fastened in three ways; by a finger bolt on each side as well as a lock. I had now unlocked the door and I also undid the finger bolt on my side.

"I peeped out into the corridor, watched my chance again, knocked at Sir John's door and entered. He was lying down, and without letting him see me, I bolted the door behind me; that was the corridor door, you understand. We began to talk and I told him how much my friend and I hoped from the invention and how long we'd been working at it and so on; just sort of padding. At last I said we should try and get a good sleep and suggested a nightcap. I brought out my flask and said I'd got some extra special old brandy that I wished he'd try. He agreed. I had the sleeping draught ready mixed in it and I poured it out with some water in his tumbler and gave it him and he drank it off. I pretended to drink out of the cap of the flask, but I didn't really swallow any. Presently he went asleep as I'd hoped he would. As soon as he was over I unbolted and opened the communicating door and went back to my berth and bolted its corridor door. That is to say, the door between the berths was open, but both corridor doors were bolted. You follow me?"

"I follow you," French said dryly. "You could do what you wanted in either stateroom without interference from the corridor."

"That's right," Joss admitted ruefully. "I started in then and had a look for the plans. I searched everywhere, through the man's luggage and his clothes and under his pillow. I even rolled him over and looked under the sheet, but devil a plan there was. He was evidently carrying the thing in his head.

"Well, as you can imagine, this pretty well upset my apple cart. The whole journey had hinged on Sir John's bringing his plans, and now he hadn't done it. I cursed till I was blue in the face, but what could I do? I sat and thought for a couple of hours, but I could see no way out. So I had to give up. I relocked and bolted the communicating door and hoped that Sir John wouldn't twig that he'd been drugged.

"When we got to Stranraer – "

French held up his hand.

"A moment, please," he interrupted. "I don't follow about that door. How did you bolt the communicating door on Sir John's side? You went out into the corridor again, I suppose?"

"No. By that time it was late and I didn't want to be seen coming out of Sir John's room. What I did was this: I unbolted his corridor door, then I went back through the communicating door to my own state-room, bolted this last on my own side and then with my skeleton key locked it."

"But that left Sir John's side of the communicating door unbolted?"

"That's so, but I couldn't help it. It was less of a risk than going into the corridor. Besides it wasn't so deadly. Anyone noticing it would have assumed it had been accidentally left open. All the same in the morning after we arrived at Stranraer and Sir John had got out, I slipped my hand in from the corridor and shot the bolt."

"Quite clear," French agreed. "I take it from all this that your friend had not solved the problem? Or had you a friend at all?"

Joss shrugged.

"I had no friend, Mr French," he answered in a low tone. "I knew nothing of linen and I had no house in Sandy Row. The thing was only a bluff. I hoped to get Sir John's idea and to make a pot out of it. I'm darned sorry for it now, but that's the whole truth."

"Very well, I follow that all right. You didn't find the plans and that saved you from stealing them. But as a matter of academic interest I'd like to understand just what you'd have done if you had found them?"

Little drops of sweat were standing on Joss' forehead. With a quick movement he wiped them off.

"I had a selection of paper and envelopes with me. If I'd got them I'd have made up a dummy so that with luck Sir John wouldn't have noticed the theft till he got to Belfast. You see, Mr French, I'm being perfectly frank with you, because as I didn't do any of these things you've nothing on me."

French shrugged in his turn.

"That's what you intended to do. Now what did you do actually?"

"Actually," Joss returned, "I did what I'd have done in any case. I looked in on Sir John just before we came into Stranraer and told him I'd met an invalid friend in the third sleeper and that under the circumstances I couldn't avoid travelling with him and seeing him to his home. I said it would only delay me a few minutes and that I'd follow him to Sandy Row. As a matter of fact when he'd gone aboard I went to Portpatrick and joined my friends. I'm not proud of it, inspector. I'd give a good deal if it hadn't happened. However, there it is. I've told you everything just as it occurred because I recognise the circumstances look suspicious. But as I say, I've actually done nothing wrong and you've nothing against me."

"I suppose drugging a man with intent to rob him is nothing wrong?"

"No good to you," Joss rejoined, shaking his head. "You can't prove it. You know that if you tried anything on I would deny the story and then you'd be in the soup. It would be your word against mine, and mine would be the probable story. You know my confession is not worth *that* in court." Joss snapped his fingers dramatically. "No, inspector, I've tried to help you because I saw it was the best thing for myself, not because I wanted to put myself in your power."

"There's only one other point, I think," French said, after a moment's thought. "You said if you didn't produce some hundreds of pounds at short notice you would be ruined. Now you say you didn't get any money from Sir John. Obviously you are not ruined. Where then did the money come from?"

A dull flush crept over the man's face.

"Victor Magill," he answered, with evident shame. "During the cruise I mentioned how I was fixed and he lent me enough to get me out."

When Joss ceased speaking there was a silence for some minutes. Finally French rose abruptly.

"You may be required to give evidence," he said, and there was a noticeable absence of his usual suavity in his manner. "Don't go away without letting me know at the Yard. I warn you that whether your story's true or false I've ample justification for arresting you, and if you attempt any tricks you will be arrested. That'll do for today."

French was profoundly disappointed. The one tangible clue that he had got hold of was that of Coates and the communicating door. And now this had been explained away. Admittedly the explanation was not satisfactory as far as the plans were concerned. But French was not interested in a possible theft of plans. It was Sir John Magill's murder that he wanted to clear up, and as a clue to this the communicating door had simply petered out. As he walked slowly back to the Yard he cursed bitterly under his breath. So far his case against Breene remained the most likely solution, and wishing again that he had a free hand to investigate it in Belfast, he went disgustedly to lunch.

12

SCOTLAND YARD

French's mood had not lightened when he returned to the Yard. He had been unfortunate in not finding anyone he knew at the restaurant, with the result that during his solitary lunch he had been unable to banish the case from his mind. Now as he settled down to work at it again it was from a barren sense of duty rather than with any hope that he might obtain results.

He began by writing to the Scotch police authorities of Campbeltown to get a report from Dr MacGregor as to the injury to Victor's knee. Then he sent a man to the Patent Office to find out if Sir John had provisionally protected his invention. Finally he set himself doggedly to review Joss' statement so as to satisfy himself that there really was nothing to be learned about it. Part of the story he believed absolutely. The scheme of getting Sir John into Joss' power in an adjoining sleeping berth and there drugging him rang true. So did the somewhat intricate operations with the doors and the search for the plans. The stories told to Sir John, moreover, must have been somewhat as stated by Joss, judging by the way in which the old man had acted on them. But where French doubted the statement was in its finale. *Had* Joss' search proved unavailing? Had he not really found and stolen the plans? To French this seemed more than likely. It might well be that Joss had actually replaced the packet with a dummy so that the old man had not learnt of his loss till he reached Belfast.

But though Joss' tale might not be entirely true, it seemed to contain enough truth to relieve himself and his friends from suspicion of the murder. Naturally, therefore, it did nothing to clear up the fate of Sir John Magill. The reason for the old gentleman's visit to Sandy Row was now known, but not what took place there. It did not explain why Sir John had gone to the Cave Hill, still less did it account for the extraordinary episodes at Larne and Whitehead. No, there was more in the whole business than he, French, had yet visualised.

He turned once again to his Breene theory. Did this statement of Joss' support or rebut it?

It didn't seem to do either. It was now clear that Breene had not been responsible for Sir John's visit to Belfast. But on the other hand might he not have taken advantage of it? French did not know. He sighed wearily as he considered the point and reconsidered it and then considered it again.

One thing at least became increasingly certain. Here in England the solution was beyond his reach. It *must* be on the Irish side. He decided that if Chief Inspector Mitchell agreed he would write to Rainey that very evening pressing his view of the situation. Then he could drop the case. There was plenty of work for him in London.

But it happened that just then the post came in with a letter from the police headquarters in Belfast. Superintendent Rainey wrote that certain discoveries which had been made by his staff seemed to indicate that the key to the Magill mystery must lie in England, and that if convenient to all concerned, he would send Sergeant M'Clung over for a consultation. At this French swore, but he sent a wire that he could see M'Clung at any time. A couple of hours later there was a reply that the sergeant was leaving that evening.

French, considerably disgruntled, swore more viciously. It was not indeed until he had reached his home and had his supper that he settled down to his usual state of complacency.

He reached the Yard next morning to find that M'Clung had already arrived.

"You weren't long in Ireland," French greeted him. "Why on earth did they send for you if they didn't want you?"

M'Clung grinned.

"They've made some discoveries, Mr French," he explained. "They sent for me to hear the details so that I might come over and tell you."

French shook his head.

"It's a bad business," he declared. "A very bad business. Do you know that yesterday I was just going to write you that the whole solution must lie with you and that I might withdraw from the case? And now you've proved that it lies over here."

"Well, we haven't just got that length, Mr French," M'Clung returned with the suspicion of a smile. "What we think is that it doesn't lie in Northern Ireland. We wouldn't like to take it on us to say just where it does lie."

French grunted.

"I suppose that means that you know nothing about it?"

M'Clung laughed outright.

"As you know, sir," he pointed out, "officially that could never be the case. But between you and me and the wall it's about the size of it."

"Well, you may take it from me that it doesn't lie over here."

"But it must lie somewhere, sir," M'Clung said innocently.

French glanced at him keenly.

"Oh, you think so, do you? Did you get my letter about Breene? No? Well, sit down on that chair and put on that filthy pipe of yours and let's hear the great discovery." ·

M'Clung told his tale well. He had the gift of narration, and French could picture the events occurring almost as if he was seeing them.

It seemed that after French's departure the authorities of Northern Ireland had concentrated on trying to trace in detail the movements of Sir John Magill from the moment he left Sandy Row until his body reached what his murderer at least believed would be its last resting place at Lurigan.

They had considered and rejected a theory that Sir John had been murdered by political enemies. Though the old man had always been a staunch Unionist, the police thought it unlikely that he had ever incurred the really serious enmity of his political opponents. Especially unlikely was it that his death, had it been decided on, would have been delayed for so long a period. The "troubles" were definitely over and had been for years. Moreover, the police knew practically all the gunmen in the city, men who in many cases were known to have committed murder, but against whom nothing could be proved. These were checked up and the police were satisfied that none of them had recently been on the warpath.

After considerable thought, Superintendent Rainey had decided to fall back on publicity. A reward for information as to the deceased's movements was therefore offered.

Advertisements were inserted in the local papers, and notices were exhibited at police barracks and elsewhere, throughout the country.

On the day of the newspaper insertions, a Mr Francis M'Comb called at police headquarters. He said that he had read the advertisement and believed he had seen the man in question.

He stated that on Thursday, October 3rd, which was the day of Sir John's visit to Belfast, he and his wife had taken some English visitors up the Cave Hill. They had climbed the Sheeps' Path from the Antrim Road to near the top, returning by the same route. On reaching their home on the Malone Road about six o'clock his wife missed an earring. It was not intrinsically of great value, but for sentimental reasons she prized it highly. She was so much upset about the loss that M'Comb volunteered to return immediately to the place where she thought she had dropped it – a slippery bit of the path on which she had had a fall. He did so and found the trinket, and it was when he was returning down the path to the Antrim Road that he saw the man.

"I'll have to explain what the path is like so that you'll understand the story," went on M'Clung. "The lower part passes through private grounds and it's fenced off from these by barbed wire palings, set back fifteen or twenty feet from each side and with laurels in patches between it and the fences. When you leave the Antrim Road the path leads through trees at first, but in two or three minutes you come to a clearing on the left side. Near the top of the clearing there's a clump of rhododendrons, about fifty feet across. It's quite a thick clump and it lies about sixty or seventy feet out from the side of the clearing and the path. I could draw it if you don't follow me."

"It's clear enough so far," French admitted cautiously.

M'Clung nodded.

"Well, M'Comb was coming down after finding the earring. When he was passing the clearing he happened to look up and he saw a man come out of the clump. The man looked round in a stealthy sort of way and then he hurried across the clearing towards the path. M'Comb was a bit surprised, but he thought it was no business of his and he went on down to the Antrim Road.

"Just near where the path comes out there is a tramway halt and M'Comb went to it and stood waiting for a car. He hadn't been there two minutes when the man appeared. He followed over to the halt and M'Comb had a good look at him. Mr French, it was Sir John Magill!"

"Good," said French, considerably interested. "What time was that?"

"About a quarter past seven. It was getting dusk, but on account of being near the man M'Comb was able to see him clearly. Then a tram came along and they both got on board, Sir John inside and M'Comb on the top."

Trams from the Antrim Road, M'Clung explained, reach the City Centre by two routes, via Carlisle Circus or via Duncairn Gardens. The Duncairn Gardens route takes a detour which brings it within a few yards of the Northern Counties station of the L M S railway, that for Whitehead and Larne. This particular car was going via Carlisle Circus, therefore had it contained passengers who wished to travel by rail, these would have alighted at the top of Duncairn Gardens and either taken the ten-minute walk down the Gardens to the station or waited for a following car.

It happened by a stroke of luck that M'Comb, who was sitting at the back of the tram, saw Sir John alight, not indeed at Duncairn Gardens, but a couple of blocks before they reached it. As the tram passed on Sir John crossed the sidewalk and disappeared into a shop.

The police at once got M'Comb to stop a tram at the place in question, and asked him to mount to the top and from there to point out the shop. This he was unable to do, but he showed them the block containing it.

Inquiries at all the shops in the block soon gave the desired information. The young lady behind the counter of a confectioner's stated that at about half past seven on an evening about the date mentioned a man answering the given description had come in and bought some fruit and nut chocolate. The price was one-and-six and he had offered her a pound in payment. She was out of change, and realising that she would have to go out for it and leave her customer alone in the shop, the girl gave him a very searching look. It was this fact that had impressed his appearance on her mind. For the same reason she had glanced at the clock and now remembered the hour. On receiving his change the man had left immediately, turning in the direction of Duncairn Gardens.

Both this young lady and M'Comb declared Sir John's photograph shown them by the police was that of the man in question. The girl had seen him in a better light than M'Comb, and she stated that he looked dishevelled and that there was moss on his coat, as if he had been lying on the grass.

It was seen at once that the hours mentioned by these two witnesses worked in sufficiently well with what was already known of Sir John's movements. He had travelled to Whitehead by the 8.0 train, and had he walked down the Sheeps' Path and bought his chocolate when stated, he would just have arrived at the station about a quarter to eight.

The police next asked M'Comb to accompany them to the Sheeps' Path and to point out the spot where Sir John had emerged from the rhododendrons. A careful search was made of the surroundings with the result that some further very interesting discoveries were made. In the heart of the clump a small space of some eight feet square was found to have been trampled down. Here twigs had been placed to make a rude couch and branches had been cut and pushed into the interstices between the bushes with the evident object of making the retreat even more invisible from outside.

But these discoveries paled into insignificance compared to M'Clung's last find. Close by and equally hidden by the bushes were traces of digging. Cut sods were piled over a little mound of fresh soil and scraps of clay lay on the surrounding grass. It was not another grave – it was too small for that. Rather it suggested treasure trove.

Spades were sent for and the soil was removed. Below was loose clay. This was lifted out and at a depth of a couple of feet the treasure was come on.

Folded into a tight roll was a cloak or garment of very peculiar shape. It was made of dark brown velvet and consisted of a complete suit and hat in one. The body portion was made like a mechanic's overalls, with full length legs and arms and an opening up the front closed by buttons. Attached to the body at the back of the neck was a helmet like a monk's cowl. The garment was roughly made, and coarsely sewn. But it was of a small size. In fact it would have exactly fitted Sir John Magill.

French gave vent to an exclamation of amazement.

"That isn't everything yet, sir," M'Clung went on, delighted at the reception his story was getting. "Wrapped up inside the cloak was a short piece of light rope ladder. It was made with dark brown silk ropes and thin rungs of dark brown cane. At one end the ropes terminated in a pair of light metal hooks, painted black. These hooks were of a peculiar shape, rather like notes of interrogation, the ladder being attached halfway down the curve. Altogether the ladder was just under six feet long."

French swore.

"What under the sun did you make of that?" he asked.

M'Clung shrugged.

"What could we make of it, sir?" he returned. "The only suggestion that I've heard was that Sir John was taking part in the ceremonial of some secret society. I'm neither an Orangeman nor a mason, but I understand the ladder is a symbol in both orders. And Sir John was high up among the Orangemen. All the same that didn't strike me as reasonable. Would it you, sir?"

French shook his head.

"More like a burglar's outfit, if you ask me," he answered. "But I'd like to think over it a bit before I make any suggestions. I've never come across anything like this before. What games that old man could have been up to at his time of life beats me."

French indeed did feel completely puzzled by this new development.

"Curse the thing," he grumbled. "There's no making head or tail of it." He moved uneasily, then went on with a change of manner. "So far as I can see, M'Clung, the one thing that comes out of it is what I said: that the whole trouble lies on the Irish side of the Channel. Why don't you go and solve it instead of coming over here and worrying me?"

M'Clung grinned.

"Och, Mr French," he answered innocently. "Sure, we couldn't do without your help anyway."

"Oh, you couldn't, couldn't you?" French grunted suspiciously. "Well, if that's so get along and tell me why you think your case lies over here."

M'Clung knocked the ashes out of his pipe and proceeded slowly to refill it. When he answered he spoke with evident seriousness.

"Well, it's what the superintendent thinks really, sir, though, mind you, I agree with him. He thinks the explanation must lie over here simply because there's nothing on our side to account for it."

"In other words a confession of failure?" French suggested.

M'Clung shrugged.

"The superintendent didn't put it just that way," he explained. "He said that though we had nothing, you had that affair of Coates and the sleeping berths in the train."

"That's a washout."

M'Clung looked startled.

"Washout, sir?" he repeated. "That's bad. You mean there's nothing on this side to account for it either?"

"That's exactly what I do mean," French growled. He glanced suspiciously at the other, then apparently satisfied, went on: "Well, I'll tell you. This man 'Coates' was really Joss, and he admitted giving the false name and volunteered all that about the communicating door as well as saying he'd drugged Sir John," and French described his interview in detail.

M'Clung was manifestly disappointed.

"The superintendent'll be sorry to hear that, sir. He was counting a lot on that Coates business."

"As a matter of fact," French admitted, "so was I; it was the only tangible thing we had. However, it's gone west and that's all there's to it."

Though French spoke despondently his manner belied his words to such an extent that M'Clung asked hopefully: "Have you anything in your mind, sir?"

For a moment French did not reply. Then he rose, and going to the vertical file in the corner of his room he took out the copy of the letter he had sent to Belfast on the previous evening.

"That's what I had in my mind yesterday midday," he said. "Since I heard Joss' story I'm not so sure about it. Read it and we'll discuss it."

M'Clung was eminently polite about the Breene theory, but he was clearly not impressed by it. "You know, sir," he said deferentially, "we went into that. Unless our people are pretty badly out, Breene was in the hotel all the time."

"Your people may be absolutely right," French admitted, "but in the light of this business about the engagement I suggest you go into it again and make quite sure."

M'Clung was agreeably reassuring as to that. Rainey, he was certain, would put the matter beyond the faintest shadow of doubt. They talked of Breene for some time, then the conversation swung back to Sir John.

"I wonder," French said absently, as if following out a private train of thought. Then he became silent as he considered an idea which had suddenly flashed into his mind. "By Jove, yes, sergeant! Sir John would hide himself all right! Look at it this way."

Keen interest once again showed in French's manner. He laid down his pipe, sat forward in his chair, and began to tick off his points on his fingers.

"Here's a problem for you," he resumed. "Would a successful robbery not involve murder? In other words, could such a secret be stolen so long as Sir John remained alive?"

"Was it protected?" M'Clung questioned.

"No, it wasn't, but it doesn't matter two hoots whether it was or not. Come now: use your grey cells, as that Belgian would say. Put yourself in Joss' place and assume you'd got the plans. Could you have used them?"

M'Clung remained silent, then he shook his head.

"Very well," French resumed, "let us consider what Joss would expect would happen if Sir John remained alive. Sir John would reach Sandy Row, and because the address he had been given proved non-existent, he would realise something was wrong. He would search for his plans and find they were missing. What then would he do? He would go to the police, report his loss, describe his process and declare his suspicions of Coates. The police would get busy and find Joss. But they wouldn't arrest him. And why? Because they would have no proof against him. The police and Sir John would be, so to speak, in a position of stalemate. They couldn't move."

French paused and looked expectantly at the sergeant, who nodded emphatically.

"Now," went on French, "Sir John would be in a position of stalemate, but there's more in it than that. So Joss would be also. Joss couldn't use his knowledge. Directly 'Sillin' or anything like it appeared on the market the police would be on to it. They would find out the process and see that it was the same as Sir John's and a short investigation would enable them to connect Joss with the manufacture. If he wasn't personally concerned in it they'd be able to trace up a sale. Anyway they'd get him. As sure as that stuff came on the market Joss would go to jail. Now Joss must know all this, so he must see that his theft could be of no value to him."

Again French paused to receive the sergeant's tribute. "What then," he went on, "would stand between Joss and his fortune? Just one thing – Sir John Magill's life. If Sir John could be kept silent all would be well. It follows absolutely."

M'Clung in his delight lapsed into the vernacular.

"Boys, Mr French, but that's powerful!" he declared. "I never heard the like of it!"

"But do you agree with it?" demanded French, who had not as yet fully grasped Ulster idiom.

"I do so." M'Clung could be comfortably direct when he desired.

"Good. Then if we're right so far something else follows. I think we can say that an accomplice must have met Sir John in Sandy Row. If Joss knew just when the old man would make his discovery, he would be bound to guard against it. Someone would meet Sir John and see to it that he didn't go to a police station."

M'Clung, with a suspicion of what was coming, agreed less warmly.

"Very well," said French, "there's the clue on your side and you've got to follow it up."

M'Clung's enthusiasm evaporated instantaneously.

"Would you not think, Mr French," he suggested craftily, "that they were all in it?"

"All?"

"Yes, the whole darned launch party."

This was no new idea to French. Again and again he had suspected it and again and again he had supposed he was mistaken. He really didn't know, of course –

"And Malcolm too," went on M'Clung.

French started. Was there any help here? What if Malcolm could have been that mysterious individual whose existence he had just postulated?

"By Jove, M'Clung. If you people can prove that Malcolm was a partner with the others it'll be the beginning of the end. What about Malcolm meeting his father in Sandy Row, eh?"

M'Clung nodded profoundly.

"That's the style, sir. That's what I was thinking myself. Malcolm. Or maybe Breene," he added tactfully. "Anyway we'll make inquiries. We should find out easy enough."

For a solid couple of hours the two men continued discussing the affair, but without reaching anything more illuminating. Finally it was agreed that the two lines they had considered were to be explored to the utmost of their capacity. M'Clung and the Belfast police were to assume that someone met Sir John in Sandy Row and were to concentrate on finding this person, whether it were Magill or Breene or someone hitherto unknown. French on his part was to assume that the whole four members of the launch party were involved and was to concentrate on the trip, trying to obtain further links between the travellers and the affairs of Sir John.

While these decisions were taken, it was without enthusiasm on either side, each of the detectives believing that success, if attainable at all, lay in the line his companion was to work.

"I'll tell you what it is," French declared finally. "You and your Belfast superintendent are the darnedest pair of nuisances I've struck for many a long day. Come out and have a bit of lunch."

13

LONDON: BARROW: NEWCASTLE

Of all the jobs that fell to French, the investigation of the life, habits and human relationships of a given individual was that which he found most tedious. His anticipations, therefore, were not particularly happy as he settled down to learn what he could of Sir John Magill's past, in the hope of getting some further connections between the old gentleman and the members of the cruise.

For some days he worked away systematically, interviewing the dead man's relatives and servants as well as such of his acquaintances as he could get in touch with, but without result. Then on the third morning a chance word gave him what he thought might constitute an additional link.

He had called on a certain Mr Aloysius Hepworth, a wealthy old stockbroker, who had been one of Sir John's cronies at the Blenheim Club. He had asked the old gentleman whether he knew of anything which might have been preying on Sir John's mind. Mr Hepworth said that some four or five months previous to his death Sir John had seemed a good deal worried, and in confidence he had explained the cause. Neither Malcolm nor Victor were doing as the old gentleman would have wished. Both were in financial difficulties and both had applied to him for help. He feared that he would be called upon to spend a considerable sum for each if they were to be kept out of the bankruptcy court.

At this French pricked up his ears.

"Yes," he answered mendaciously, "we knew that Major Magill had been badly hit by the depression in the linen trade and we knew that Mr Victor Magill was also in a bad way. Sir John didn't happen to mention the cause of Victor's trouble?"

Mr Hepworth shrugged.

"The usual thing," he said contemptuously. "Horses. Hundreds on every big race. Owing money all over the place. A cool thousand to some blighter called Mallace and the Lord knows how much to others besides."

"And was Sir John going to meet it?"

"He hadn't made up his mind when I saw him. He didn't want the family disgraced. He talked of debts of honour and all that. Bunkum, I call it."

"People feel strongly about that sort of thing all the same."

"Sir John did. But he'd helped Victor before and to do it again seemed like pouring good money after bad."

"The money wouldn't have meant much to Sir John."

"That may be. But no one likes being bled."

French did not see how a temporary debt to Mallace could have affected the case. However, the matter would leave to be looked into. He had to interview Mallace in any case, and with this matter of the debt fresh in his mind, the present seemed as good a time as any.

Maurice Mallace, he had learned from Victor, was an agent for the "Lowe" oil engine. A short investigation with a technical directory informed him further that the makers of these engines were Messrs Potter & Lowe and that their

offices were in Bedford Street off the Strand. Having telephoned an appointment with Mallace, French walked
across.

Mallace was a short, jolly-looking man of about forty,
with a bright manner and a knowing eye. He led the way
into a small private office.

"I am investigating the death of Sir John Magill," French
began, "and as you can readily understand, I am trying to
find out whether the late gentleman had any special worries
preying on his mind prior to his death. In fact, I am looking
for a motive for suicide."

"But I thought a verdict of murder had been brought
in?" Mallace returned.

"By the coroner's jury, yes. But at the Yard we don't pay
much attention to coroner's juries. The truth is that the
circumstances of Sir John's death are rather mysterious and
we are really not yet in a position to say whether he
committed suicide or whether he was murdered. I was
hoping that you may be able to help me to a conclusion on
the point."

Mallace's features indicated a slight surprise. He glanced
keenly at French, then laughed shortly.

"I'm afraid you've come to the wrong shop," he declared.
"Beyond the fact that he was the uncle of Victor Magill,
who is a friend of mine, I know nothing whatever about the
man."

"None the less I think you can help me," French
persisted. "As you doubtless know, Sir John had a son as
well as this nephew, Victor. According to my information
both were involved financially and both were worrying Sir
John for money. The son's trouble arose through the
depression in the Irish linen trade, Victor's because he was
supposed to be in debt – to you, amongst others, to the

extent of a thousand pounds. It is confirmation or otherwise of this last matter that I want from you."

Mallace's features now showed as much surprise as French imagined they could.

"Bless my soul!" he exclaimed. "I never heard anything like that. So that's the way rumours get about, is it? I'd be interested to know where you heard that?"

"Then it's not true?" French asked.

"True? Of course it's not true. A thousand pounds! I only wish it were. No, but I'll tell you what's true, inspector. Victor and I were betting together – horses. Victor lost – but only a hundred. One hundred; not ten. We were very good friends and I did not press him about it, but he seemed anxious to square it off and he did so."

"He paid?"

"Every penny."

"And when was that?"

"Let's see." Mallace hesitated. "Between three and four months ago, I should say. I can turn up the exact date if you like."

"You don't happen to know where he got the money?"

"From Sir John, at least so he told me. I said when he gave it to me, 'Look here, old chap,' I said, 'don't you worry about this if it's not convenient. I'm not in any hurry.' 'Oh,' he said, 'that's all right. I pitched a tale to my respected uncle and he turned up trumps as I knew he would.' He spoke very appreciatively of Sir John. All the same, inspector, Victor's no charity. He's far better off than I am."

"There was some story that he owed a lot beside his debt to you?"

"I believe he did owe a little, I don't know how much, but I understood there were a few small sums. He said that Sir John had cleared the whole business off. But if you want to know about it, why don't you ask Victor? He'll probably tell you everything, though he may wonder what business of yours it is."

French laughed.

"Quite right, Mr Mallace," he said good humouredly. "And if I asked you about your launch trip to Scotland you'd probably wonder the same. But I really am interested in that trip," and he told his yarn of his own efforts in that direction. Mallace thawed immediately. Motor launching was evidently a pursuit which lay close to his heart.

"Yes," he said, "we had a jolly fine time. We had a comfortable boat and good weather, the two things that make the difference. Of course the launch was both old and slow: she would only do about nine knots, though we rarely ran her above seven to keep down noise and vibration. But she was broad in the beam and steady and dry, a thorough good sea boat. One man could run her, in fact I ran her myself from off the Isle of Man to Portpatrick, for Victor damaged his leg after we left Barrow and took to his bunk, while Joss and Teer, our other two men, didn't come aboard till Portpatrick."

"Joss and Teer," said French. "Were those not two more of the men to whom Victor owed money?"

Mallace looked at him curiously.

"I couldn't tell you," he answered, "but I should say it wasn't at all unlikely. We four were together a good deal, and Victor probably gambled with them as well as with me."

On the pretext of wanting a launch for the trip he hoped to carry out in the following summer, French obtained the name of the firm in Barrow from whom Mallace had hired his. Then he stood up to go.

"There is one thing you shouldn't do that we did, inspector," Mallace said as he walked with French to the door, "and that is, don't travel at night. We did that because I was combining business with pleasure. We have a number of agencies for the Lowe engines in Western Scotland, and I called at these as we passed. We left most of our ports in the small hours, got to the next place in the forenoon and I did my business while my friends played around. It suited everybody except that some of us came off rather short of sleep. Well, good day, inspector. I hope you'll get all you want."

Had French spoken his thoughts as he walked back to the Yard, his language would have been more than unparliamentary. Curse this darned case! Was he never going to get any information without having it contradicted in the next breath? Had Victor owed Mallace a thousand pounds, or had he not? Had he paid his debt, whatever it was, or had he not? Was he badly off or well off? In short, had he a motive for assisting to steal the plans, perhaps not recognising the terrible end of such a scheme.

From his own observation French would have said that Victor had plenty of money, at least in the restricted sense in which the term is used by ordinary middle class people. Certainly he had shown no evidences of financial stringency, and it was impossible to imagine him in such desperate straits as to be driven to crime.

However the matter must be put beyond doubt and the first thing was to confirm that gift from Sir John some three or four months previously. It was too late to visit the old man's bank that night, but early next morning French called and asked for the manager.

On showing his credentials the matter became simple. A clerk was summoned who led French to a small private office and produced the records covering Sir John's account. But there was nothing even remotely resembling the transaction mentioned by Mallace. The last money which had passed between uncle and nephew was a cheque for 500 guineas dated December 23rd, and as similar cheques had been issued on the same date on previous years, French took this to be merely an annual Christmas present.

Of course the fact that there was no record of it did not mean that the transaction had not taken place. The money might have been paid in cash. There was simply nothing to confirm or disprove its existence.

On returning to the Yard French found that two important letters had come in. The first was a reply from the Campbeltown police. The sergeant wrote that he had called on Dr MacGregor, who remembered visiting Victor Magill – the original of the photograph enclosed – aboard the launch on the date and at the hour mentioned. Victor was suffering from a contused injury to his left knee such as might have been caused by the fall on the companion steps which he described. The injury was genuine beyond the slightest possibility of doubt and the doctor estimated that it must have been incurred at about the time stated by Victor. Its results would be practically total disablement for a couple of days, followed by three or four weeks of lameness.

French gave a sigh of relief. That settled the launch party. Whether or not its members might have been indirectly connected with Sir John's murder through the theft of the plans, it was now certain that none of them had taken any actual part in the crime itself. Certainty on any point in this troublesome case was a new and a pleasant experience for French and he felt that to have obtained so much of it was nothing short of a triumph.

The second letter was from Rainey. He was – he said – profoundly interested in French's theory about Breene. He had for the second time gone into the matter of his alibi and – reluctantly – he had been forced to the conclusion that it was good. There was definite evidence that Breene was in the hotel during lunch, tea and dinner on the Thursday and breakfast on the Friday. This evidence was not dependent on a single waiter, who might have been squared. The head waiter had seen him also. In the morning the chambermaid had gone into his room to pull up the blinds and swore that he was in bed.

Admittedly Breene was not seen between the close of dinner at about 7.40 p.m. and the call next morning. But that he remained in the building during this critical period was proved by two things. First, if he had been out all night, Rainey's men believed it would have been impossible for him to have returned unobserved to his bedroom. Second, the chambermaid had seen that the light was on in his room for about half an hour between eleven and twelve. Rainey appreciated French's idea greatly, but…and so on.

French sighed again, this time from disappointment.

The Breene theory, then, was a washout. He turned his thoughts back to the quartet.

Would not the discovery that Victor's alibi also was good end his investigation into the movements of the quartet? Personally he thought so, then he saw that Superintendent Rainey would not be satisfied unless the complete activities of the four were demonstrated. As a matter of fact it would not take so long to finish the thing up. He had already interviewed Victor, Joss and Mallace. It would be necessary only to see Teer. He would do that at once and then be done with the whole wearisome affair.

But when he reached Teer's rooms in Rudolph Street, Hampstead, it was only to find the man was from home on a business tour. It appeared that he also was the travelling representative of a London firm – Messrs Livesay & Pullman, the paint manufacturers. French therefore called at the firm's head office in Queen Victoria Street and obtained Teer's itinerary. From this he learned that the man was at present in Edinburgh and was working slowly southwards through Berwick, Newcastle and the great north-eastern towns to York and the Midlands.

French decided that as he had to go to Barrow, he would do so first, then cross the country and intercept Teer at some convenient centre.

He took the afternoon train from Euston, slept at Barrow, and in the morning was early at the establishment of Messrs Thos. Wivell & Sons. There he saw the senior partner, showed his official card and stated his business. A Mr Maurice Mallace had recently hired a motor launch for a cruise to Scotland. Would Mr Wivell kindly tell him all he could about the transaction?

Mr Wivell was not communicative. He remarked impassively that he would be pleased to give the inspector any information in his power, then dropped into silence.

French accordingly fell back on questions. By dint of a rigorous examination he learned that some three weeks prior to the date of the cruise, Messrs Wivell had received a letter from Mallace asking if the *Sea Hawk*, which he had once before had on hire, was available for a fortnight's cruise from Wednesday, October 2nd. The *Sea Hawk* was a most comfortable boat, eminently suitable for the purpose. Though admittedly old, she was a fine sea boat, steady as a rock and dry in all weathers. Her cabins were roomy and well fitted and all her equipment was first-class. She would do ten knots or more at a pinch.

On writing Mallace that he could have her, he replied that he would come down to make the final arrangements.

He had done so a week later, had looked over the boat, had paid half the hire and had given Messrs Wivell a note of several stores which he wished to have put on board. His instructions had been carried out.

On the Wednesday night Mallace and a friend, whose name was believed to be Magill, had arrived at Barrow station at 8.0 p.m.; that was by the 1.30 p.m. train from Euston. There they had been met by Messrs Wivell's clerk and driven to the wharf where the *Sea Hawk* was lying. She had been brought in there by a mechanic, who had remained to hand her over to Mallace. On reaching the wharf, Mallace had again examined the boat, and had checked over the stores from his list. Everything appearing in order, he had taken over and started forthwith. A fortnight later he had returned the launch and paid the balance of the hire.

French said he was obliged for all this information, but would like to see the clerk and mechanic.

The clerk, who first appeared, had little to add to his employer's statement. He had met Mallace and Victor off the London train on that Wednesday night and had driven them in Wivell's car to the *Sea Hawk*. There he had checked over the stores and seen the two men start. That was at 9.15p.m. exactly. He knew because Mallace had discussed the probable time of their arrival at Portpatrick and the calculations had depended on the hour of leaving Barrow. The launch had headed north. He recognised both men, Mallace from his description and Victor from his photograph. No, Mr Magill was not then lame.

The mechanic was next summoned. He confirmed what had already been stated as to the start and agreed that the hour was 9.15 p.m., remembering it for the same reason.

So far, then, Mallace and Victor had spoken the truth. There could be no doubt that the cruise had started exactly as they had stated. According to their story they had called next at Portpatrick and then at Campbeltown. Their statements as to the Portpatrick call were true, for French had already investigated that, and in the case of Campbeltown the sergeant's letter provided an adequate check.

Teer, therefore, was French's next care. Looking up the man's itinerary, he found that next day he would be quartered at the Boar's Head Hotel in Newcastle. To Newcastle therefore French booked, arriving just in time for dinner.

He had no trouble in getting in touch with his new quarry. That huge bulk seated at a table near the fire could be no one else. French, after waiting till the man had settled down to smoke in a corner of the lounge, dropped into a chair beside him and presently got into conversation.

French was not prepossessed by his appearance. Though good-looking enough in a rather coarse way, Teer's face was unattractive. Except, when wearing a conventional smile, his mouth was harsh and cruel, his jaw too heavy and the expression in his eyes more than a little sinister. He was immensely big and powerful, a man, French felt, who would take a strong line and who would not be easily turned from his purpose.

In considering his method of approach, French found himself at a disadvantage. His suspicions of Teer were vague and unsubstantial. Of actual fact there was nothing against him except that he was a member of a suspect party. It was true that, instead of reaching the King's Arms at Stranraer in the evening, as he had written to the manager, he did not turn up till the following morning, but this was not in itself suspicious, and the delay might well have a satisfactory explanation. It was obvious that he might be entirely innocent and it therefore behoved French to move cautiously.

From the man's appearance French believed his only chance of learning anything was by directness. Therefore after they had discussed a heavy shower which had deluged the city just before dinner, and a street accident by which two lorrymen had lost their lives, he drew his chair closer, glanced round as if to make sure that they were not overheard, and asked confidentially if he was not addressing Mr Dennis Teer.

"My name," Teer admitted. His manner was slow and impassive and he showed neither curiosity nor interest at the question.

"Mine is French – Inspector French of New Scotland Yard. I came and sat here with a purpose, Mr Teer. I wanted a word with you in the hope that you could give me some information about a case I'm working on."

Teer neither moved nor changed his expression, but French thought his eyes flickered and they certainly took on a wary look. In spite of the man's outward calm, French felt sure he was inwardly keenly alive to what was taking place. Teer puffed deliberately at his cigar, then asked quietly: "What do you want to know?"

"A rather impertinent question, I'm afraid, Mr Teer," French smiled. "I want to know what sum, if any, you were owed by Mr Victor Magill during the last four or five months and whether such debts, again if any, have been paid?"

Teer turned slowly round and fixed French with a stare which gradually became aggressive.

"Well, you haven't half a cheek on you, have you?" he rumbled. "What blanked business of yours is that?"

French glanced round again as if anxious for secrecy. Though he lowered his voice, he answered briskly: "My business all right, Mr Teer. I'm on a murder case – the murder of Sir John Magill in Northern Ireland. No doubt you've read of it? The relations between Sir John and his nephew, Victor, are being investigated. It had been alleged that Sir John paid Mr Victor a large sum four or five months ago to clear off certain gambling debts. It is further alleged that part of these debts were to you. We want to check up the whole affair, hence my question."

"Who told you Victor Magill owed me money?"

" 'Acting on information received.' That's the phrase, as you doubtless know. But seriously, Mr Teer, I want this information. It is my duty to inform you that you are not bound to answer my questions, but if you can see your way to do so I shall be obliged."

The big man remained silent, staring at French out of his small, shifty eyes. French sensed an inimical intent which might have boded ill for him were he in the other's power. Presently Teer seemed to come to an unwilling decision, and his words showed that this was for conciliation.

"I'm hanged if I can see what business of yours my money transactions with Victor Magill are, or what they have to do with Sir John's death," he said at length, continuing reluctantly: "However there's nothing secret about them and I don't want it to look as if I was holding anything back. We did a bit of betting and gambling, both of us, in one way or another, horses sometimes, but mostly poker. Sometimes he won from me, and sometimes it was the other way round, but the amounts about balanced. During the last few months the luck was more with me than otherwise and in settling up he paid about a hundred. It was a game, you understand, and we were always friendly about it. At the present moment we're all square. That what you want?"

French admitted that his question had been answered, and with a confidential air proceeded to discuss the murder, pointing out incidentally that in his view the explanation of the whole affair lay in Ireland, hinting that Malcolm's conduct seemed far from satisfactory, and saying that if he himself had a free hand he would be operating at Larne and not in Newcastle-on-Tyne.

Whether Teer swallowed all this he could not tell, but he seemed to do so and after some further chatting French made a move to go. Then he paused and said: "It's a funny thing, Mr Teer, that I should be speaking to you today. I once ran you to earth, though it was entirely by mistake. Rather unusual, that, you'll admit."

Teer answered casually, though the wary look remained in his eyes.

"Ran me to earth by mistake? I've not the least idea what you're talking about, inspector. I'm not conscious of having been run to earth by you or anyone else."

"I ran you to earth at the King's Arms at Stranraer on the morning of Thursday, the 3rd instant. But I wasn't really looking for you. It was Mr Joss, and curiously enough it was on this same case. Mr Joss had travelled from Euston in the same sleeper as Sir John and I wanted to know if he had seen him *en route*. He had left the train at Stranraer, so I naturally tried round the hotels. I got on his track at once, as I thought. 'Oh, yes,' they said, 'a big man. Yes, he came in time for breakfast that morning you speak of.' That seemed all right until I found that he had dark hair and had come in his car. It was you, Mr Teer. When I mentioned red hair they said: 'Oh, yes, he came here also, about half an hour earlier.' That was Mr Joss. I've seen him since, but though he travelled in the same sleeper as Sir John they didn't meet."

Teer murmured vaguely.

"You had trouble that night, had you not, Mr Teer? They said at the hotel that they had been expecting you on the previous evening, but you hadn't turned up."

Here was the crisis of the conversation. French had spoken in the most off-hand manner he could achieve, but he was nevertheless keenly anxious as to the fate of his sally. A tiny thrill shot through him, as once again he saw the flicker in Teer's eyes, and felt alert tenseness behind the man's impassive features. His instincts, extraordinarily keen through long practice, told him the other had realised danger and that the battle between them was joined. For a moment Teer hesitated, then he replied easily; too easily, French imagined.

"I should just think I had trouble that night. Curse it, I feel annoyed even now when I look back on it. You know those occasions when everything goes wrong, one thing after another. Well, that was one of them."

French had an overwhelming suspicion that the tale he was about to hear had been prepared for just such an emergency as the present. He controlled his feelings, however, and showed merely a conventional interest.

"For some days before joining my friends in the launch," went on Teer, "I was touring in my car just as I am at present. I suppose if you were talking to Joss and Victor Magill you know that four of us went on a launch tour to Scotland? I was in this part of the world, in fact on that Tuesday night I slept here in this hotel. I was to join the launch at Portpatrick on the Thursday morning, and it was my intention to drive my car through to Stranraer on Wednesday. I reckoned it would take me about five hours to do the run and I intended to leave here about four, have an early dinner at Carlisle and push on about seven or later, arriving at Stranraer about eleven.

"I carried out this programme, except that I delayed longer over my dinner than I had intended, and it was eight o'clock as I turned out of Carlisle. Then my bad time set in. I passed Dumfries all right, but a few miles farther on I had a puncture. It was not a serious matter for I had a spare wheel, but when I tried my torch I found it was run down and I had to do everything by feel. The pressure was low in the spare and I had to pump it up. This was all in the day's work and I only mention it because I lost time over it. I daresay I was the most of an hour fumbling about there in the dark."

"That would bring it to about ten when you got started, I suppose?"

"Later than that. It was easily half past ten when I got away again. However I reckoned on being into Stranraer by one o'clock. I made pretty good running past Castle Douglas and Newton Stewart, but on the high ground between there and Glenluce my engine stopped.

"I don't know if you are familiar with the country there, inspector. It's wild open moorland, very lonely and deserted. You wouldn't pass a soul there after dark. Just the very worst place for a breakdown. However, that's the place a breakdown would naturally happen."

French admitted that such was also his experience of life.

"Well, I worked and worked at my engine, but it was all no use. Every now and then it would go a few revs and then stop again. I guessed my jet was choked and I tried to take it out in the dark, but I couldn't manage it. I dropped bits of the carburettor on the road and I had the devil's own job finding them again. You see, I was afraid to use matches,

180

even if I had had anyone to hold them for me. At last after trying, I suppose, for a couple of hours, I gave it up and settled down to make the best of it for the night. I walked about a mile each way along the road, but I couldn't find a house, so I rolled myself up in the car and slept there. Fortunately it was a saloon, but even so it was darned cold. As soon as it was light I had the carburettor out and found, as I expected, that the jet was choked. I soon had it in again and off she went as right as rain. I got to Stranraer about seven o'clock, as you already know."

French was impressed by the recital, and that in two ways. First as to the actual story. It was one of those statements which might so easily be true or false. Such a run of bad luck and such a breakdown were eminently possible, and if it had taken place Teer's action was reasonable, if not inevitable. Judged on the probabilities there would be no difficulty in accepting the statement.

On the other hand if Teer had been up to any games, it was just the sort of story he would tell. And French could not forget his feeling that it had been prepared for use in emergency.

But it was not the details of the story that most strongly impressed French. It was the fact that Teer had thought it necessary to tell it. From what he had seen of the man, he was convinced that Teer's normal reaction to his approach would have been to tell him to go to hell and mind his own business. Teer had made an evident effort to be polite. French was strongly of opinion that it was because he was afraid. The more he thought over the whole interview, the more convinced he became that Teer's story was false and that he had told it to prevent the further investigation of his actions. Well, if so, the ruse wouldn't succeed. This was the first interview in the whole confounded case which had left

French definitely suspicious and he would take no risk. He would follow the affair up to the bitter end. He turned his attention back to Teer.

"Very hard lines, all that," he declared sympathetically, "but just what would happen. I'm surprised all the same that you could get no help when your jet choked. Do you mean to say that no vehicle of any kind passed you during the night?"

Teer replied that there was none. The inspector surely didn't imagine that if there had been he would have sat there quietly and let it pass? No motorist would have refused him the loan of a torch to get his carburettor fixed.

French wondered if he could get anything further.

"Where exactly did this breakdown of yours take place?" he asked sharply. "I want to know the exact place. It you can't describe it I shall want you to come and point it out."

If Teer were innocent French felt he must resent such a tone. But Teer to all outward showing did nothing of the sort. He answered civilly, even anxiously.

After this experiment French did not suppose he could dispel the idea that he was suspected from the man's mind. However he did his best. After a few minutes' friendly chat he thanked Teer for meeting him so pleasantly and took his leave.

He had next a word with the manager. Unquestionably on that eventful Wednesday, 2nd October, Teer had left the hotel in his car about four in the afternoon, ostensibly for Carlisle.

A good, but obvious beginning! French decided that next morning he would take an early train to Carlisle and begin the checking in detail of Teer's movements.

– 14 –

CASTLE DOUGLAS

At half past ten next morning French stepped down on to the platform at Carlisle. The County Hotel at the station was his first objective, and five minutes later he was talking to the manager.

But here he drew blank. No one remotely resembling Teer, so far as he could ascertain, had dined on the Wednesday in question. This of course was not conclusive; no member of an hotel staff can remember every chance visitor. But French reasoned that if Teer had been laying a trail he would have done something to impress his presence on those with whom he came in contact. He therefore left the station and began the round of the remaining hotels in the hope of having better luck elsewhere.

He tried the Crown and Mitre and the Red Lion without success, but at the Adelphi he struck a satisfactory vein. Teer had arrived about six and had ordered dinner. He had chatted at some length to the reception clerk, saying he was driving through from Newcastle to Stranraer and therefore did not require a room. He had then taken his car to the garage and insisted on having it greased. During dinner he had conversed with the waiter about his drive, the weather and the roads, and on leaving at a few minutes past eight he had explained to the garage man where he was going, and asked his advice as to the route. In short, from French's point of view he had acted in the most satisfactory manner possible. It was hard to doubt that he had intended his call to be discovered by the police, should suspicion become aroused.

One other useful fact he learned. The number of the car was 1905. The garage man remembered it because 1905 was the year of his marriage. The letters, however, not being connected with any event in his own life, he had forgotten.

So far, so good, but when French turned to consider the checking of Teer's journey between Carlisle and Stranraer he realised that he was up against a very different proposition. During that whole period of twelve hours the man appeared to have met no one from whom confirmation of his story could be obtained. Nor was it likely that the mere passing of his car should have been noticed. For some time French felt at a standstill. At last he decided to put out a general call over the entire area. For this he had to get in touch with the Scottish authorities, but eventually he managed it and before very long every man in the district was presumably racking his brains and probing his memory in the effort to produce something useful.

All the remainder of that day French haunted police headquarters in Carlisle, a nuisance to himself and everyone else. Officers to whom he applied suggested tactfully that their colleagues were in a better position to help him than themselves. At intervals he would disappear for a meal or a stroll round the town, returning hopefully to make fresh inquiries and to suffer further disappointments.

He arranged for telephonic communication with his hotel to be kept up during the night, but in spite of it he was back at the police station before breakfast next morning. Still the same blank silence reigned. It was Sunday and the

184

slow passage of the day got badly on his nerves. On Monday he was again early at the police station, once more without result.

Fretting impatiently at the delay, he returned to his hotel for breakfast. There he determined that if he received no news by twelve o'clock he would go himself to Dumfries, Castle Douglas, Newton Stewart and the other towns *en route* in the hope of picking up information. Accordingly, after fruitlessly waiting until midday, he went to the station and took the 1.26 train.

One of French's greatest pleasures was travelling through new country. He had never before gone by this route during daylight and now as the train pulled out of Carlisle, he looked forward with pleasurable anticipation to the journey. The day was fine and the country smiled under the thin autumn sunshine. The trees had turned coppery, and already the ground bore streaks of russet and brown where the wind had blown the fallen leaves into swathes. Presently on the flat lands approaching the Border, French noticed the ruins of the great munition town which had sprung up during the war and which now, save for those slight traces, had as completely disappeared. The name board at Gretna Green Station turned his thoughts into another channel, and he mused over the breathless and passionate pilgrimages with their hopes and fears and alarms which this famous little place must have seen. So, enjoying himself hugely, he passed Annan, and after a peep at the Solway Firth and the Cumberland Hills beyond, reached Dumfries.

At Dumfries it appeared that something unusual was afoot. On the platform there were three police constables who seemed to be searching the train for a suspect. Two in turn approached French's compartment, regarding him with a cold stare as he prepared to alight. Immediately they transferred their activities elsewhere, but as he began to move down the platform one of them came back and spoke to him.

"Ye wouldna be Mr French o' London?" he said encouragingly.

"Ah would so," French returned, relaxing into the vernacular.

The man nodded and felt in his pocket.

"Ah hae a wee note for ye," he explained, handing over a thin buff envelope. It contained a sheet of flimsy paper bearing the words:

To Det. Insp. French, CID.
SIR,
Carlisle phones your car believed seen at Castle Douglas and recommends that you proceed there immediately.

ANGUS M'TAVISH,
Sergt, Dumfries.

The train was on the move, but French, to the indignation of the station officials, hurled himself into a compartment. As the men's scandalised faces slowly faded from sight he could not help giving a few breathless chuckles. He did not see exactly how the discovery that Teer's car had been seen at Castle Douglas was going to help him, but he felt cheered at the prospect of renewed action. And if Teer had been up to anything he ought not – why then his, French's, luck was holding in a way he could scarcely have believed possible. He was so much taken up with the possibilities which were opening out that he scarcely even saw the beauties of the country through which the train was now running, and it was with but slightly veiled eagerness that he alighted at Castle Douglas.

The sergeant was expecting him and told his story with gusto. On receiving French's general call he had gone over in his mind everyone who might possibly have been out of doors on the night in question. Amongst others, he had remembered that certain of the railway staff were on duty to pass the night trains. Upon these he had concentrated. Getting into conversation with each in turn, he had made his inquiries. The fortunate circumstance that an engine had been derailed on the Kirkcudbright Branch on the previous afternoon enabled him to fix the night, and before long he had his clue.

It seemed that there were three men on duty when the down boat trains passed at about four in the morning, a signalman, a platform porter and a booking clerk. None of these had himself seen the car, but the porter unwittingly put him on to a man who had.

The sergeant had naturally asked whether any passengers had joined or left the boat train, and the porter had answered that though no one had joined it, one man had alighted. This was a friend of his own, a young fellow in the motor trade, who had been to London on a holiday. The porter had seen him getting out and had passed the time of day – or night – with him. It had not taken the sergeant long to run the young holidaymaker to earth and to hear his story.

"Ye best see him yoursel' an' get the tale first hand," the sergeant went on. "But forby that, ye'll need to see the lie o' the land, if ye're to onderstand it right."

French, recognising sound sense when he heard it, agreed and they set off in quest of the youth.

"Aye," said the young worthy, when at last they had tracked him to his lair. "I saw a car all right, but I didna see ony one wi' it. Ye see, I came off the Lonnon train an' walked home. I live half a mile out along the Dumfries Road. Well, when I came to yon wee wicket gate on the far side o' the railway – ye ken the place, sairgent? – the car was there. It was parked up against the side o' the road, headin' for the toun."

French's questions elicited the fact that the car was a new-looking Morris six saloon, and so far as the youth had observed, it might well have been Teer's.

"Good," said French heartily. "We'll go and see the place."

Castle Douglas station is of the ordinary roadside type of a double line passing between two platforms. The town lies on the "down" or south side of the railway, the side for Stranraer, and on the down side also are the station buildings. At the west end of the station, beyond the platforms, and close to the junction for Kirkcudbright, there is a bridge over the railway. This carries the main road from Castle Douglas to Dumfries. A row of houses fronts this road on the station side, being separated therefrom by a field and narrow belt of trees. Some hundred yards or more beyond the bridge the road takes a slight bend and at this bend was the wicket gate.

French stopped at the gate and looked about him. Owing to the bend, the car, parked on the far side of the wicket, was out of sight of the bridge leading from the town. Moreover, while between the wicket and the bridge the adjoining houses were close to and overlooking the road, opposite the car's position there was a larger house, set back from the road and well screened by trees. The car, therefore, could not have been overlooked.

"Let's see where this wicket gate leads to, sergeant."

They passed through, to find a footpath, a mere track, running across the adjoining field in the direction of the station. It led to a wire paling, apparently the railway boundary, edging the belt of trees. There was no gate in this fence, but the track passed on beneath it and through the trees. At the opposite edge of the belt was the station, and the path led across a couple of goods lines to the up platform. The whole distance from wicket gate to platform was not more than some 120 yards.

When French had assimilated these details he experienced a sense of profound disappointment. There was no proof that this was Teer's car. There was no reason why Teer should have stopped it in a place which, if not actually overlooked, was near a town where people might be abroad at night. There did not seem to be much help here.

"Umph," he grunted, "this is all very interesting, sergeant, but I'm afraid it's not much use to me. We can't prove that this is my man's car. As a matter of fact it's about the last place I'd expect him to park. I'm obliged to you and all that, but I'm afraid we'll have to try again. No car was seen passing through the town?"

The sergeant answered stiffly that no car was seen passing through the town. The sergeant's feelings were hurt. He had done, as he imagined, extraordinarily well and this was his reward. He had never thought much of these English upstarts at New Scotland Yard. Now he thought less.

French saw that he had blundered and in his kindly way hastened to remedy his mistake. He was beginning to explain how much he appreciated the sergeant's action, and in what a rosy light he would paint it to the man's superiors, when suddenly he came to a halt. For a moment he stood motionless, staring at the sergeant, while something more than his usual little thrill of excitement ran through his nerves. Illumination had come!

"By heck, sergeant," he cried, beaming on the surprised officer, "you've got a bull's eye after all! It's the man I want right enough. Congratulations! I know now what he was doing here."

He remained standing on the pavement while delightedly he followed out his new idea.

This train by which the young motor mechanic had arrived, this boat train from London to Stranraer which had passed Castle Douglas while the new Morris six was parked beside the station, this was the train by which Sir John Magill had travelled! It was the train in which Joss had carried out his evolutions with drugs and doorlocks! Here with a vengeance was the connection for which French was seeking. And in another moment a swift flash of insight showed him the underlying motive. Joss had drugged Sir John in order to get his plans. He had got them. But when Sir John awoke he might discover his loss. He might wire forward from Newton Stewart or Glenluce. Police might be awaiting the train at Stranraer. There might be a search of the other passengers' luggage. Joss must be in a position to submit to that search; in fact, he must be in a position to demand it. And how could that be done? Obviously only by getting rid of the package. And once more, How? *By handing it out of the train to Teer.*

Delighted now, French looked about him with new interest. Why, the place seemed to have been specially created to facilitate thefts from trains! He felt there could not be much doubt as to what had taken place on that night when Sir John Magill passed through on the down boat express!

In his mind's eye he seemed to see the little drama being enacted. Shortly before four in the morning a car arrives at the wicket, a new brownish-yellow Morris six. From it a man steps. He passes through the wicket gate, like a flitting shadow he crosses the field and reaches the up platform. There – possibly lying on the ground between the rails and the up platform wall – he waits unseen for the arrival of the boat express. The train arrives, he goes to the sleeping car, a bundle of plans is pushed out of the window of a berth, the man returns to his lair and the train starts. When the station has settled down again he picks himself up, retraces his steps, reaches the car and drives off with the precious documents.

All surmise! Surmise truly, but French could have sworn that every detail had happened just as he had pictured it.

"Heartiest congratulations, sergeant," he said warmly. "I believe, thanks to you, I've got my man. I have only two other questions to put. First, is the station quiet when the boat train is passing: I mean, is there any other train there? Second, is there any way in which we can trace the further movements of the car? If you can answer those I'll trouble you no further."

An inquiry at the station soon produced the information that the station was otherwise entirely deserted during the passage of the boat express, but French's second question was not so easy to dispose of. The sergeant could only repeat that he would not rest on his oars, but would continue his inquiries in every possible direction.

As French further considered the matter two corroborative facts emerged. One was that Castle Douglas was the first station, the nearest to London, at which the plans could have been got rid of by such a scheme. South of Carlisle the train stopped only in big well-lighted stations. The same applied to Carlisle itself and in a lesser degree to Dumfries. At all these places shunting on adjoining lines might have been in progress during the halt, involving the presence of shunters and engine men. Carriage examiners also might have come to investigate the sleeping car wheels at the critical moment. But at Castle Douglas, on a branch line, the station at that hour was quiet.

The second was even more convincing. Here was the explanation of that extraordinary question which Joss had asked the clerk at Euston when reserving the sleeping berths. He had wanted the berths to be on the right side of the coach. Why? Because the right side was the side away from the platform at Castle Douglas. It was the side at which Teer would be waiting for the plans.

But in spite of these highly promising considerations further thought produced the usual reaction and French's enthusiasm waned. He saw that once again he was on to the wrong crime. Again he was investigating the theft of the plans, not the murder. And though, as he had thought before, the one might involve the other, this could only be very indirectly.

However, his undertaking with Superintendent Rainey was to investigate the movements of the launch quartet and he must go through with it. Obviously, therefore the first thing was to get proof that this parked car really was Teer's. Such proof could only be obtained by tracing the car. How was this to be done?

French was not at all clear, and the more he thought of it the less clear he became. The problem was the more exasperating as when put into words it sounded so extraordinarily simple! A motorcar had left Castle Douglas at about four in the morning – he felt he was sure enough of his ground to postulate this. Either the same car or another had reached Stranraer about seven that same morning. Where had this car or these cars been between the hours named?

Mentally French writhed. He could not see his way. Then at last a possible solution occurred to him and he returned to the station and took the first train for Stranraer.

15

KIRKANDREWS BAY

French's idea was a very ordinary one after all – publicity. As a general rule the policy of the Yard was to avoid publicity and with this policy he was fully in agreement. But this case was exceptional, firstly, because he could see no other way in which the information could be obtained, and secondly, because his suspects could scarcely have avoided knowing that they were suspects, and publicity could not therefore put them more on their guard than they already were.

As a result of his further cogitations French called next morning at the police station at Stranraer. For half an hour, he and the sergeant in charge put their heads together, finally producing the following advertisement.

POLICE NOTICE – In connection with a recent case of burglary the police are anxious to check up the traffic on the road from Stranraer to Castle Douglas between the hours of four and seven on the morning of Thursday, 3rd October. They would be glad if any motorist or other person who was on any part of this road between these hours would kindly communicate with the police at Stranraer (telephone, Stranraer 0271) or with any police station.

Copies of this notice were sent to the papers read in the surrounding areas and bills were printed and posted at every police station, while French enclosed copies to the secretaries of the Automobile Association and the Royal Automobile Club, asking them to draw them to the attention of any of their members who were known to be touring in the district at the time.

There was nothing then to be done but wait and hope for the best. French, therefore, decided that for a day or two he would remain at Stranraer. With a clear conscience he could make a holiday of his enforced idleness and indulge in some of those long country tramps which he so greatly enjoyed.

But – on the whole to his delight – his time for exploring the country was soon cut short. On the afternoon of the following day a reply came in.

He was finishing lunch at the hotel when a telephone message came from the police station, asking him to step across as soon as possible. He did so, to find a hatchet-faced man in purple tweeds talking to the sergeant.

"Here's Mr Andrew Macpherson," the latter explained. "He's come in from three miles oot tae tell us he drove from here tae Carlisle that Thursda' mornin'. Maybe, Mr Macpherson, ye'll tell the inspector aboot it?"

"Pleased to meet you, inspector," said the hatchet-faced man in nasal tones and holding out a long thin hand like a bird's claw. "I reckon we don't see a man from Scotland Yard every day."

"You're not sorry for that, I dare swear," French rejoined. "You read our notice?"

"Sure I did, and as I've always aimed to be on the side of the cops, I thought I'd come right along and put the sergeant wise to anything I could."

"Good," said French heartily.

"Sure. Well, I'd best explain that I'm a farmer. Been in Amurrica for years, then got tired of it and thought I'd like to see the old country again before handing in my checks. So I came back and started in farming right here. Yuh. Well, sir, on that Thursday I'd business in Carlisle, and, as I wanted to get back that same night, I started early. I left home at five thirty, long before it was light, and I got to Carlisle round about nine. So I guess I passed that stretch of road between five thirty and say seven thirty. Yuh."

"That's pretty valuable to us, Mr Macpherson," French declared. "You can tell us what we want to know in a moment. Did you pass any cars between here and Castle Douglas?"

"Nope," Macpherson returned concisely. "Not a car nor a horse nor a hobo nor a cow nor a hen. No, sir; nothing at all."

"I'm surprised at that. Surely one would expect some traffic at that hour of the morning?"

Macpherson nodded gravely.

"I certainly was surprised myself. Yuh."

French hesitated.

"I'm not questioning your statement," he went on "but the matter is too important for there to be any doubt. Are you quite certain you would have noticed a passing car? Might not one have slipped past, seen no doubt and avoided, but not consciously observed? Remember what a frequent thing the passing of a car is."

Macpherson nodded approvingly.

"That's all right, inspector. If I was you I'd feel the same way myself. Yuh. But I tell you what I say is OK. I've a good memory. I guess if I passed a car I'd have it in mind. Sure I would."

French remembered Teer's story.

"Our information is that there was a broken down car on the road – show me that map, sergeant – just there. Now we were informed positively that a car stood there, pulled in to the side of the road, from about midnight till nearly seven. Suppose there had been a car there, could you not have slipped past without noticing it?"

Macpherson's slow emphasis was convincing.

"Say, quit it," he drawled. "Guess if I say there was no car there, there wasn't one, and that's all there's to it. Yuh."

As French looked at the man's dependable face with its alert expression, he felt that wherever Teer's car was at the time, it was not on the road from Castle Douglas to Stranraer.

But if not, then where was it?

He turned again to the map. If Teer had not gone by the main road was there any other route he could have used?

"You went of course by Newton Stewart, Gatehouse of Fleet, Ringford and Bridge of Dee?" he asked Macpherson.

"Sure I did; by the main road."

"There seem to be other possible routes?"

"Yuh, sure," Macpherson answered. "You could go by Wigton and cut the stretch between Glenluce and Newton Stewart, or you could cut Ringford by going through Laurieston, or you could cut the whole road between Castle Douglas and Newton Stewart by going north through New Galloway. Yuh. And that's not to speak of by-roads that you might be able to work your way along. That OK, sergeant?"

The sergeant agreed and French made a grimace.

"We don't seem to be so far on as I had hoped," he lamented. "It looks as if our friend had avoided the main road. I'm afraid we've got a bit more work to do before we're through."

When Macpherson had gone, French and the sergeant settled down with the map to make a list of the possible roads by which a driver from Castle Douglas to Stranraer might have deviated from the direct route. As the car was assumed to have been seen at Castle Douglas at four and as it certainly reached Stranraer at seven they limited themselves to those which could be covered in three hours or less. But even within this limit they found a surprising number of possibilities. Investigation along all these roads would be a big job. French indeed was aghast at the amount of work indicated, particularly as he realised that all this energy might easily go for nothing. Teer, on that night, might never have been near Castle Douglas railway station, in fact he might have been a perfectly law-abiding citizen and he, French, might be on a wild goose chase.

But he determined to carry on with the inquiries for the very good reason that, however doubtful their result, no other line promised any result at all.

"Some work, this, sergeant," he remarked. "How on earth are we to do it?"

The sergeant, with the Scotch equivalent of a shrug, said that "gin the warrrk was ordered it mun just be done" that it "wouldna tak so long neither," and that the men of the force in these regions were "a braw lot o' boys" who would do it fine.

French said he was glad the sergeant thought so and they went into committee of ways and means. The scope of the previous inquiry was to be enlarged to take in all these new roads, and the police, coastguards, doctors and others who might have been abroad during the night, were to be interviewed. French, however, remembered that the similar inquiries already made had not revealed the fact of Macpherson's journey, and he pressed for still more energetic measures. It was finally decided that a house to house visitation should be made of those living along selected lengths of all the roads. Some one of all these might have been awake and heard the car. This was not so big a job as it seemed, as most of the roads ran through a sparsely inhabited country.

French was not hopeful of the result, as his previous difficulty, that of fixing the night on his hearers' minds, was now greater than ever. For two days he and his band of helpers scoured the roads, stopping at every likely house and questioning its inmates. And then, just as he was doing one of the last stretches and coming to the conclusion that the inquiry would prove a washout, he struck luck and struck it rich.

How rich he did not at first realise, but when he did so he became lost in wonder. It was not often that so great a lift was vouchsafed him.

With the local sergeant he was driving along a road which led from Kirkcudbright to Gatehouse of Fleet, through the little hamlet of Borgue and along the coast. Near Kirkandrews Bay they came down close to the shore, a grass field alone separating the road from the rocks at the water's edge. Below, the sea stretched away to the hard line of the horizon, a deep blue plane, flecked with white.

A few hundred yards before they reached the point nearest the sea they had to slack. A bridge was being rebuilt and only half its width was available for traffic. The place was picturesque in a mild way and as the sergeant steered carefully over the narrow path French turned an appreciative eye to either side. Then it was that the sergeant made a chance remark which as it were touched a reservoir and their luck poured out.

"Gey an' bad place at night, that," said the sergeant casually.

It was not an illuminating remark, but it gave French the necessary idea. Quickly he swung round and ran his eye over the contractor's plant.

"Hold on a minute, sergeant," he said. "I see a watchman's hut there. Perhaps we'll find someone who can check up this road for us."

"By heck, Mr French, but I should ha' thought o' that," the sergeant declared as he pulled into the side of the road. "Thaur's been a nightwatchman on for the last month. There's no that mony cars pass here but he'll be able to tell us if yon one o' Teer's went by. I'm weel acquainted wi' the foreman." He pulled up and the two men got out and walked back to the bridge.

"Andy aboot, Jock?" he asked a labourer, evidently also an old acquaintance.

Jock gave his head an upwards sidelong twist which indicated even to the Londoner in French that his foreman was to be found beneath the partially constructed arch. The latter proved to be an immensely stout man with a round red face like a setting sun. He also gave his head a sidelong twist, but downwards. As clearly as Jock's upward twist this indicated: "Good morning. How are you?"

"You're gettin' on fine wi' the job," began the crafty sergeant, looking round appreciatively at the litter of planks and materials with which the ground was strewn.

The stout man monosyllabically admitted that things might have been worse.

"This is Mr French from London," went on the sergeant. "Scotland Yard," he said impressively. "But that's for yer ain ear, Andy. Don't you be lettin' on."

A nod without any side twist indicated that the foreman appreciated the situation, was impressed thereby, and would keep it a profound secret.

"We're lookin' for a bit o' information, Andy. Tryin' to trace a burglar. He got awa' from up the country wi' a car an' we want to know if he passed here. It's a while ago – early on the morn o' Thursday, the third o' the month. Ye had a watchman on then, had ye no?"

"An' have still," the foreman declared firmly. It's M'Leod. Lives in yon wee house." A back jerk of the head fixed it geographically. "Ye could see him the noo."

"Thanks, Andy. We'll go right on."

Another nod did duty as farewell, and the two detectives walked across the fields to a small whitewashed cottage which stood on the side of a hill some half mile away. A knock brought an elderly, decent-looking woman to the door.

"He's in bed, but he'll come doon," she explained. "Come in an' bide a wee."

"Thank ye, missus, we'll no go in. We'll just sit here on the wall an' wait."

Alexander M'Leod was not overpleased at being awakened, but so soon as he understood the sergeant's suggestion that his trouble might be productive of siller, his annoyance faded. French listened passively to the conversation, but as he suddenly realised that M'Leod had something to tell, his easy indifference fell from him like a cloak, and he became the Scotland Yard officer at his very keenest.

Yes, M'Leod had heard a car. In fact he had seen it, though only as a dim shadow passing in the darkness. But he couldn't tell whether it was on the night the sergeant said. But the sergeant could find that out for himself, for he, M'Leod, minded well that it was the night that Bob MacTavish's "auld red cow had deid."

MacTavish lived at the adjoining farmhouse, and before hearing the details of M'Leod's story the three men walked across to see the owner of the deceased animal. MacTavish remembered the night well. The death of his best milker had been a serious blow which he was not likely to forget. The date was early on Thursday, 3rd October. To fix this he produced after some search the receipted account from the vet, for a visit to the cow on the previous day.

So far so good. M'Leod had heard a car on the morning in question. Now for details.

These, extracted by the sergeant after exhausting and highly praiseworthy efforts, proved much more convincing and far-reaching than French could have hoped.

It appeared that shortly before five on the morning in question M'Leod was seated in his sentry box thinking of nothing in particular, when he heard the sound of a motor. He thought at first it was an approaching car and he had a special look round to see that his lights were burning brightly. Then he realised that the sound came from the sea. Idly curious, he left the road and walked across the rough grass towards the water. He could see neither the boat itself nor its lights, but he heard its engine a good deal more distinctly than he thought he should. Fearing that the boat had mistaken its position, he hurried forward to shout a warning. But just then the motor stopped. It was calm and M'Leod listened intently. Presently he heard the faint sound of oars. Someone was coming ashore.

From this it became evident that the strangers were in no danger. M'Leod was a good deal puzzled as to what anyone could want in this bay whose coast was so sparsely inhabited, but he felt it was not his business. His business, however, lay at the bridge and he turned slowly back there.

When he was still some hundred yards from the road he heard another motor, this time a car. It was coming quickly from the direction of Kirkcudbright. He ran forward as fast as his bad leg would allow, but before he reached the bridge the car passed. It slowed for the lights and got across the bridge safely. M'Leod could not see it in any detail, but he was sure it was a saloon and fairly large. He heard it pass on and saw its red tail lamp. It disappeared round a bend and the sound suddenly ceased.

M'Leod was surprised that it should get out of earshot so quickly, but he knew how tricky noises were and he supposed the vehicle had gone behind some hill or bank of shrubs which had cut off the sound. All the same he could not think of any such which might have had this effect.

However, there it was, and he began congratulating himself that no accident had happened while he was away from the job, and thought no more of the car. His surprise, therefore, was considerable when he heard it again. Far away, but quite distinctly, he heard it start, gain speed and slowly die away in the distance.

He pondered the affair and came to the conclusion that one of the tyres must have picked up a nail when passing the bridge and that the stoppage had been to enable the spare wheel to be put on. He did not at this time connect it with the arrival of the boat, though what followed suggested this to his mind.

The car had stopped, he supposed, for some fifteen minutes, and ten minutes or more later he once again heard the boat. Its engine was also started up and the sound of it also died gradually away. He did not hear the row boat return, but he would not in any case have heard this from the road.

"Just whereabouts do you think the car stopped?" French asked when the story had come to an end.

"Awa' yonder," M'Leod pointed, "just there forenenst the auld ruin, Castle Haven, they call it. Ye see the place?"

"Let's go down."

When they reached the spot indicated French saw that, if there really was any connection between the boat and the car, a more suitable place for secret communication could scarcely have been found along the entire coasts of the British Isles.

Immediately to the west of the ruined castle was a little cove. It was well protected, on the left by the rock on which the castle was built, on the right by another rock which after running straight out to sea, curved round like a breakwater across half the mouth. A sloping beach led up across rough grass to the field. Some hundred and eighty yards from the water's edge was the road, bounded here by a stone wall. The whole place was extraordinarily deserted. It was true that some distance farther on two or three houses appeared, but close by there was no human habitation.

French wondered if he dare assume that the car was Teer's. He had an unhappy feeling that, in this matter of the car, he was gradually leaving the realms of ascertained fact and approaching those of speculation, but he could think of no better way to proceed. In difficult cases, such as the present, truth was more frequently reached by bold assumptions than in any other way. With misgivings, therefore, he decided to complete the investigation in hand, and if no trace of any other car was come on he thought he would be justified in assuming this one to have been Teer's.

But if so, whose could have been the boat? Where could it have been coming from, where going to? Why this stealthy approach to the shore without lights? What could have been Teer's business with those on board?

At once Mallace's launch occurred to French, not because he had any reason to connect it with the mysterious visitor to Kirkandrews Bay, but because it was a launch already connected with the case. But he didn't think it could be Mallace's. It seemed too big a round for it to have made in the time. However, its speed was known, together with the hours of its departure from Barrow and its arrival at Portpatrick. An examination of the atlas and a simple calculation would therefore clear this point up. In vain French continued to question M'Leod in the hope of getting some further fact. The man had clearly told all he knew. Nor did detailed inquiries among the other residents of the district lead to anything. Puzzled, but more determined than ever to unravel the tangle, French returned late that night to Stranraer and after a long delayed meal, turned in.

16

CUMBERLAND

By that same evening, the whole of the alternative roads from Castle Douglas to Stranraer had been combed by the police, and French sat down in his room at the hotel to consider the information he had obtained.

This was certainly meagre enough. In addition to his own discovery at Kirkandrews Bay, the car – or what might have been the car – had been seen only once. At a little place called Girthon, a labourer who had been up on that Wednesday night attending to his sick wife heard a car and saw its lights about half past five. It was running quickly from the direction of Kirkandrews Bay and towards the main road from Castle Douglas to Gatehouse of Fleet and Stranraer. Girthon was about five miles from Kirkandrews Bay, and if the hour given by the watchman was correct, the car he saw should just have passed Girthon at the time stated.

That this was Teer's car French was inclined to believe, though he saw that pending the receipt of further information he could not be sure. In the meantime he wondered whether anything could be deduced about the launch.

A good map was his first requirement and he rang up the police station and enlisted the sergeant's help. Soon a constable arrived with a first rate atlas which his superior had borrowed from a friendly neighbour.

Retiring once more to his room French set methodically to work. First he scaled the distance from Barrow to Portpatrick – 84 sea miles he made it. The launch had left Barrow at 9.15 at night and arrived at Portpatrick at 9.40 the next morning, that was 12 hours 25 minutes. Twelve hours 25 minutes into 84 sea miles gave a speed of about 6¾ knots – 6¾ sea miles per hour – which was just about the speed Mallace stated they had run the launch.

Now, if the launch had called at Kirkandrews Bay, how much faster must it have travelled? French again began scaling. From Barrow to Kirkandrews Bay was about 54 sea miles and from Kirkandrews Bay to Portpatrick about 45, a total of 99 miles. The launch which had called at Kirkandrews Bay had waited there for about half an hour, so that if this were Mallace's, only about 12 hours could be taken as running time. Ninety nine miles divided by 12 hours gave a speed of only 8.3 knots.

Wivell, French remembered, had given 10 knots or more as the launch's speed. Mallace had said about 9, which agreed as nearly as the varying points of view of the two men might be expected to allow. In either case it followed that, so far as speed was concerned, the Kirkandrews Bay launch might well have been Mallace's.

For a moment French wondered why, if there had been anything underhand about the trip, Mallace should have made that admission about not running at full speed. Then he saw that Mallace could have done nothing else. The speed he gave – 7 knots – would check in well enough with his hours of departure and arrival and so would not arouse suspicion. But supposing that from some other cause suspicion were aroused, an inquiry from Wivell would at once obtain the launch's real maximum. The fact that

Mallace had kept this back would therefore tend to confirm the suspicion.

As French continued turning the matter over in his mind, he suddenly saw that still further evidence was in his hands. If the launch were Mallace's, between what hours must it have called at Kirkandrews Bay? These, he saw, would be fixed by the hours at which it left Barrow and reached Portpatrick. Taking Wivell's figure of 10 knots as maximum, he found that to do the 54 sea miles between Barrow and Kirkandrews Bay would have taken about 5 hours 25 minutes. Five hours 25 minutes after 9.15 p.m., the time of leaving Barrow, would bring it to 2.40 a.m. According to M'Leod the launch had actually arrived at Kirkandrews Bay at about 4.45. Therefore, so far, the launch could not only have done the journey, but done it at a speed far below its maximum.

Eagerly French went on to the next stage of the journey, from Kirkandrews Bay to Portpatrick. From, say, 5.10 a.m. to 9.40 a.m., the hours of departure and arrival, was 4 hours 30 minutes. The distance was 45 sea miles, which gave a speed of exactly 10 knots, just within the boat's capacity.

While this looked satisfactory enough, French was aware that the run of tides, currents and wind might entirely invalidate his results. Next morning, therefore, he sought out the local coastguard officer, put the case before him and asked his advice. He was overjoyed to find that while his speeds required some slight modification, his conclusions stood.

It was at least possible, therefore, that Mallace had put into Kirkandrews Bay and had there been met by Teer. If so, it was not hard to guess the motive. In the event of the theft of the plans being discovered it was desirable that they should at the earliest moment be passed onto a secure hiding place. And what hiding place could be more secure than the launch, which obviously could not in any way have come in contact with Sir John?

But possibilities were no use to a CID inspector trying to build up a case for a jury. Could he not anywhere get proof?

It occurred to him to work out the speed at which the launch had travelled on the next section of its journey.

According to the Portpatrick longshoremen it had left there about midnight on the Thursday night. The Campbeltown sergeant had stated that it had arrived at his port at 7.15 the next morning. The distance between the two places was 41 sea miles and this gave an average speed of 5¾ knots.

French scratched his head thoughtfully. This did not work in with the theory of the call at Kirkandrews Bay. On the contrary, it looked as if the party really had travelled at a greatly reduced speed throughout. From his conversations with the quartet he had the departures and arrivals of three other trips, and of these he next worked out the speeds. They were 7½, 6¼ and 6½ knots respectively.

French swore. At first it had certainly looked as if he had hit on something vital, but now he began to doubt it. Brooding morosely over the problem, he racked his brains to find some further test which might differentiate truth from falsehood.

The running of the launch at something over half speed, Mallace had stated, was to reduce the noise and vibration. The reduction must surely have been considerable to make it worthwhile putting up with the slower speed. Mallace admitted he could not get enough sleep owing to visiting his agents during the day and running the launch at night. Surely under these circumstances he would have put up with a little discomfort in order to complete the run quickly and so get to bed? French shook his head. It looked fishy. Undoubtedly, the whole business looked fishy.

Suddenly he brightened up. Here at last was something that he could test. Was a speed of 6 knots really much more pleasant than one of 10? He wondered if it would be worthwhile going back to Barrow and trying.

The result of his cogitations was that two days later – the next day was Sunday – he walked once more into Messrs Wivell's office and asked for the senior partner.

"It's the *Sea Hawk* again, I'm afraid," he apologised. "Could you hire her to me for a couple of hours?"

Fifty minutes later he was aboard.

"I want," he explained to his crew of one engineer navigator, "to run her all out and see what she'll do. Then I want to run her at ten knots and then at six. I want to feel the vibration. Is there a measured mile we could test her on?"

The "crew" suggested that they should run between two buoys, whose distance apart he knew. Accordingly very carefully they made their tests. First they ran the distance a couple of times at six knots until the motor got well heated and until French's internal mechanism had registered the resultant amount of noise and vibration. Then the crew suddenly put his throttle to full open. The motor responded promptly and the launch began to slip at nearly twice the speed through the water.

For a moment French's internal mechanism suspended judgment and then it gave a report which sent a little shiver of delight down his spine. The noise and vibration were increased truly, but only to the most trifling extent! The launch was old and massive, even clumsy, and the motor was small, too small to send more than a tiny tremor through the heavy timbers.

So Mallace had lied! If he had reduced the speed of the launch it was certainly not because of its unpleasant vibration. At full speed it had no unpleasant vibration. Would Mallace then – short of sleep as he was – have spent twelve and a half hours going from Barrow to Portpatrick when he could as easily have done the distance in something over eight?

French did not think so. Suddenly he became sure – as sure as it was possible to be without proof – that Mallace had done nothing of the kind. The man had taken twelve hours because he had called at Kirkandrews Bay and met Teer, and his speed from there to Portpatrick had been the maximum the boat would do.

With the throttle open they were now slipping through the water at quite a reasonable rate; not in it with modern speed boats, of course, but not bad for a heavy boat like the *Sea Hawk*. They had timed their start and with some eagerness French waited till they had completed their course to learn their speed. It proved to be just under 10¾ knots.

This was eminently satisfactory, and as that evening he sat puzzling over the whole affair in the corner of the hotel lounge, the questions he returned to again and again were: Did Mallace call at Kirkandrews Bay, and if so, how can proof be obtained?

His thoughts returned with some misgivings to the speeds on the subsequent nights, also far below maximum. What games were the quartet up to on these later trips? Then he saw that the slow running involved no evil activities. It was simply a matter of ordinary precaution. If for some nefarious purpose they had run at half speed on one lap of their trip, they must do so on all. If the vibrations were too great to run at full speed on Wednesday night it

211

would not do to ignore it on Thursday. They could not afford to discount their own explanation.

There being nothing, then, in this matter of the speed on subsequent nights, French turned back to the troublesome question, how was proof of a visit to Kirkandrews Bay to be obtained?

He began slowly pacing the room, now happily deserted. Then an idea occurred to him, and as before he borrowed a map and began to pore over it.

Barrow to Kirkandrews Bay would be a coasting trip, at least as far as St Bees Head. He ruled a line along the course. After rounding the projection at Annaside, where Mallace would pass as close to the shore as was safe, he would run from three to four miles off shore till he reached St Bees Head. Whitehaven, which was well round the shoulder of St Bees, he would pass within seven miles. That was of course unless he deliberately deviated from the direct line.

On the other hand, if he had gone straight to Portpatrick he would have headed well out to the north west, passing indeed not far from the Point of Ayre, the northern promontory of the Isle of Man.

French's idea was that it would be worthwhile having inquiries made along the shore at all these places in the hope that the launch might have been seen or heard. Admittedly it was a long shot, but he didn't see any other line of investigation.

Accordingly he got in touch by telephone with the police authorities in Cumberland and the Isle of Man, explaining what he required. To the former he added that he was going to Whitehaven and would himself work from there along the shore to the south, and asking for any help that could be given.

Then commenced a slow and wearisome inquiry. Next morning he began by interviewing the harbour masters at

Maryport, Workington and Whitehaven in order to learn whether any vessel had reached or left their respective harbours which might have seen the launch. This involved looking up records and working out distances, but all three men did their best for him and he got the information without undue delay. But it was all negative. No steamer had passed at the desired hour.

Starting then at Whitehaven, French began calling at police and coastguard stations, gradually working his way south. In each new district he began his inquiries with fresh hope, each he presently left with an increased sense of futility and disappointment. The further he went the more hopeless his quest seemed to grow. It was, he admitted to himself, a pretty thin chance on which he was banking. A launch three or four miles from the shore would be out of earshot from the land except under the most favourable conditions. On a dark night, moreover, it would be utterly out of sight, particularly if Mallace had run without lights. French indeed believed that his only hope was the remote possibility that the launch's path had crossed that of some other vessel, though even in this case the chances were enormously against his finding the vessel in question.

For several days, however, he worked steadily on, until indeed he had nearly reached the end of the available stretch of coast. And then just as he was preparing himself for failure, he heard something.

It appeared that the police at Bootle had learned that a young farm labourer who lived at Easkmeals had visited a friend at Bootle on the night in question, and had set out to walk home at about half past ten o'clock. Bootle, which is not to be confused with the place of the same name near Liverpool, is a Cumberland village lying within a couple of miles of the sea and nearly halfway between Barrow and St Bees Head. From it the road leads down to the coast near Tarn Bay, then turns north and runs, at first close to the shore, to Easkmeals.

When the labourer, whose name was Ritson, had left Tarn Bay half a mile behind him and was walking parallel and close to the sea, he noticed in front of him a red light. This, as he approached, resolved itself into the rear light of a saloon car, standing on the sea side of the road and facing north. It was a fine night and though there was no moon the stars were brilliant and Ritson could dimly see the surrounding country.

He had come within about fifty yards of the car when a man appeared like a shadow from the shore. It was too dark to see him distinctly, but he was hurrying and Ritson thought there was something furtive about his movements. He appeared suddenly mounting the slope from the sea, and running to the car, got in. Just as Ritson reached it the car moved off and disappeared rapidly towards the north.

Ritson thought the whole affair unusual, but it was not his business and he dismissed it from his mind. But not more than five or ten minutes later he heard another sound, also a motor being started up. This time it came from the sea. Ritson stopped to listen and he soon became satisfied that a launch, which evidently had been lying close inshore, had restarted. The sound grew gradually fainter, at last dying away in a northerly direction.

The more French thought over this story, the more interesting he found it. Here were a car and a launch, admittedly both unknown, but all the same the combination thrilled him. Was it possible that he had found not only what he wanted, but vastly, enormously, unbelievably more? His excitement grew as he asked himself if by any incredible chance it could have been Teer's car which the labourer had seen and Mallace's launch which he had heard? He whistled softly. Here were possibilities with a vengeance!

When he came down again to earth he saw that there was a test which he could immediately apply. Once again, distances, times, speeds! Was it possible for Mallace and Teer to have been in the district at the time in question! If not, it ended the matter. But if it was possible…It seemed to French that the possibility of this would be mighty near to proof. Once more he took out his map.

If Ritson had left Bootle at 10.30 he must have reached the meeting place about 11.00. Now first as to the launch.

The *Sea Hawk* had left Barrow at 9.15. Assume it had reached Tarn Bay before 11.00, say at 10.50. The distance scaled about 15 sea miles. This gave a speed of just under 10 knots.

French breathed more freely. Nothing could be more satisfactory. He had crossed his first fence. Now for the car.

It was not so easy to find the distances by land, but by dint of careful scaling, French got what he believed must be approximately correct – near enough to settle his immediate problem at all events.

From Carlisle to Tarn Bay scaled 61 miles, about, he reckoned, two and a half hours' run. Teer had left Carlisle at 8.10, so that he should have been easily able to reach Tarn Bay at 10.40. So far, so good.

From Carlisle to Castle Douglas, French estimated at 52 miles; say a two hour run. In other words it should be possible to drive from Tarn Bay to Castle Douglas in about 4 hours. Four and a half hours after 11.00 p.m. brought one to 3.30 a.m. But Teer presumably had reached Castle Douglas only in time to meet the train at 3.59, therefore he could easily have done this run also.

His second fence! French felt absolutely triumphant. He hadn't achieved proof of course; all the same he would have staked his reputation that he was right.

As he considered the matter further he saw that if true it would clear up a point which had puzzled him a good deal, namely, why Mallace had not sailed more quickly from Barrow to Kirkandrews Bay. Now he saw the reason. The whole trip from Barrow to Portpatrick had been done at the maximum speed possible. From Barrow to Tarn Bay and from Kirkandrews Bay to Portpatrick the launch had done its full ten knots. On the intermediate section from Tarn Bay to Kirkandrews Bay the speed of the launch had been low, but here the launch had not been the ruling factor. The distance by sea between these two places was only 39 sea miles while by land it was 113 miles. Therefore over this section the speed of the car had ruled. And this – 25 miles per hour or more – was reasonably fast for night travelling.

There were therefore pretty strong reasons to believe that Teer and Mallace had been in communication at Tarn Bay as well as at Kirkandrews Bay. But why? What under heaven had been their object? For the Kirkandrews Bay meeting, French had been able to suggest a motive, but this earlier one at Tarn Bay completely knocked him out. He couldn't form even the faintest idea of their purpose. Curse it all! The only thing that seemed certain was that there must be some deeper factor in the affair than he had yet imagined.

All that night French racked his brains over the problem, but without result. In vain he took a three hour walk, in vain he drank large cups of strong coffee: he could get no light anywhere. What he should do next day he didn't know. And then suddenly his problem was solved for him. Superintendent Rainey wrote raising a question which set him off next day hot-foot on a fresh phase of the inquiry.

17

GLASGOW

Superintendent Rainey's letter, which was to the Yard and which had been forwarded, ran as follows:

Re Sir John Magill Case.
Since discussing this affair with Inspector French a discovery had been made relative to the presence of a motor launch in Northern Ireland waters on the night of Sir John's disappearance. This may or may not have a connection with the case, but at all events I think it should be considered by Inspector French.

There is a further point upon which I should be glad to have some inquiries made in Glasgow. If you could conveniently arrange for Inspector French to proceed to Glasgow I would send Sergeant M'Clung to meet him there, when the two points in question could be discussed between them and such action taken as might be considered desirable.

The letter was accompanied by an instruction from Chief Inspector Mitchell for French to arrange the meeting as and when he thought proper.

French, being for the moment at a dead end, hailed the letter with delight. He wired to Belfast making a rendezvous for the following morning at the St Enoch Hotel and that night travelled up to Glasgow.

He was not displeased to see the rugged features of the sergeant in the lounge next morning. Though he had not known him very long he had formed a high opinion of him as well as growing to like him personally.

"Did you have a good crossing?" he greeted him, determined for once to say the right thing.

M'Clung had had a fine crossing and he was glad to get to Glasgow for he had a sister married on a Glasgow man and he hoped maybe he'd be able to see her.

"Sure you will," said French heartily. "Come and have a bite of breakfast and then let's have the great news."

"Not so great maybe as you think, Mr French," the pessimist answered doubtfully, though he threw himself into the breakfast plan with no lack of enthusiasm.

"Those two things the superintendent wrote about," he went on, when a little later they were ensconced with pipes in a deserted corner of the smoking-room, "those two things came out of the one inquiry. The superintendent was still going on about that XYZ letter, you understand, and he was annoyed that we couldn't get any word about it or the car passing or anything. So he arranged to have a house to house visitation along all that bit of Coast Road from Larne to Glenarm to find out if anyone had heard the car pass. There were a couple of us on it for three days. Well, we got these two points.

"The first one we got from people who live close to the shore just on the Larne side of Lurigan. There's a daughter, a woman of about thirty, and she sleeps in a room looking out over the sea and keeps her window open at night. Well, that night of the disappearance she happened to wake up and it was some time before she dropped off again. While she was lying awake she heard what she first thought was a car on the road, but afterwards she realised it must be a launch out at sea. She'd never heard such a thing before and she remarked it specially. It sounded close in shore and seemed to be coming from the Larne direction and going north. We tried to shake her statement every way we could, but she was quite certain about it."

French was growing more and more interested.

"What time was that, sergeant?" he asked.

"It was just coming on to two-thirty, because she heard the half-hour strike almost at once and then after a while three o'clock."

"Just a minute; let me check that up."

French dropped once more into his old pastime of scaling distances and calculating speeds. He had had so much of this to do that he had bought some four-inch Ordnance maps of the whole district. Presently he announced his results.

"Since I saw you, M'Clung, I've been going into the matter of Mallace's launch – I'll tell you directly – and I've found she'll do 10¾ knots maximum, say 10 knots for ordinary full speed. Well, see what I've just found. The distance from Portpatrick to Ballygelley Head is just 26 sea miles. At 10 knots she would do it in about 2½ hours. She left Portpatrick about midnight, so what time would you expect her to pass your friend's house?"

M'Clung was profoundly impressed. While the idea that the Ballygelley launch might be Mallace's, had naturally occurred both to himself and Rainey, neither had really accepted it seriously. The sudden likelihood that it was indeed the truth therefore struck him as of the first importance.

French had become equally excited.

"By Jove, M'Clung!" he cried, "if that was Mallace's launch it means we're getting warm in this inquiry. By Jove, yes!"

He remained silent while visions of progress floated illusively before his eyes. What if the launch really had called at Lurigan during that tragic night? What if its party had gone ashore? What if they had there met Sir John, who had walked from Whitehead to keep a prearranged appointment? What if the party had then and there murdered him? And lastly, what if they had buried his body on Malcolm's ground so that, were it found, Malcolm and not themselves might be suspected?

Here was the first theory of the crime which seemed to offer any shadow of consistency. As French thought over it he grew more and more impressed. By Jove, yes! Here certainly was something that must be thoroughly gone into. He turned back to M'Clung.

"That's good as far as it goes," he declared. "But you had a second point?"

M'Clung once more took up his tale.

"After we left the young woman who heard the launch we pushed on to the houses beyond Ballygalley Head, on the bay, you remember, where the road from Carncastle comes down. Well, we'd been through the most of them when we came on one where they told us something; you can believe it or not as you like. A man and his wife and a sister-in-law lived in it and the man had been ill, in fact he wasn't quite better yet. But that night he'd been bad, so bad that they hadn't expected him to last till the morning. So the wife and the sister-in-law had both sat up all night. Well, neither of them had heard any car pass, and what was more, both of them swore no car had passed at all. I said one would easy slip by and they never hear it, but they said no, if one had passed they'd have heard it for certain. They said the man was disturbed by noises and they were afraid that if a car had startled him it might have been fatal. That's how they were so sure there was no car, and they couldn't have helped hearing it if one had passed for the road was just about twenty feet away from his window. Well, there you are, Mr French. If what those women said was true no XYZ drove past at two-thirty in the morning. On the other hand there might have been a dozen cars and they not notice them."

"What do you think yourself, sergeant?"

"It's not easy to say, Mr French, but I don't mind admitting that I was impressed by their manner. They seemed to be quite certain, and if they were both there, and were frightened about noises, why then they ought to have heard a car if there was one to hear. But you couldn't say for sure."

"Did Superintendent Rainey take it seriously?"

"He did, sir, and that's what I'm coming to now. It occurred to him that maybe that letter was not written by any public-minded citizen out to redress wrongs, but by somebody who wanted the body to be found." M'Clung turned his head on one side and slightly closed one eye. "Did it occur to you, sir, that the legacy wouldn't be paid if the body wasn't found?"

French nodded.

"Not without a considerable delay," he amended. "Yes, that occurred to me. Go on."

"Well, there were two men that were due legacies and both of them wanted the money pretty badly." M'Clung looked indescribably sly.

French felt slightly puzzled.

"You mean Malcolm and Victor? But we've suspected both of them and we've been rather forced to admit their innocence."

M'Clung nodded.

"That's right, Mr French. But this tale of the two women's has reopened the question. At least with Superintendent Rainey it has."

"But this tale of the two women's doesn't alter the facts that made us conclude they were innocent."

French spoke to pump the other's brains. So far as he himself was concerned he was ready enough to suspect either, or both of the cousins. Victor he suspected as it was. M'Clung 's voice broke in on his thoughts.

"You may be right enough about that, Mr French; probably are. But the superintendent would like it gone into a bit further, that is, if you agree."

"I'll agree all right," French assured him. "Anything that may help I'll agree to. What exactly does he want?"

"Well, sir, about Malcolm and Victor and the letter there were two things. The first was that seeing where the body was buried it wasn't very likely that Malcolm wrote drawing attention to it."

French agreed with a nod and M'Clung went on.

"But there's a funny thing about Victor. That XYZ letter was posted in Belfast. Now Victor got to Belfast that very morning off the Glasgow boat. And it was the first time he'd been in Belfast for long enough. And what's more, the letter was received at Chichester Street by the afternoon delivery. That means it must have been posted between say 10 a.m. and 1.30 p.m. But by 1 p.m. Victor had seen Malcolm and seen you and me and the superintendent, so he had learned how the case stood and what was known and therefore the sort of letter that would be wanted to get the body found.

And from 1 to 1.30 he'd have had plenty of time to type it. So you see, sir, there's a bit of a case against Victor."

"Well, what does Superintendent Rainey want me to do?"

"It's this way, sir." M'Clung was not to be hurried. "Suppose Victor wrote the letter, where would he get a machine to type it on? If we're right so far he must have had it in Belfast. Now he wouldn't get a typist to do such a letter. He would do it himself. And what's more, he wouldn't use his own machine, supposing he had one. Therefore what would he do?"

French felt his usual thrill.

"Good man, M'Clung! I get you. He'd buy one. Now let's see. He'd have to buy it either in Oban or Glasgow or Belfast, wouldn't he? Oban's too small a town for that – such a sale would be remembered. And Belfast is too near home. Therefore try Glasgow! Eh, M'Clung, I begin to understand why I was asked to meet you here."

"Yes, sir, and besides we've done Belfast thoroughly and it wasn't bought there."

"Good. By the way, did you bring the XYZ letter with you?"

"I've got it here, sir. The superintendent said we'd want it if we had any luck."

"Your superintendent's a man after my own heart. Well, sergeant, that's very good. And now unless we're going to spend the entire day sitting here, we'd better get a move on. We'll have to make a list of the typewriting places and go round them. Get hold of that directory and we'll begin."

A few minutes later the two men turned into Argyle Street.

"We may as well start with this big place here near the Central, Frazer's."

Frazer's was one of those establishments which deal with one or two makes of new machines and any class of old ones they can get their hands on. French asked to see the principal.

"I want you, if you'll be good enough, Mr Frazer," he said, "to tell me what type of machine this was done on."

Frazer examined the letter carefully, first with the naked eye and then with a lens.

"It'll be a Corona Number Three," he said at last. Then as French would have spoken, he held up his hand. "Wait till I ask my foreman. He knows the types better than I do."

The foreman was sent for and in his turn unhurriedly scrutinised the document.

"Yon's auld Coronatype," he pronounced. "A Number Three Corona. Ah ken it well."

"Kind of miraculous," French declared, feeling that a judicious compliment might smooth the remainder of the interview. "To me all type looks very much alike. Do you mean to tell me that they're all so different that you can distinguish them at a glance like that."

Frazer picked up the paper again.

"Some letters are the same in most makes," he explained, "and some are different. The difference is bigger perhaps in the figures than in the letters. For instance, to take an obvious case, some makers carry the lower loops of the 3's and 5's down while others curve them round like print. Then again in most makes the small 'l' does duty for a '1', but with some others there is a special key for the one and the figure is a different shape to the small '1'."

"A matter of elimination, I expect?"

"That's so. The shape of one letter may limit the machine to half a dozen makes, a second letter may knock out two of those six and so on."

"I can understand that," said French. "I'm always using the same method. In fact, your spotting the machine is just a bit of detective work. We'll be appointing you consultant to the Yard next."

Mr Frazer's forte was not humour. He replied that he would always be glad to be of use and was that all?

French assured him that it was not all, that it was in fact only half of what he wanted.

"That letter," he explained, tapping it with a long forefinger to emphasise his point, "that letter which you tell me was typed on a Number Three Corona, is believed to have been written by a murderer. We think he bought the machine, obviously a second-hand one, here in Glasgow on Tuesday, the 8th of October last. Now the other thing that I want to know is – Did he buy it here?"

Mr Frazer was mildly interested. He did not know anything about such a purchase, but he would do his best to trace it. Would Mr French mind waiting a moment?

In ten minutes he came back. No No. 3 Corona had been sold on the day in question.

"We may just settle down to it," French said when he and M'Clung were once more in the street. "I'll tear my list in two and you may do one lot and I the other. Ring up the hotel at every even hour."

All day French worked hard, visiting shop after shop where second-hand typewriters were to be had. At twelve and two he returned to the St Enoch Hotel and took M'Clung 's call, but the latter had nothing to report. And then when he got the four o'clock message there was news.

M'Clung believed he had got it. Would Mr French come to Farquharson's in Queen Street?

Ten minutes later French reached the shop. M'Clung introduced him to Mr Farquharson himself. A third man was hovering in the distance.

"Yes," the proprietor said, "I think we must have sold the machine you are looking after. This is Mr Duncan, who handled the transaction. Tell him anything you can, Duncan."

Duncan was a little rat of a man with an extraordinarily stupid face. His evidence was disappointing. On the afternoon of the day on which Victor Magill had passed through Glasgow a man had called and said he required a second-hand typewriter, a portable. Duncan had shown him two or three, among them a No. 3 Corona. This the man finally bought, carrying it away with him. Duncan was able to fix the date from the sales record.

"Was the man among these?" asked French, producing his photographs of Sir John, Malcolm and Victor.

Duncan hesitated, not indeed without excuse, for the three portraits were not unlike. Finally he admitted that he could not tell.

"Well," said French, keenly disappointed, "describe him in your own words."

But this was just what Duncan could not do and it soon became evident that for all he remembered of the stranger he might as well never have seen him.

For a moment French was baffled, then he turned back to Mr Farquharson and with a good deal of trepidation asked where his firm had got the machine.

A moment later he breathed more freely. All was not necessarily lost. Mr Farquharson admitted that he kept records of his purchases as well as of his sales. If they would excuse him a minute...Yes, he had turned it up. The machine had been taken in part payment for a new one from Mr Jabus Montieth of 136A Strathpeffer Street, off the Great Western Road.

"It looks well, M'Clung, it looks well," French exclaimed as the two men drove to Strathpeffer Street. "This is one for you and your superintendent! If only we find this Montieth we may get what we want tonight."

Still their luck held. Montieth was at home.

"Yes," he confirmed, "I sold my old machine to Messrs Farquharson. A right good machine it was too, but it was getting worn and out of adjustment. I write a good deal and thought I might treat myself to a new one."

"I'm glad we've come to the right man," French said in heartfelt tones. "Now, Mr Montieth, if you can only answer one other question I'll trouble you no more. Do you happen to have any of your writings there, those that were done by the old machine? If I could get hold of anything typed by that machine I could tell whether it's the one I want."

"I can do that easily." Mr Montieth turned to a shelf. "Here is the manuscript of a short story done on it – rejected, I'm sorry to say."

French did not trouble to hide his eagerness as he took the papers. Very little more than a glance was necessary. Here in the manuscript were the same type defects as in the XYZ letter, the same worn letters, the same types out of adjustment. A short examination through a lens put the matter beyond doubt. This machine had been used for both. Though without a formal identification by Duncan there was as yet no legal proof, there could be no doubt on the main point. Victor unquestionably had typed the XYZ letter!

18

CAMPBELTOWN

As the two detectives regained the Great Western Road their minds were full of a happy satisfaction. M'Clung was conscious not only of a piece of work well done, a vital forward step taken in the case, but he was also pleasantly aware that the credit for this step was due to himself and his superintendent. The detective force of Northern Ireland had abundantly vindicated itself, in fact it had shown the way to this experienced officer of the CID. Altogether things were going well.

French was even more pleased. Not only was there this important success about the purchase of the typewriter, but there was the even more vital suggestion that the launch had put in to Lurigan on the night of the murder. If this latter could be proved it would be the beginning of the end.

With satisfaction he reconsidered the theory which this story of the launch had suggested to him. Sir John Magill, robbed of his plans, reaches Sandy Row in search of Coates' friend and his linen – silk machinery.

There he is met by a confederate – possibly Malcolm or even Breene – who somehow induces him to lie low for the day on the Cave Hill and then in the evening to go to Whitehead. There possibly the same or another confederate meets him and in some other way – perhaps by promising

228

negotiations for the return of the plans – persuades him to walk to Lurigan. At Lurigan the stage is set for the tragedy. He is captured and murdered by the gang, who bury his body on Malcolm's ground. Supposing this were all true, would the gang, French wondered, have had time to murder him and bury the body?

It was part of the theory that the launch arrived at Lurigan at 2.30 a.m. Assuming it ran full speed to Campbeltown, at what hour must it have left Lurigan?

Maps again! The distance scaled 37 sea miles – say, a journey of 3¾ hours. To reach Campbeltown at 7.15, therefore, meant leaving Lurigan at 3.30. From 2.30 to 3.30 was an hour, surely time enough for the sinister work. No snag here at all events. Then another point occurred to him.

He had already realised that the theft of the plans would have been valueless so long as Sir John lived; the moment "Sillin" was put on the market, under whatever name, the theft would have been traced. The murder, therefore, must necessarily have been a part of the thieves' programme. And now French saw why an interval was necessary between the theft and the murder. The gang required an opportunity to examine their booty so as to make sure it contained the genuine plans. Considering their extraordinary value it would have been a reasonable precaution for Sir John to have sent the real plans to Belfast in some other way while carrying a dummy set for the use of thieves. If the gang murdered the old man for a dummy set, goodbye to their chance of getting the genuine ones.

After dinner French settled down with M'Clung to discuss the case in the smoking-room of the St Enoch Hotel. First French told of his discoveries at Kirkandrews

Bay and in Cumberland. Then he turned to their more immediate achievement.

"If we assume Victor typed that letter, as we must, can we not reach some further conclusion? The thing is bristling with clues. Is there nothing that we missed?" M'Clung replied vaguely.

"Let us think," French went on. "To have been delivered at the time it was, you tell me the letter must have been posted before about one-thirty on that Wednesday. If we admit your suggestion that Victor didn't write it until *after* his visit to police headquarters – which I think exceedingly likely – we see that he could not have written it before one. He left the police station, if I remember rightly, about ten minutes to one. Therefore on the balance of probability it was written between one and one thirty. Now, M'Clung, where must that have been done?"

"An hotel, sir?"

"That's what I think. What was to prevent Victor calling at an hotel on his way from police headquarters and in the secrecy of a bedroom typing the letter? It seems to me that the thing to find out now is – Did Victor go to an hotel at that hour on that day, and if so, what did he do there?"

"That's easy done," M'Clung pointed out. "A phone to Superintendent Rainey would get the information in an hour or two."

"I daresay," French admitted, "but I haven't done yet. If we're right so far a much more important thing follows. See what it is?"

M'Clung slowly shook his head.

"He must have had something with him," French prompted.

M'Clung slapped his thigh.

"The typewriter!" he exclaimed. "That's a fact. And where did he put it?"

"Right, M'Clung. That's what I have been coming to. He must immediately get rid of such a dangerous piece of evidence. Where did he put it? Or in other words, can we find it?"

"If we did, it would prove your whole theory," M'Clung declared with evident admiration.

"Job for the Belfast force surely," French suggested blandly. "Do you think, M'Clung, if we wired to Superintendent Rainey asking him to find the typewriter that he would do it?"

M'Clung grinned, then scratched his head thoughtfully.

"Where do you think we should look, sir?" he asked innocently.

French took him seriously.

"Well, where?" he said. "You know the locality. Where would you have hidden it, M'Clung?"

M'Clung was of the opinion that there were plenty of places, but when pressed to name them he hesitated.

"He could have thrown it off the Queen's Bridge into the Lagan," he suggested at last. But French ridiculed the idea.

"In broad daylight, with crowds on the bridge and boats on the river below? I don't think, M'Clung. Try again."

"It could have been done at night."

"It could, but not by Victor. Remember he went down to Lurigan in the early afternoon."

"That's a fact," M'Clung admitted.

Evidently it was not such an easy thing to get rid secretly of a typewriter. M'Clung put forward other suggestions, but all were ruled out after consideration. At last French made his contribution.

"Well, I'll tell you what I think," he declared. "Sir John had found a hiding place at Belfast already, up the Sheeps' Path. Now that's not a place that would occur to everyone and if Sir John chose it it might – *might*, I say – be because some previous happening had suggested it to him. Now is it too much to assume that this previous happening might have been known to Victor also – perhaps known to the whole family? Say some childish escapade known to them all. Of course all this is an absolute shot in the dark. But let us assume it for argument's sake. If it's true something may follow?" French paused interrogatively.

"I get you, sir." M'Clung now made no attempt to conceal his admiration. "Victor used the same place?"

"May have used it," French amended.

"It's worth trying anyway, sir."

Next morning French put through his call. Rainey was keenly interested and within a few minutes men had left headquarters to go the round of the hotels and to start a new search for buried treasure on the Cave Hill. French and M'Clung strolled out to get what amusement they could from the city's somewhat drab life. But the streets were filled with a dank fog and they soon gave up their quest of entertainment and returned to the more comfortable boredom of the hotel.

Before long there was a telephone call. Victor Magill had engaged a room at the Grand Central Hotel on the day on which he had crossed from Scotland. After breakfast he had gone out, but the chambermaid remembered that he had returned about one and remained for some minutes in his room. She had heard a clicking sound that might have been a typewriter. Victor had not been seen leaving his room, but his bill showed that he had lunched. After lunch he had cancelled the room, stating that he had met a friend who had asked him to stay at his house.

This information seemed to French to prove his theory, irrespective of whether or not the typewriter were found. But he was very keen that it should be found. He therefore wired a message of congratulation to Rainey, asking him at the same time to continue his efforts on the Cave Hill.

As the evening drew in he found himself at a loss as to what he himself should do. Should he go to Belfast and discuss the affair with Rainey or go to London to report in person to Mitchell, or again should he remain where he was in the hope that news would come from Ireland?

Finally he decided to remain in Glasgow for another twenty-four hours. By that time the more promising parts of the Cave Hill would have been searched and perhaps the machine would have been found.

Next day he realised with enthusiasm that his decision had been justified. As he and M'Clung were lunching gloomily in the dining-room of the St Enoch Hotel he was again called to the telephone.

It was Superintendent Rainey and he had great news. There was a ring of quiet triumph in his voice as he told that the search on the Cave Hill had been successful. Lightly buried in another part of the very same clump of bushes in which the cloak and dagger had been found, was a Corona typewriter. Moreover it was *the* machine, that on which the XYZ letter had been typed. The truth of French's theory had therefore been demonstrated and Rainey returned with interest the congratulations he had received from French on the previous day.

To say that French was overjoyed would be sadly to understate the situation. Quite apart from the very material progress in the case the discovery represented, it was one of those instances of the justification of an enlightened guess, which are so soothing to the self-esteem of the person responsible. French felt that a more thoroughly satisfying demonstration of his own efficiency had seldom been vouchsafed.

Victor Magill then, was the author of the XYZ letter. Victor therefore knew the true facts of Sir John's death and burial, and Victor was out to get his share of the spoils. Victor, there could no longer be any doubt, was party to the murder.

So, unquestionably, were Joss, Teer and Mallace. So possibly was Malcolm. So possibly was Breene. While the greater part of this awful tragedy was still shrouded in mystery, it was at least becoming clear that in some way the unhappy Sir John had been inveigled to Lurigan in the small hours of that fatal morning and had there been brutally done to death.

Was there no way, French asked himself, in which he could arrive at the truth? His optimism slowly evaporated as he came to grips with the many difficulties still left unsolved. Then he suddenly remembered a remark of M'Clung's and stopped short.

"Look here," he said, "that's all I want. Get away and see your sister or your young lady or whoever it is that you want to see. Only call at the hotel before your train. If there's anything I'll leave a message."

In a dream French settled down once again to his struggle with the problem. What was wrong with him? He had got plenty of clues and why couldn't he use them? He *must* do better! His whole career was at stake. He *must* get somewhere with this wretched business!

Setting his teeth he determined to sit down and for the nth time think the whole thing out from the beginning. He swore great oaths that nothing would induce him to move until he had reached some conclusion.

He made his way to the smoking-room, which at that hour was deserted, and sitting down in the most comfortable chair, got his pipe going satisfactorily. Then he gave himself up once again to collating and marshalling his facts.

For upwards of two hours he sat pondering over what he knew, trying to imagine what he didn't know, seeing if he could not find the missing link, which would cause his isolated facts to drop into place, and form one connected whole.

In vain he twisted and turned, and sucked vigorously at his pipe, in vain he consumed cups of strong coffee, in vain he cursed as each avenue he tried brought him up against still another blind wall. And then – French's heart seemed to miss a beat and he sat for a moment breathlessly. His pipe slipped from his half opened mouth and dropping to the floor, ejected a little heap of red hot ash on to the carpet. But French saw neither it nor anything else. He was gripped by a sudden new idea, which like a blinding flash of lightning in the murky blackness of a hurricane, had illuminated the whole of his thoughts.

He got up, automatically picked up the pipe and tramped the red ashes into blackness, and with growing excitement began to pace the room. Yes! Tremulously he began to admit to himself that he had got it! Yes, at last it worked in! The visits of "Coates" to Sir John, the plans of the linen – silk machinery, the journey to Ireland, the movements of the launch and of its four passengers, the velvet coat and its accompanying symbolic ladder. As he ran over the details in his mind he saw that at last they fitted! Now he knew why Teer had called at Tarn Bay and just what had taken place on the Cave Hill. He saw in his mind's eye the strange happening on the road where the bloodstained hat was found, he realised the true inwardness of what Cleaner M'Atamney had seen at Larne and visualised the hideous consummation at Lurigan. At last he understood Malcolm's part in all these manifestations. In short – oh, could it be? – at last he had solved his problem!

He moved impatiently. Drat that fellow M'Clung! Would he never come? French wanted someone to share his triumph.

But M'Clung was away visiting his friends and French had perforce to keep his transports to himself. He fell to pacing the smoking-room, continuing to turn the affair over in his mind.

Yes, it was great! His solution was great and the problem that he had solved was great. Gosh, but the facts would make a stir when they became known! One of his most spectacular triumphs! Once again his thoughts turned hesitatingly to a chief inspectorship. The last time there had been a vacancy he had been passed over. Now he was older and promotion was more probable. It was true that there was no immediate vacancy, but you never knew...Old Rolleston's heart was none too good...

"Turned wet, sir," said a voice and M'Clung, bearing evidences of weather, entered the room. French glared at him.

"M'Clung, you black-faced son of a gun," he roared, and then in answer to the sergeant's look of surprise, he chuckled. "Ah, something's happened since you've been out," he declared. "Something big! Something huge, immense, prodigious! I've got it!"

"Got it?" M'Clung repeated dully. "I don't just – Got what, sir?"

"Got *it!*" French yelled. "*It! It! It!* The whole blessed thing! I've got the *Solution!* Now do you understand?"

M'Clung gaped.

"Boys o' boys!" he murmured weakly, then subsided into a chair and begged for details.

"Details?" French shouted, striding vigorously up and down. "I'll not tell you a blessed thing! Just think for yourself! You know the whole confounded business. You know as much as I do and you've everything you want to give you the answer." He halted and spoke with immense impressiveness. "You've – got – every – darned – fact – you need – to give you – the solution! Sit down and for once in a way use that fat head of yours and you'll get it. Meantime go to the telephone and reserve a couple of berths in tonight's London train. I'll want you up with me to see the end."

Great business! The end of the case, and the end brought about by him, Joseph French, and not by these darned Irish! Well, it was just another triumph to add to the long list that had gone before.

And then suddenly French stopped as if he had been shot, while an expression of blank dismay formed on his usually not too expressive features. For a few seconds he remained motionless, and then in low tones of extreme and concentrated bitterness a stream of oaths began to pour from his lips.

It was not often that French's self-control gave way, but the truth was that he had just seen a snag of such devastating proportions that it completely swept away the whole of the magnificent theory of which he had been so proud. The reaction from triumph to despair was too acute.

"Beg pardon, sir?" M'Clung's voice broke in on the blasphemous monologue.

"Here," said French gruffly, "did you get those blasted reservations? Well, you can cancel them again. We're not going to town tonight."

M'Clung opened his mouth to reply, then catching sight of French's expression, he closed it quickly and vanished.

"Reservations cancelled, sir," he reported a few minutes later. He sat down without further remark, and taking out his notebook, busied himself with its contents. French glared at him. Then he spoke.

"A snag, M'Clung; my fault, not yours. I overlooked it and it's upset my theory. But it'll come right. It must." He paused as the other nodded thoughtfully, then beginning once more to pace the room, he went on: "An object lesson, M'Clung. Don't count your chickens! Nothing's certain till you've got it in your hand, and not always then. I have a gorgeous theory: it explains everything, clears up all our puzzles and leaves the whole affair complete. It's so good that I can't doubt its absolute truth. But here's the snag. It requires all four men to take an active part in it, Mallace, Joss, Teer and Victor. And there's Victor's bad leg! I was so pleased I got temporary swelled head and overlooked Victor's bad leg."

M'Clung twisted his head and half-closed his eyes and looked sly.

"If that's all it is, Mr French, you know very well that bad legs can be faked. Sure we were doubting that bad leg anyway."

"Not since we got the doctor's report, I wasn't. Let's turn the blessed thing up." He rummaged in his bag. "Here's what the sergeant says: 'I then called on Dr MacGregor and questioned him. He stated as follows: "About nine o'clock on the morning of Friday, 4th October, a man called at my surgery. He gave the name of Teer and stated that he was one of a party of four who were on a motor launch tour. He stated that one of his companions, a Mr Magill, had had a fall and hurt his knee. He asked me to go aboard the launch and have a look at it. As soon as I had finished my breakfast I went down to the harbour. The launch *Sea Hawk* was moored alongside the wharf and I went on board. Magill was in his bunk. I examined him and found a contusion on the inside of the left knee at the head of the tibia. The joint was swollen and inflamed and must have been painful. In my opinion Magill could not have walked, or at best could only have hobbled with the aid of a stick, but I believed that in three or four days he should be able to do so. The injury was absolutely genuine and could not by any possibility have been faked. I asked Magill how it had occurred, and he replied that owing to the launch giving a sudden lurch he had fallen while carrying some cocoa up the companion steps, striking his knee on the sharp edge of a step. That was early on the morning of the previous day. In my opinion the injury might have been incurred at the time and in the manner stated. I attended to the knee and then left." 'The sergeant goes on: 'Dr MacGregor is reputed to be a very skilful and reliable doctor and bears a high character in Campbeltown.' There you are, M'Clung. Unless this doctor is a much bigger fool than the sergeant believes, there's our snag."

"Dr MacGregor wasn't looking out for any fake and so he didn't find one, and now he's not going to admit he made a mistake," M'Clung declared stoutly.

French shrugged.

"I hope you're right." He paused, then added: "You must be right. At all events we'll have to make sure. There's nothing for it but a trip to Campbeltown. You might go and find out how you get there."

"You go by steamer from Greenock," M'Clung explained after another brief disappearance, "but you can't go and come on the same day. You leave the Central at 8.35, change to the boat at Greenock, and get to Campbeltown at 1.30. Then you're stuck there for the rest of the day. Coming back you leave at 7.45 in the morning and you're in Glasgow at 1.15."

"Good Lord! What'll we do there for a whole afternoon? And we can't go tomorrow for it's Sunday. Well, we needn't worry; we can't help it. Ring up your superintendent, will you, and ask him if you can remain with me for a day or two. Then you can go and see your young woman again, or anyone else you want to. But be at the train on Monday morning."

It was an immense though minor disappointment to French that on Monday the bad weather should hold. Enveloped in waterproofs, he and M'Clung sheltered precariously behind deck houses on the Clyde steamer, trying to appreciate through driving mist and rain the beauty spots of one of the best coastal trips in Europe. But all they could see were dripping and windswept piers, with occasional cheerless-looking houses in the background, and bleak shores rising grey and smudgy to the dim outlines of mountains above.

They were fortunate in catching Dr MacGregor before he went out on his afternoon's rounds. He was big and shrewd-looking with a breezy manner, and French felt instinctively, a man to be trusted. After a few words of introduction French saw the line he should take.

"You mustn't misunderstand the object of our call, Dr MacGregor," he declared with a smile. "At first sight it looks like an inept kind of joke, but I need scarcely say that that is not the fact. You remember the sergeant calling on you relative to a visit you paid to a man named Victor Magill, who had hurt his knee while on a launch cruise?"

The doctor nodded decisively.

"Now this is very strictly between ourselves," went on French. Again the doctor nodded and French continued impressively: "From certain facts which have come into our possession we have reason to believe that this launch trip was undertaken to cover up a serious crime. Indeed I needn't make any mystery about it, we believe the members, all four, guilty of the murder of Sir John Magill near Larne. You may remember seeing the case in the papers?"

"Aye, I think I saw it," Dr MacGregor answered, with more than a suspicion of the Doric. "And was that what the sergeant was after? He wasna over ready with his explanations."

"A good man, the sergeant," said French. "Well, from information received we believe these four ruffians went ashore near Larne between half past two and half past three o'clock on that same morning, all four of them, you understand. That of course raises the question of Magill's knee."

"I see it does," the doctor returned dryly.

"So then," went on French, "it follows that either they didn't all four go ashore as we suppose, or else that the injury was faked. And the last is what I firmly believe was done. I've come to you, doctor, to ask your help in finding out how."

French spoke earnestly and MacGregor, who seemed at first inclined to get on his high horse, remained silent.

"Well," he said at last, "you may suggest that the injury was faked if you like, but if you do you'll be wrong. There was the swelling and the heat and the colour. You might heat up the knee with mustard and paint on the discoloration and pretend it was painful, but you couldn't fake all the symptoms together, at least not well enough to deceive a qualified doctor. No, inspector, you may take it from me there was no fake about it. I'll swear that in any court of law."

French felt, and looked, terribly disappointed.

"That's a pretty heavy blow, doctor, and no mistake. It about leaves me in Queer Street so far as my case is concerned. I could have sworn you'd be able to help me."

Dr MacGregor intimated that he was sorry, but that he couldn't alter facts to suit the inspector's cases. French tried again.

"The man would be lame, I suppose?"

"Lame? Aye, he'd be lame. I doubt for the first day or two he wouldna do any walking at all."

"He told you how the injury was supposed to have occurred?"

"He did."

"And the appearance of the bruise agreed with that?"

"Absolutely."

French made a gesture of despair.

"Then you can't help me at all, doctor?" he almost implored. "If I were to take up enough of your time to tell you the whole facts you'd see how extraordinarily strong is the suggestion of a fake. You can't tell me anything more?"

For the first time the doctor began to show impatience.

"I can tell you again what I've told you before and what I'm not bound to tell you at all," he said, "and that is that there was no fake about it. If you don't like to take my word for it you needn't. I'm afraid I must wish you good day. I'm behind already with my calls."

"It's not your word I doubt, doctor," French returned, rising. "There's my address. If in thinking over the thing you see a way out I'd be obliged if you'd let me know."

Dr MacGregor took the card with evident rising anger.

"I'll tell you what I'll let you know," he said harshly. "If you bring a case against the man on the lines you've mentioned, I'll go into the box and swear that your case is false. Goodbye."

"Pity people are so beastly touchy," French grumbled as he and M'Clung turned away from the doctor's gate.

"It's what I said, Mr French. He's not sure about the thing, but he's not going to admit any mistake."

"You think so? Now I don't agree with you, M'Clung. I believe he's sure enough. And he looks competent. I can't picture him making a mistake of that kind. It's an abominable puzzle and I don't see the way out. And yet I believe there must be a way. Here, let's go for a walk somewhere."

At another time and under other circumstances French would have been delighted at the prospect of a ramble along a new and fine stretch of coast, but for the moment he was past scenery. His case and his case alone occupied his mind. For the next couple of hours as they trudged along through what had become merely a damp mist, he proved a poor companion. Then he suddenly stopped and faced M'Clung.

"I believe I've got this too!" he declared, with a kind of cold excitement. "Look here, that doctor gave the thing away himself. Don't you see? Come back and let's see him again."

He hurried M'Clung along till once more they were in Dr MacGregor's consulting-room.

243

"Sorry to trouble you again and all that, doctor," French said with eagerness, "but I believe I've got it!"

MacGregor looked at him with cold eyes.

"Got it? Got what?" he asked none too graciously.

"How that knee evidence was faked. As a matter of fact you told me yourself, though neither you nor I recognised it at the time."

The doctor looked as if his temper might get the better of him at any moment, but he was evidently interested.

"Well?" he said.

"You said that in your opinion the injury took place at the time and in the manner stated?"

"Might have taken place," MacGregor corrected.

"You're absolutely sure of the time?"

MacGregor rapped out an oath.

"I'm not absolutely sure of the time," he declared angrily, "nor no man living could be sure of the time. What I'm sure of is what I said: that it might have taken place when stated."

French had the self-satisfied air of a conjurer who has just successfully produced a lady's vanity bag from a consequential old gentleman's coat pocket.

"You think," he suggested innocently, "it couldn't have taken place that same morning?"

M'Clung started and French thought he heard a smothered "Boys o' boys!" But MacGregor dashed his hopes.

"I don't believe it," he answered sharply. "Admittedly it's a point you can't be so sure of. You go by the discoloration and one person discolours more quickly than another. But in this case discoloration was well marked. It could scarcely have taken less than thirty hours to develop, though it might easily have taken a lot longer, several days in fact."

"Now, doctor," said French in evident excitement, "here's my last question. Excluding discoloration, could the injury in your opinion have occurred that same morning, say six hours before you saw it?"

Both he and M'Clung waited almost breathlessly for the reply. This time it was satisfactory. MacGregor admitted that in this case it might.

"Then," French cried triumphantly, "there we have it! Suppose, doctor, the injury was done six hours before you saw it *and the discoloration was painted on!* What about that?"

French sat back and beamed at the other. MacGregor returned his gaze earnestly. Then his manner changed.

"Sorry, inspector. I see what you are driving at, and you may be right. You mean that, while there was no fake of the injury, as I said, there may have been a fake as to the time it occurred?"

"That's it, doctor. I suggest that the injury was deliberately produced *after* the launch left Ireland, say about three-thirty in the morning. You saw it about nine-thirty, say six hours later. By that time the swelling would be there all right, but not the proper discoloration, not the discoloration, that is to say, which might be present if the injury had taken place thirty hours earlier as Magill stated."

MacGregor, now quite thawed, admitted the possibility. All the same it was only a guess on the inspector's part and there wasn't any proof of its truth.

French agreed, but pointed out that if his case stood as a whole it would automatically provide sufficient proof. The doctor saw this for himself. He even obscurely hinted that it was "smarrrt" of French to have thought of it and they parted friends.

"Now we for London as soon as we can get there," French exclaimed as they turned towards their hotel.

"What time does that blessed boat get to Glasgow tomorrow?"

"It goes to Greenock. The train gets to the Central at 1.15."

"Well, we should get up to town that night. We'll have a shot at it any way and then the great experiment will begin."

"We can get the Midday Scot at 1.30, into Euston at 9.50," returned the travel expert.

French looked at him.

" 'Pon my soul, M'Clung, you're not doing so badly. How do you know that?"

M'Clung sniggered.

"Thought we might need it, sir, and looked it up before we came away."

"Huh," said French. "If we don't pull this case off after the amount of brains that have gone into it it'll be queer an' strange, so it will. That right?"

Something almost approaching a wink hovered for a moment near M'Clung's left eye.

"Ain't 'arf a bad shot, sir," he responded encouragingly.

That night they travelled to town and next morning French had a long interview with Mitchell. The chief inspector was profoundly impressed with French's theory and congratulated him warmly.

"I believe it's the truth," French admitted modestly, "but I'm not sure that it's good enough as it stands. I think, sir, with your permission we should have a reconstruction."

Mitchell thought over this.

"I agree," he said at last. "It's a thing I'm not usually keen on, but this certainly seems a case for it. Very good, French, go ahead. You can have what you want."

"Any chance of your coming along, sir?"

"I'd like to, but I can't get away: that Brighton burglary."

"Sorry, sir. Well, I'll carry on and fix up my arrangements."

"Good. Who would you like?"

French hesitated.

"I want a small man," he said, "for Sir John's part. We've no one small enough really, but I think Ormsby would do. He's middling small and very handy. Carter and Harvey will do for Victor and Teer, for Harvey's a good man with a car. I shall want a witness also, I think. M'Clung would do for that."

"Right, French. Good luck to you."

When French left the chief inspector's room his movements became mysterious. Calling Ormsby, Carter and Harvey, he gave them certain instructions. Then with M'Clung in tow he left the Yard and called at a large clothing establishment on the South Side. There he gave orders for three cowled cloaks of very dark brown cloth of the cheapest quality, two to fit large men, the other slightly smaller. Then at a ship chandler's he described the rope ladder found on the Cave Hill, and ordered a similar one to be sent to the Yard. By dint of a good deal of persuasion the shop people agreed to have all four articles completed and delivered by the following afternoon.

"Now to Euston," he said, leading the way to the nearest tube station.

Half an hour later they walked for the second time in the inquiry into the reservation office on No. 6 platform. The clerk greeted them as old friends.

"Well, gentlemen," he began, as if prepared for a long conversation. "I suppose you're not looking for sleeping car attendants this time?"

French regretted it was nothing so dramatic. On this occasion, he and his companion were mere humble members of the travelling public. In fact, they only wanted a reservation. Could the clerk fix them up with two communicating berths to Stranraer for the following night?

The clerk's comment took the form of a low whistle. But he was able to reserve the berths.

"Now I want something else," French added. "I want the corridor on the left side of the carriage."

Again the clerk whistled as he shook his head.

"So that you can wave to little Albert?" he said with a grin. "You're not trying to make me an accessory before the fact, I suppose? Neither of you gentlemen going over to Ireland to be murdered, are you?" Then seeing that French was not overwhelmed with the humour of his remarks, he returned to business.

He could not tell on which side the corridor was, but he could ask the stationmaster's people to ring up and find out. Some time was spent in telephoning and then French learned that once again his luck was in. The berths were on the right side of the train. He therefore took the necessary tickets and half an hour later he and M'Clung were back at the Yard.

"Good enough for today," French declared. "We'll knock off now. You can amuse yourself as you like tomorrow, but meet Ormsby and me at Euston in time for the Stranraer train. Tomorrow night'll settle our hash."

M'Clung duly vanished. But French did not go off duty. Instead, he called his three men together and spent a solid hour posting them in their duties for the following night.

19

LONDON TO STRANRAER

Shortly before 7.40 next evening French and his two companions arrived at Euston. In the little drama which they were about to enact French was taking the part of Joss and Ormsby that of Sir John Magill, while M'Clung acted as observer. French and Ormsby carried suitcases, and in French's lay the smallest of the brown cloaks and the rope ladder.

Carter and Harvey, who were playing the parts of Victor and Teer respectively, had left on the previous night for Dumfries. There they were to hire a car and drive it to where Teer's car was seen near the station at Castle Douglas, arriving shortly before the boat train was due. For rightly or wrongly French believed that Victor had not spent the night on the launch with Mallace, but instead had been with Teer at Castle Douglas. With these two went the other brown cloaks.

French did not consider it necessary to reproduce the movement of the launch or to appoint anyone to act as Mallace. If his theory were correct there could be no doubt as to the movements of the launch, and as he was satisfied that Mallace had remained with it during all its voyages, his movements were therefore also known.

By a fortunate chance it turned out that their former acquaintance, Pugg, was the attendant in charge of the sleeping cars. French called him aside.

"We're going to try a little experiment tonight," he explained, "and we want you to give us your help. It's a simple matter. We want you to act as nearly as you can in the same way in which you acted on the night Sir John Magill crossed. For the purposes of the experiment, Mr Ormsby here will sleep in the berth corresponding to Sir John's and I in the next berth, corresponding to Mr Coates'. Mr M'Clung, whom you met before, will travel in my stateroom. I want you to satisfy yourself that the communicating door is not only locked, but bolted on each side. Do not keep any better or worse watch than you kept on that night, but, of course, if you see anything wrong, let me know."

Pugg assured them he would act as desired, but as French pointed out to his companions, his request was really weighing the scales against their success. "He says he'll act as on that night," said French, "but, of course, he won't. You bet he'll keep his eyes skinned. So if we can succeed under this handicap Joss and Co. won't have had much difficulty."

They left their suitcases in their staterooms and came out for a final stroll on the platform.

"I should remind you two," French went on, "that Coates has already twice visited Sir John. On these calls he has told him of his friend's success with the linen – silk fabric, and has got him to agree to go over to Belfast via Larne to see the process with a view to putting money into it; all much as Joss stated. On some pretext, such perhaps as hearing details of further experiments, he had doubtless also led the old man to expect a call at his stateroom after the train has started. Either of you see anything wrong so far?"

Ormsby and M'Clung both thought that a plausible man could have convinced the deceased on all these points.

"Very well then, we'll leave it at that," French concluded. "You Ormsby, expect a call from me after we start."

They took their places and presently the train began to glide slowly from the station. The network of roads at the end of the platforms passed before them and the train wormed its way into a tunnel. As it did so Attendant Pugg appeared.

"I'll just see your tickets now, gentlemen," he said, "then you won't be disturbed till we get to Stranraer. Thank you, sir: thank *you*, sir. What about a call in the morning?... '*Alf* an hour before we get in? Right, sir. And two cups o' tea? Thank you, sir."

He noted the particulars in his book and vanished, closing the door. Immediately they heard him repeating his formula to Ormsby.

As soon as he had gone on to the next stateroom, French got busy. Bolting the door to the corridor he took an instrument of bent wire from his pocket and inserted it in the lock of the communicating door. For some minutes he worked, then a faint click, and a satisfied expression on his face announced that the bolt had been shot back. Next he did the same with the finger bolt. The door was now fastened by the handle and the bolt on Sir John's side only.

By the time this was done both men estimated that Pugg would have moved on to the third-class sleeper adjoining. French unbolted and slowly opened the corridor door.

"All clear," he whispered and knocked at Ormsby's door. "Come in," they heard faintly above the roar of the train, which by now was running at a high speed. Both men squeezed in and closed the door.

"Get over there on to the luggage stool," French directed M'Clung. Ormsby was sitting on the bed near its foot and he moved slightly up so that the Irishman might pass him and take his place at the window. French also sat down on the bed.

"Now first," went on French, "without letting you see me, Sir John, I bolt your corridor door." He suited the action to the word. "Next I talk to you and I am as pleasant and interesting as I know how. I tell you about my friend's experiment or whatever you are expecting to hear, and then I probably say that I must go back to my stateroom, as no doubt you are tired and wish to be alone. At all events, at the end of my interview I produce my flask.

" 'I happen to have here some really choice old brandy,' I say. 'I hope you will join me in a nightcap?' I unscrew the top of the flask, hand you the glass from the toilet rack and use the cap for myself."

French paused to let his companions appreciate the situation.

"Whether Sir John wants the drink or whether he merely takes it for politeness' sake, we don't know, but we know that he accepts it. And when he does so Joss has taken his first fence. For, as I presume, you have grasped that brandy contains a safe, but powerful and quick-acting sleeping draught. Lastly, I wipe my finger marks off the flask and leave it here on the rack."

French took out his watch.

"You have now drunk the brandy, Ormsby, and we shall give you fifteen minutes to be asleep. In order not to arouse your suspicions I go on talking to you. But presently you drop over. We shall suppose you have done it. I now unbolt the communicating door. This enables me to open it and I return through it to my stateroom, bolting it behind me on my own side. You may go to sleep now, Ormsby. There'll be nothing more until we're near Castle Douglas. But before I go I want you both to appreciate the situation.

"Sir John is lying here asleep with his door bolted. Should anything go wrong and the door has to be broken open everything will be found normal. The flask – a new one – containing the dregs of a mixed sleeping draught will be found. To get a good sleep in the unusual circumstance of a train journey, it is quite reasonable that Sir John should have taken a draught. You follow me? Up to the present there is nothing to arouse suspicion."

"The communicating door is unlocked," M'Clung suggested.

"That won't arouse suspicion," returned French, because my side of it is bolted and therefore it cannot be opened. If any trouble arose I should of course lock it."

"It's not bolted on Sir John's side," M'Clung persisted.

"I agree," French admitted, "but that would be put down to an oversight on the attendant's part, no matter how he denied it. Besides if one goes in for crime one must take some risk."

Both men agreed. French and M'Clung then withdrew according to plan, bolting the communicating door behind them.

"There's an extra rug and I told the old chap to leave in a second pillow. Make up another bed on the floor, M'Clung, and we'll take it in turns."

But neither French nor his companion felt like sleep. Though neither would have admitted it, both were consumed with a lively excitement, to which in French's case was added not a little anxiety. For him, this was a serious matter in which they were engaged. After what had seemed an endless period of effort and suspense he had at last taken the plunge. He had stated his theory and now it was under test. If the thing went well it would help him at headquarters as surely as the converse would be to his disadvantage. To a certain extent his reputation and prospects were at stake.

To M'Clung the affair was simpler. His interest came from curiosity, and from the mere fact that he was assisting at the reconstruction of a big murder case with officers of the far-famed Yard. He only wished a certain young lady, Mrs Adam M'Clung that was to be, could see him moving in these exalted circles.

The train was running well. French presently giving up the pretence of sleep, raised the blind and the two men gazed out into the black night and watched the lights appear at intervals, singly or in groups, twinkle for a moment and hurry by. Bridges hurled themselves backward with a quick "Wha!" while the rhythmic beat of the wheels on the rail joints ran on relentlessly, occasionally, indeed, grumblingly broken by the crossings at some station, but immediately dropping once more into its endless song.

After a time they reached Rugby. A halt there and off again. Crewe. Wigan. The long pull up Shap. The rush down on the other side. Carlisle.

"No good making a move till we pass Dumfries," said French, and they settled down again.

For a while they lay listening once again to the rushing noises of the night, and then at last the great moment was upon them. French slowly got up, switched on the lights and bolted the door into the corridor. Then unbolting that into the next berth, he opened the door and passed through.

Ormsby was asleep, but he roused himself as French turned on the lights here also.

"Now, Ormsby, ever been murdered by a knock over the skull?" French said cheerily. "Because you'll see what it's like now."

He took a pencil from his pocket and held it up.

"This," he explained, "I obtained some days ago in London. It is, I imagine, a short tube of very soft, thick rubber, sealed at the end and filled with shot. Soft, but very heavy; would crack a man's skull without cutting the skin. Or it may be a sandbag. At all events you appreciate the fact that I have arrived here with my weapon and that you, Ormsby, are asleep from your drug and therefore helpless."

The men nodded, keenly interested.

"I now," went on French, "crack your brainbox. You are lying on your side, so I do it at the correct place." He touched the man's head lightly with the pencil. "There, the deed is done. You're a dead man and I'm a murderer. Well, it'll not lie heavily on my conscience. Now with the help of my friends I have to cover up the evidences of my crime. This is how I do it."

From the other stateroom he produced the brown cloak. "Remember, Sir John," he continued, "that you are undressed. We shall suppose your clothes are there on the rack. Now I dress you in this brown cloak. You put it on and we'll suppose I've done it for you. All I want is that you should both be satisfied that Joss could have dressed the body in the cloak."

Of this neither man had any doubt.

"In that cloak of dark and dull material, you would be invisible on a dark night, and that's what you've got to be now. Let me explain to you just what Carter and Harvey have done, remembering that Carter is playing Victor and Harvey, Teer."

They sat down, Ormsby swathed to the eyes in the cloth and with his hood drawn down low over his forehead, while French, demonstrating with outstretched finger, continued his tale.

"They were told to travel last night by this same train to Castle Douglas. When they got out they were to note the position in which the sleeper stopped. As you know, trains stop pretty well at the same place every night. Next day they were to explore the station and surroundings. From there they were to go to Dumfries, hire a car, and run it during the night to Castle Douglas, arriving shortly before this train. Dressed in their cloaks, they should be waiting for us on the line – probably lying down between the rails and the far platform wall."

Both his hearers were listening with an eager intensity. While they no longer had any doubt as to the denouement of the affair, they were none the less anxious to follow it to its inevitable end.

A whistle, followed by the grinding of the brakes, warned them that the moment was upon them.

"That's Castle Douglas," said French, who now held the rope ladder in his hand. "Now, Ormsby, look sharp and do as I tell you."

The speed began to slacken and French turned off the light in both staterooms. Then he opened first the shutter and then the window.

"The opening is only 24 inches wide by 15 high," he explained, "and you have to go out through it. If you really were that corpse we talked about I should throw you out; as it is you must go out yourself. But for any sake be quick, for the train only stops for one minute and Carter has to get in."

They were now drawing up at the platform and French put out the ladder, hooking it to the window. Its query-shaped terminals made it stand out from the side of the carriage so that its rungs could be grasped. The train came to a stand.

"Now, Ormsby!" came in a sharp whisper from French.

With considerable difficulty Ormsby pushed himself feet first out of the window and disappeared into the darkness. The rope ladder shook and then suddenly hung loose. French, looking out, could see nothing. A wave of misgiving swept over him as he stared anxiously down. If Carter didn't hurry up…What if the thing had miscarried? And then French heard the whistle of the guard, and the train began slowly to move. Curse! Something had gone wrong! No, it hadn't though! The ladder shook again and the ropes strained tight. With the train moving quite rapidly, Carter's head appeared at the window, followed by his shoulders.

Carter was a bigger man than Ormsby, and, for a few seconds, it looked as if he wasn't going to get in. But with a prodigious thrust he managed it, falling in a heap on the floor. French swore in his relief. If Carter could do it, Victor, who was a much smaller man, could do it easily. With muttered benedictions, French pulled up the window, closed the shutter and turned on the light.

"What kept you, Carter?" he demanded. "You gave M'Clung and me the fright of our lives. We thought something had gone wrong."

Carter sniggered.

"I'll tell you, Mr French. We wanted to get the body away from the six foot way in case some of the station staff should take it into their heads to cross the line. So we lifted it across the other line and laid it up against the platform wall. It would have been all right only Ormsby was a bad corpse, he struggled when he felt us lift him. He nearly made me miss the train. But I got it all right," he added with satisfaction.

"No difficulty up to the present?"

"None, sir. We got down here last night and fixed the place where the sleeper stopped. Then in the morning we looked over the ground and saw how you got from the station to the road. It's a fairly long carry, Mr French. If Harvey carries Ormsby all that way, he'll wish he was in London." Carter sniggered again at the prospect.

"A man trying to cover up a murder won't worry if it's a bit tiring," French reminded him. "Along that path through the trees, and across the field they're not likely to be seen, and that's all that matters."

Carter agreed. "There's not much chance of being seen so long as they're in the field. It's getting into the car on the road that's the difficulty. However, I expect there'll be no trouble. The place was deserted when we left the car, and it's unlikely there'll be anybody around."

"Harvey understands to leave the body in the field until he prospects, I take it?"

"Oh, yes, sir. Harvey knows his way round all right."

"Very well, that's the end of our experiment so far as those two men are concerned. Now with regard to ourselves. You understand, Carter, that you're Victor and that you've got to be Sir John. You and I must get busy. I have in my bag the white wig which, you remember, you bought some time ago in connection with some amateur theatricals. I have also an actor's make up set and I know how to use it. You may remember Joss was on the stage in America. Very well, I make you up with a white wig, a few lines on your face and glasses. I'm careful not to overdo things: a very slight application of the pencil is enough, for you are like Sir John to begin with. The attendant is the only person you are likely to meet who has seen you within the last seven years, and he will suspect nothing. You agree?"

Both men agreed. M'Clung indeed was "certain sure" the thing could, and had, been done.

French glanced at his watch.

"This old boy will be coming to call us pretty soon," he observed. "We'd better get ready. Carter, you bolt your door after us and unbolt the corridor one. Come, M'Clung, we'll get home."

A few minutes' work with the bent wire shot the lock of the communicating door. French then bolted it with the finger bolt, and unfastened the bolt on the corridor door. Presently a knock came and the latter opened.

"*Good* morning, Mr French. *Good* morning, sir. Your tea, gentlemen."

French could not repress a grin as the two sat, listening intently. They heard the knock next door and the unctuous "*Good* morning, Mr Ormsby." Then there was a startled oath, and a little crash, suggestive of a falling tea-tray. French opened his door.

"Hush, Pugg, don't make a noise. It's only the experiment we wanted to try. We'll tell you about it afterwards, but just now try this communicating door."

Finding the door locked and bolted on each side seemed to add to the man's mystification. He had a quick look round, then excused himself on the ground that he had to wake his other passengers.

"That's all right," French said in satisfied tones, "we may call this a success. If Harvey and Ormsby carry off their part the possibility of the thing is demonstrated. Jolly good, M'Clung, what?" He could not refrain from smiling.

M'Clung seemed equally pleased. But he admitted that there were still many details he hadn't got the hang of and he wondered if Mr French could give him some further explanation.

"Surely," French said amicably. "But we'll wait till those other two join us. We'll see the sights of Stranraer until they turn up, then we'll have breakfast and after that we'll go into the thing thoroughly."

Pugg put his head into the stateroom.

"Are you crossing over, gentlemen?" he asked. "Because if not I'd like to 'ear 'ow that was done. I shouldn't 'ave believed such a thing could 'ave 'appened, not no matter 'oo said it."

"I'd like to 'ear 'ow it was done," he repeated, when they had the car to themselves. "I'm sure this 'ere gentleman," he pointed to Carter, "is not the gentleman 'oo started from Euston. I don't believe as 'ow any make up could alter 'im like that. But I'll swear there weren't no change made neither. It's got me fair mazed, it 'as, and I'd like it explained."

French seemed better pleased than ever.

"You're quite right about the gentleman," he agreed, "but you're wrong about no change being made. Mr Ormsby got out at Castle Douglas and Mr Carter, here, got in."

Pugg slowly rubbed his chin.

"If so be as you say so, sir, I must believe it, that is," he hesitated, "if you're not pulling my leg. But I kept an extra good look out all the way and I saw nothing. And what's more, I tipped the wink to the guard that something was up and 'e 'ad a look out too. And 'e saw nothing. I tell you, sir, 'owever you did it, it was well done."

French smiled.

"I thought you'd do something like that. That's why I gave you the hint. It's made our experiment all the more convincing. Just call the guard, will you?"

"Now," French went on to the two officials, "you two men in the course of your business have got to know a police secret. The gang that did this did it as part of a scheme to murder a helpless old man, Sir John Magill. We're on to them, but we haven't got them yet. If they get to know that we've learned their trick they'll find it unhealthy here and make tracks. Perhaps we'll lose them. So they haven't got to know. Do you see what that means?"

The two men smiled.

"Right," French went on. "That's it. You hold your tongues. Not a word to a single soul. Hard lines, I know, because it would make a good story; but it's only till the gang are caught. Have I your word?"

Both men gave it, but Pugg added complainingly that he didn't yet know how the thing had been done.

"You know a darned sight more than you should," French returned. "But I'll make you this promise: when the gang's arrested you'll hear the whole thing. Now," he turned to Carter, "for that walk and then breakfast."

20

STRANRAER

Shortly after French and Carter reached the King's Arms, Harvey and Ormsby turned up in the car.

"No trouble, Mr French," Ormsby declared. "The whole thing went like clockwork. Just as easy as falling off a log."

"Tell me about it."

"I slid down that ladder," went on Ormsby, "like as if it was greased and when I got to the ground I found myself lifted and carried across the rails. I hadn't known that was in the programme, but Harvey whispered it was to get me close under the wall of the other platform, so I'd not be so conspicuous if anyone started to cross the line. So I lay quiet while the train went out and until everyone left the down platform. Then Harvey whispered to come on, but I thought that was hardly the game, me being a corpse, so I didn't make any move and – "

"The lazy blighter just lay there like a log and I had to carry him the whole way," broke in Harvey indignantly. But he'll not do it again," he added, with more satisfaction. "I dragged him over the rails by the feet."

"Excellent," French approved. "I expect you children made twice the noise Teer did, so if you were able to get clear away, he certainly could. You saw no one?"

"Not a soul. We got to the car and drove to Kirkandrews Bay, waited there half an hour, and then came on straight here. No trouble anywhere."

"Well, you deserve your breakfast."

For some time conversation waned under the stress of more serious matters. Then pipes and cigarettes were lit and desultory remarks began to be made. Presently exchange of ideas became normal.

They discussed the weather, their tobacco, the great adventure and similar experiences of the past, until at last French, glancing at his watch, declared that the hour for conference had arrived.

"I want to go right over this affair as it now appears to me," he said. "You will all hold watching briefs and pull me up if I say anything you think not quite OK."

He settled himself more comfortably in his chair, stopped his pipe with the end of a pencil, and began: "I'd better make it clear right at the start that there's a lot in this affair that I've not yet got the hang of myself. There's a doubt about the motive, there's a doubt about the linen – silk plans and there are doubts about Malcolm Magill. All these and other things have still to be gone into and that'll be our next job. What I'm going to discuss with you now is simply the method of the actual murder – what we tested last night – together with one or two things leading up to it or following from it. First I'll tell you what I believe these people did, then I'll explain why I believe it, and lastly we'll consider whether my reasons are sound."

He stopped and looked round while his hearers, each in his several way, expressed approval.

"We begin with these four, Teer, Mallace, Joss and Victor Magill – for that is the order I should put them in – being desirous of Sir John Magill's death. Let us leave their motive in the meantime. Well, they meet and work out their scheme. The first thing is to get Sir John to travel by the Stranraer boat express. We may take it that is done with the silk – linen story as stated by Joss.

"It is a tale well calculated to fetch Sir John and it fetches him all right. He agrees to visit Belfast. Doubtless by dilating on the rough weather and the short sea passage, Joss gets him to decide on the Stranraer route, and to clinch the matter and to enable him to engage communicating berths, Joss undertakes to make the sleeping car reservations.

"Whether, therefore, Sir John has solved his problem and has agreed to take his plans to compare with those of Joss' friend, or whether, as I am inclined to imagine, he has not solved it and has no plans, doesn't really matter. In either case the alleged Belfast process is used to induce the old man to travel to Ireland by the Stranraer route. We know further, both from Joss' admission and our own inquiries, that this story of Joss' is a pure fabrication – he has no friend in Belfast, nor has he ever worked at a scheme for combining linen and silk. Joss then goes to Euston and engages communicating berths on the right side of the train, that is, the side which will be away from the platform at Castle Douglas."

"How does he know, sir, which side of the train the berths would be on?" Ormsby inquired.

"That's another thing we've still to find out," French admitted. "He asked the reservation clerk, but the clerk was not able to tell him. However he must have learned it somehow.

"After the train starts Joss carries out the actual murder as we reconstructed it. He drugs Sir John, kills him, wraps the body in a dark cloak and pushes it out of the train at

Castle Douglas. Victor gets in by means of the ladder and Joss helps him to make up to personate the dead man. So much for Joss. His act is now over and he meets Teer at Stranraer and they join the launch at Portpatrick."

There was a little murmur of appreciation as Joss passed from the stage and interest focused on his successor.

"Now let us take Mallace," went on French. "Mallace is the nautical member of the quartet and he concerns himself with the launch. He arranges its hire and its start from Barrow in such a way that these can be checked over by inquisitive detectives. He had two witnesses of the start, the clerk and the mechanic, and he calls their attention to the hour in such a way that it is not likely to be forgotten. These two, furthermore, will swear to Victor's departure and so lay the foundation of his alibi.

"Mallace presumably leaves Barrow at the slow speed of six or seven knots, but as soon as he has passed out of observation he increases to the maximum of ten or more. At Tarn Bay he goes inshore, anchors, puts Victor ashore in the dinghy, returns on board and runs the launch single-handed to Kirkandrews Bay, taking care to arrive about a quarter to five. There he again anchors and goes ashore in the dinghy. He meets Teer, who has just arrived with the body of Sir John. They put the body into the dinghy and while Teer returns to the car Mallace rows back to the launch, gets the body aboard, hides it and then runs at full speed to Portpatrick. At Portpatrick, by making remarks with muffled replies, he tries to establish Victor's presence on board. As soon as Joss and Teer have arrived he goes to Stranraer to visit his firm's agents, thereby supplying a reason for the selection of that particular itinerary for the cruise."

"Very clear, sir," M'Clung remarked in answer to French's pause and look of inquiry.

"Good. Then let us take Teer. Teer's business is land transport. He is actually on a business tour in the north and he has a car. Under the circumstances it is only reasonable that he should use this car to join his friends, so his arrival at Stranraer and his subsequent garaging it there are unsuspicious.

"Teer's movements are pretty clear. He starts from Newcastle for Stranraer, leaving a good trail. He establishes firmly his visit for dinner to the hotel in Carlisle. Again, after giving his destination as Stranraer he starts off in the Stranraer direction. But he circles round and runs down through Cumberland to Tarn Bay, picks up Victor and runs him to Castle Douglas, parks the car, comes down with Victor to the station, takes over the body of Sir John from Joss and when the station is quiet carries the body to the car. Then he runs to Kirkandrews Bay, carries the body down to the sea, and helps Mallace to get it aboard the dinghy. He returns to the car, drives to Stranraer, picks up Joss, reaches Portpatrick and goes aboard the launch."

As far as attention and interest were concerned, French had no reason to complain of his audience. The four men sat eagerly drinking in his exposition. M'Clung, of course, already knew most of it, but to the others it was new and they found it as thrilling a tale as they had listened to for many a day. Carter indeed had let his pipe go out in his absorption, a signal compliment to the narrator.

"Now for Victor," French went on in satisfied tones. "It is after Victor leaves the train at Stranraer that his movements become interesting, but for the sake of completeness I will begin at Barrow with him also.

"Victor travels to Barrow with Mallace and accompanies him from there to Tarn Bay. He goes ashore, drives with Teer to Castle Douglas, and wearing a dark cloak, climbs into the train. With the assistance of Joss he makes up as Sir John. On reaching the boat he virtually is Sir John. The light at that hour is not good, and as Sir John had not been that way for seven years, those who remember the old man do not question Victor's identity. All the same he is taking no risks. He engages a private cabin, goes to it at once, and remains there until the boat reaches Larne. At Larne he is practically safe. No one remembers his uncle and he acts the old man's part with assurance."

Ormsby moved uneasily.

"What about his clothes, sir?"

"His clothes? Whose clothes?"

"Victor's clothes, sir. When Victor got into the train he undressed and went to bed and when he got up he dressed in Sir John's clothes. What about his own?"

French shrugged.

"A matter of guesswork, I'm afraid," he answered. "Either Victor left his clothes with Teer in the car and climbed into the train wearing only the dark cloak, or he gave them to Joss to pack in his suitcase. In either case the clothes must have been taken ashore at Lurigan for Victor, as Sir John's were wanted to reclothe the body. I don't think that's a snag, Ormsby. It could have easily been got over."

Ormsby, slightly apologetic, agreed, and French resumed.

"At Larne, Victor lays a satisfactory trail, as he does also at the Station Hotel in Belfast. The call there enables him to order a taxi in a way which will enable it to be traced – through the hotel porter. Incidentally there was a hint of the truth in that, if we'd had the wit to see it. If this had really been Sir John, he'd have gone to the Grand Central Hotel, not to the Station. He would never have made a mistake about a thing like that. Well, Victor drives to Sandy Row, and that for two reasons. Firstly, if suspicion be not aroused, it will suggest that he is about to visit the engineering firm who have previously worked for Sir John, and consequently that the latter's visit to Belfast really is about the invention. On the other hand, if suspicion be aroused, it will provide corroboration of the story that Joss will tell later to account for his actions in the case.

"He has now to put away time until the evening. Belfast is full of people who knew Sir John, so he cannot remain in any public place. Nor at this stage can he go where he might he traced, such as to an hotel. Nor yet can he remove his disguise, as he will want it again later on. What then is he to do? Only one thing is possible. He must hide. And so he hides. He hides until the exigencies of his plot call him again to action." French grinned. "A good phrase that, eh?" he pointed out. " 'Called to action by the exigencies of his plot.' I'll remember that for my report."

The others smiled and French went on.

"Victor chooses what is perhaps the best hiding place within a dozen miles of Belfast, and it is for him a pure accident that he should be seen both going to it and coming away. But this, as you all know, is just the kind of accident that happens to such plans.

"He has with him in Sir John's dispatch case the dark cloak and ladder he used for getting into the sleeper. These he now buries, and it must be admitted that it was only one chance in a million that they were found."

"He made a mistake there all the same," M'Clung declared.

"Why?" French asked curiously.

"Sure weren't they found where he hid them? He should have given them to Joss to throw into the sea."

French considered.

"I don't know that you're right," he said at last. "If he threw them into the sea the chances that they'd never be found were a million to one. But there was the millionth chance. They might have been brought up in a trawl. No. He may have committed an error of judgment, but it was certainly no worse than that."

"Well, that was what he did anyway and lucky for us," M'Clung conceded. "What do you think he dug the hole with, sir?"

"Guesswork again, M'Clung. Probably in the dispatch case he also had a trowel. However he buries them somehow, and then he spends what we may be sure was a very cold and miserable day."

French paused as if at the end of a chapter, and a little wave of movement ran over his audience as they changed their positions and settled down once more to listen. Carter, his curiosity considerably assuaged, leaned forward surreptitiously and relit his pipe.

"A minor mistake in Victor's staff work was that he allowed himself to run short of provisions and therefore had to lay a trail on the way back to the station. He could not, of course, foresee that his visit to the shop at the head of Duncairn Gardens would become known. Well, he reaches the Northern Counties station, travels by the eight o'clock train to Whitehead and there once again begins to lay a deliberate trail. He impresses his personality – or rather Sir John's – on the stationmaster by asking for some-one who he knows is not there, and rings up Malcolm, mimicking Sir John's voice. Then he walks out along the road towards Larne, presumably hides until Malcolm has passed in his car and then stages the struggle. Doubtless, he cuts his arm, or perhaps his gum to get the necessary blood, and he tramples the grass and breaks the twigs and throws the hat into the hedge.

"Remember that we are not so far considering motive, but only putting up a theory of what actually happened. Victor's next object is to get to Lurigan and his only way is on his own feet. The distance is about fourteen miles and he has from, say, half past nine to half past two – five hours. As he is now presumed to be dead, he is naturally anxious to do the journey unseen. To walk by the railway, deserted at that hour, is his obvious plan, and here again he has a stroke of real bad luck in being seen by the cleaner at Larne. However, in due course, he reaches Lurigan.

"In the meantime the launch with the other three conspirators and with Sir John's body on board has left Portpatrick. It runs at full speed to Lurigan. There it is anchored and the party come ashore with the body and spades. Soon the burial is complete and the party – all four of them this time – regain the launch and head full speed for Campbeltown.

"Victor has already begun to pay for his misdeeds and now his payment continues. He must hurt his knee. That, we may be sure, is done for him and done thoroughly. Joss' theatrical knowledge again comes in handy and he colours it up to show the necessary age. This colouring has doubtless been very carefully studied beforehand. The knee looks after its own swelling. The party arrive in due course at Campbeltown and Dr MacGregor is called in to confirm the alibi. Some scheme, isn't it?"

There were further shiftings of position with congratulatory and appreciative murmurs, but few

constructive comments. Then French invited the others to
trot out their views.

At first it didn't seem as if they had any, but gradually it
began to appear that the sergeants were not really so
satisfied with the theory after all. For some minutes they
hedged, then Carter cleared his throat with emphasis and
expressed what seemed to be in all their minds.

"It's a good theory and you could put up a strong case
for it and all that," he began, "but there's a thing I don't
altogether follow. Maybe, sir, you'd say what you think
about it."

"Right ho," French approved. "A chain's weakest link.
Forge ahead, Carter."

Carter moved restlessly as if not quite sure of himself.

"It's this way, sir," he said at length. "All this movement
seems to me to be more complicated than is needed. If they
only wanted to kill Sir John would they not just have put a
bullet into him or given poison instead of a sleeping
draught? Why bring in all this business of the launch and
the car?"

French nodded.

"A point, Carter; quite a point. I'm glad you've raised it."
He thought for a moment, then went on: "I don't think I
agree with you, Carter. It seems to me that these people's
scheme was good, in fact, I don't see how you could well
get a better. Sir John was murdered in the train. We may
start with that, because if we suggest something else we
begin to discuss an entirely different murder which did not
take place. Now if he was simply shot or poisoned as you
suggest, it would be immediately evident that the murderer
was among the passengers or train crew. Elimination would
be undertaken by the police, with the result that the
reservation of the communicating berths would come out,

Joss would be identified with Coates, and the necessary motive would be found. The thing would end with a nine o'clock walk for Joss. Joss wasn't having a risk of that kind, so he and his friends adopted a safeguard: they decided to conceal the fact of the murder. And how could it be concealed? Only surely in the way they did it – by removing the corpse and providing a living substitute. If Sir John travelled through to Belfast, he obviously couldn't have been murdered in the train. His murder was then staged at Whitehead at a time when the launch and presumably the whole quartet were in Portpatrick Harbour. Now that appeals to me as being a thundering good scheme. And for the life of me I don't see how it could have been done more simply than it was. No, Carter, I don't agree that it was too elaborate. If I had been in their place I should have considered such a safeguard well worth the trouble."

Carter agreed. He had not looked at it like that, and he thought now that the inspector was right.

"I agree with that, Mr French," M'Clung said in his turn, "and also that you've got a fine theory, but the worst of it to me is that it's only theory. They may have done every single thing you say, and probably did, but you can't prove it. There's no case so far to put before a jury."

French smiled.

"Now, M'Clung, what do you bet that you don't eat your words inside ten minutes? Proof! Of course there's proof. And you know what it is as well as I do. Use your brains, man! Here, I'll give you a hint. Two facts prove it, both given by verbal testimony. I may tell you that was the connection between these two facts that occurred to me that afternoon in Glasgow and that gave me the solution. Think, man! Can you not see it? I'm not saying anything about Carter and Harvey and Ormsby, because I don't think they know the facts."

M'Clung's confusion was only surpassed by the delight of the other three sergeants. But French did not give them long to develop the situation.

"You don't see it? Well, look here. The whole crime was given away by Joss, and what's more – a tragedy for the man, but really poetic justice, I suppose – it was given away unnecessarily. Not knowing what he was doing, he volunteered the damning statement. Now do you see?"

This did not tend to cure M'Clung's embarrassment, but still he couldn't grasp French's point.

"You don't get it? Then I'll tell you. He volunteered about the drugging. No doubt he thought that such a confession would tend to strengthen the remainder of his story. But instead it has done him in. See it now?"

Poor M'Clung had still to confess bewilderment.

"Don't you worry about it," French said, pitying his confusion. "I didn't see it myself for long enough. The reason the statement conveys nothing to you is that you've forgotten to put it alongside the testimony of that doctor at the inquest. You remember what he said? In his evidence he said that in his opinion the sleeping draught had been taken within eight to ten hours of death. That'll give it to you."

This time light not only dawned on M'Clung but on the other three also. French gave them no time for remarks, but hurried on.

"Now, if you think, you will see that the entire case follows from those two statements. Let us run over it. If Joss gave the sleeping draught shortly after leaving London, as he said, and if Sir John was murdered within eight to ten hours of receiving it, death must have occurred before six o'clock in the morning. If this were so it follows absolutely that the murder took place in the train. There is no escape from this conclusion, except by assuming that Sir John got a *second* sleeping draught on the next evening – a bit too far fetched a coincidence for real life.

"Now, if this is correct, it is obvious that it was not Sir John who crossed to Ireland, and therefore that he was impersonated by the traveller to Sandy Row, and second, that in some way his body was removed from the train before the latter reached Stranraer. Where could these changes have been made? The affair at Castle Douglas at once gives the answer. This view is confirmed by the brown cloak, and the ladder, as well as by the insistence that the sleeping berths should be on the right-hand side of the train, all of which were necessary for the exchange.

"So much known, we come to the question of the identity of the impersonator. We know that he must have been like Sir John from the evidence of the stewards on the boat, and as only Malcolm and Victor fulfilled this condition, we may assume it was one or other. It was not Malcolm, because at that hour Malcolm was at his home in Ireland. Therefore it was Victor. Victor, it must be remembered, is already suspect as the author of the XYZ letter.

"When we examine the details we find instant confirmation in the Tarn Bay call. If this was not to let Victor go to Castle Douglas, what was it for?

"There is similar proof as to the removal of the body. It was taken from the train at Castle Douglas and was buried at Lurigan. How was it conveyed? There can only be one answer. It *must* have gone by the launch, and the launch *must* therefore have called at Lurigan.

"This last point is proved by a second consideration. If Victor went to Belfast instead of Sir John, and, if he reached

Campbeltown on the following morning, the launch must have touched the Irish coast to pick him up. There is no other way in which he could have made the journey.

"You see it now, M'Clung? There is practical proof for every stage of the entire affair. We can and will make a perfectly watertight case to put before a jury."

French's hearers were a trifle awestruck. Seldom had they heard so convincing an exposition. They discussed the affair for some time, Ormsby finally expressing the general sentiments.

"They're as good as hanged, the whole four of them," he declared, "and it's going to be one of the biggest triumphs ever made for you personally, sir, as well as for the Yard and the detective force of Northern Ireland. With your permission, sir, I think we should celebrate."

French, nothing loath, rang for the waiter and the healths of the two detective organisations were duly drunk. Then French returned to business.

"Before we separate I want to say a word about motive. I'm inclined to believe that the entire business of the linen – silk plans was an invention of the quartet's. I doubt that Sir John had any plans; the most careful search has failed to reveal any preliminary sketches, and even if he took the finished plans with him, such sketches must have existed. There is no question Sir John was working at the problem, but I doubt that he had solved it. We have only Victor's word for it and we know now that Victor's evidence was tainted.

"In the meantime I'm disposed to assume that Sir John was murdered by the quartet in order to get Victor's legacy of £50,000. I think that Malcolm is wholly innocent, but that the others intended that he should be suspected, found guilty and executed. This would have brought Victor the command of £400,000 more. To me this explains the episode at Whitehead and the burial at Lurigan. Admittedly we have no proof of this, but I'm sure we shall get all the proof we want after we make the arrests."

He paused in thought, then went on: "Now, with regard to Malcolm's guilt or innocence, I'm going to suggest a little test. I suppose, M'Clung, Superintendent Rainey would make a few arrangements for me?"

M'Clung was reassuring on the subject.

"Very well. Now I want you to go over to the superintendent and tell him this," and French gave him detailed instructions. "You get my idea? Kind of Mahomet and the mountain. If we can't get this extra proof ourselves why not get our friends to supply it for us?"

His hearers grinned delightedly. It was a plan after their own hearts. Being what they were, they did not say much, but French read their approval in their eyes.

Excited over what they thought would be the last move in this tragic and lengthy drama, French and the three Yard sergeants returned to town by that night's boat train, leaving M'Clung to travel by the morning steamer to Belfast.

21

LONDON TO PLYMOUTH

Before they left the train at Euston French put the first stage of his new scheme in operation.

"I want," he said to Carter, "to meet Victor Magill accidentally. You get along to his office and find out his movements so that I can have a chat with him without suspicion of ulterior motive."

Later in the day Carter returned to the Yard. He reported that in the guise of a rate collector he had called at Victor's office. Victor was out, but by judicious pumping of the staff Carter had learned that he was going to Plymouth by the 10.30 Cornish Riviera Express on the following Monday morning. This was Saturday.

"It's the devil of a distance," French grumbled, "but I suppose that's not your fault. All right, that'll do."

For once French went off duty and that afternoon and the next day he spent in the bosom of his family. But on Monday he was early at Paddington. He saw Victor arrive, unexpectedly accompanied by Teer.

At first French swore, thinking that Teer's presence would spoil his experiment. Then he realised that so far from spoiling it, it would vastly increase its value. In good heart, therefore, he shadowed the two men to their compartment, afterwards putting his own things in another carriage. Finally he sought out the restaurant car attendant and purchased his help.

"Come down the platform," he said confidentially. "Now," he went on when they were close to the other compartment, "walk on there and glance into that second compartment as you pass. You'll see a small man in grey clothes in the far corner and a big dark-haired man opposite. I want you to fix it that I sit with them at lunch. A four-place table, you understand. I sit down and when those two come along you put them with me."

The attendant, mindful of past favours and hopeful of others to come, promised to do what he could. As a result, some hours later Victor and Teer were shown to the table at which French had already taken his place.

"Hullo, inspector, this is an unexpected pleasure!" said Victor as he sat down. "I didn't see you join the train."

Teer muttered a short greeting and looked annoyed.

"Nor did I see you gentlemen," French returned mendaciously as he also murmured his surprise and delight at the meeting.

"What's it now?" went on Victor. "Some new tale of blood and agony?"

French smiled.

"Nothing so dramatic," he declared. "Merely a visit to the prison at Princetown?"

Victor shook his head.

"Ghastly place," he murmured. "It should be closed. No poor devil has gone far enough wrong to deserve that hell."

"That may be, Mr Magill. It's a thing I have no say in. But it's not as bad as it was. As you know, there's been a deal of improvement in prison conditions in recent years."

Victor said it was not before it was due and they discussed the penal systems of this and other countries for some minutes. Then after desultory conversation in which Teer took a small and sulky part the talk came round to the Magill case.

"I suppose," Victor said, "that you people have pretty well given up hope? You're not doing anything about it, are you?"

This gave French his opportunity.

"We are and we aren't," he answered, leaning forward and speaking confidentially. Though the speed was high, the coach was running silently, and French could talk without fear of being overheard. "We've got a number of clues which have almost led us to what we want, but they've all just stopped short of doing it. The most promising is what I may call the Cave Hill clue, because it really is likely to lead us to something."

In spite of themselves, a startled glance passed between the two men. French watched them unobtrusively. Victor covered his emotion by a slight fit of coughing, while Teer found a bone in his fish which required his attention. The bone removed, Teer asked disinterestedly for further details.

"I don't know how much you've heard," French went on. "I suppose Rainey told you of our find on the Cave Hill?"

"Not a word," said Victor.

"Probably he hasn't seen you since we made it. It seemed an important enough discovery, but really instead of clearing the case up it makes it even more mysterious. We found that Sir John spent the day on the Cave Hill."

"Good Lord!" Victor exclaimed. Both men registered surprise with commendable efficiency, but French could have sworn their real emotion was relief.

"He was seen both going up and coming down a rough path which leads from the Antrim Road to the top; the Sheeps' Path, it's called."

Victor nodded with obvious interest.

"I know every inch of it," he declared. "Many a time I've climbed it when I was a kid. You've heard me speak of it, I'm sure, Teer?"

"Well, we made a search and we found that Sir John had camped out in a clump of shrubs in a field adjoining the path. There was a rough bed of soft twigs in a small trampled clearing. He must have spent the day there from 10.30 in the morning until after seven at night."

"But whatever for?" Victor queried with an air almost of incredulity, while Teer suspended mastication and stared bovinely at French.

"Ah," the latter answered, "if we knew that we'd be a few steps further on. We think that for some reason he may not have wished to meet any of his old Belfast friends. We made another very strange discovery that suggested to some of my colleagues that he was present at a meeting of some secret society, though I do not myself share their view. In searching round we came on what looked like a tiny grave. We opened it and we found, what do you think? You'd never guess."

"If so there's no use in our trying," said Victor, whose temper seemed to be wearing a trifle thin under the strain.

"I don't think there is," French agreed. "We found a brown cloak with a cowl and a short piece of rope ladder. The cloak was just what one might expect some order of masons or Orangemen to wear – I'm neither a mason nor an Orangeman so I may be blaspheming the orders – and the ladder is, I believe, a symbol in both fraternities. This secret society theory may be correct enough, though it seems to me to be far-fetched. But I admit it's very difficult to account for these things on any other hypothesis."

Victor shook his head helplessly.

"I'm blessed," he declared, "if that isn't as queer a business as I ever heard of! The more you think about it the stranger it seems. A cowled cloak and a ladder! Good Lord!"

"Darned odd," said Teer woodenly.

French was delighted. There was now no question as to the relief of both. With satisfaction he recognised that his foundation had been well and truly laid and that he might now proceed with the superstructure.

"Ah, but that's not the important clue," he went on, leaning forward and speaking with increased interest. "Sir John buried something else up there which we've not found, but which we hope to get in the course of the next four or five days. I'll tell you about it."

He paused to heighten his effect.

"Some time ago a constable belonging to the Belfast force was making inquiries into this affair on the Cave Hill when he heard a story of a boy having seen something being buried near the Sheeps' Path. He called at the boy's home, but found he had been knocked down by a bus on the Antrim Road and was now in hospital. The constable therefore went to the hospital. There he saw the boy, who confirmed the story. He had been, he said, up the hillside near the Sheeps' Path, when among some bushes he saw a man burying a box. From the description there could be no doubt that it was Sir John. The only thing that puzzled the constable was that the date didn't agree; it was three or four days too late. However he assumed that the boy had made a mistake. After the man went away the boy found the place and tried to dig up the treasure trove. But he couldn't do so with his fingers and he ran home for a shovel. But his eagerness proved his undoing. He crossed the Antrim Road without looking where he was going, with the result that he was struck by the wing of the bus. Fortunately he's getting all right and the doctor has promised to let Rainey carry him up the Sheeps' Path on Thursday next, so that he may point out Sir John's second hiding place. Whether the box will contain anything to help us remains to be seen, but we are living in hope."

Victor and Teer were still simulating a surprised interest, but French could see that they were profoundly impressed by his story.

"I'm surprised that Rainey didn't tell you all this," he said to Victor. "When were you last in Belfast?"

"Not since that day we met in the superintendent's office."

French nodded.

"That explains it," he said easily. Rainey would have told you if he had seen you, but I expect he didn't care to put the thing in writing. You can realise that in our business it is better to be sure than sorry."

Victor agreed and after lighting cigarettes they continued their discussion. French talked round the subject with an air of the utmost candour, but actually he gave away no further information. At last by slow degrees he led to his second point.

"Yes," he said in answer to a remark of Teer's, "it certainly has been an exasperating case. And perhaps one of the most exasperating points in it, is that we have been quite unable to find XYZ.

"XYZ?" Teer repeated doubtfully, while Victor looked up sharply.

"Yes." He turned to Victor. "You saw the letter, didn't you, Mr Magill?"

Victor shook his head.

"Don't even know what you're talking about," he declared.

It was now French's turn to show surprise.

"But, bless me, it was when you were with us in Rainey's office that it arrived." He paused as if to consult his memory. "No, I beg your pardon, I'm wrong. We didn't get it until later that day. You had gone, of course, so you didn't see it. All the same I'm surprised that Rainey did not tell you or at least Major Magill."

"Perhaps he told Malcolm. I've been back in town for some time."

"Probably that's it. Still I should have thought you would have heard about it."

Teer drew the attention away from Victor.

"But what is the letter anyway?" he growled.

French became even more confidential. He glanced round, then bent forward and spoke in a tone which could just be heard above the murmur of the train.

"It was that very day that Mr Magill was in with us or the following, I'm not sure which, that we got a most interesting letter. It was addressed to Rainey, and it said," and French went on to give its contents.

Both men dutifully registered the necessary amazement.

"And you could find no trace of the writer?" Victor asked.

French made a gesture of annoyance.

"That's just the trouble," he explained. "We made the most detailed inquiries, but all to no purpose. We've never had the slightest hint as to the writer's identity. Nor could we find that any car had passed along the road that night. I can tell you, gentlemen, that these seemingly simple things are the very devil when they go wrong. You keep on worrying and worrying and feeling what a fool you are and you *can't* get to the bottom of them."

"It must be annoying," Victor agreed. "What you tell us is certainly very extraordinary, but I don't see why it is so immensely important. You've got your information. Of course it would be interesting to know where it came from, but why does it really matter?"

This was what French wanted.

"Why," he said, "don't you see? The object of the letter was clear; at least both Rainey and myself thought so. It was not written by a disinterested passer-by whose sole concern was to aid justice. No, sir." French brought his finger down on the table with meticulous accuracy. "That letter was written by the murderer. And why? That surely will be clear to you, Mr Magill. The murderer wanted the body to be found there on Major Magill's ground, so that suspicion against the major might be clinched. You remember suspicion was already aroused by the finding of the hat. Well, the murderer wanted it clinched. And why again? Obviously because if the major was found guilty he himself would be safe."

Victor had another troublesome fit of coughing, while Teer took a gulp of hot coffee. This view, put forward so resolutely, clearly disquieted them. They expressed a suitable interest and then Victor turned to the crucial point.

"I follow you," he admitted. "But of course it's only a question of time. You'll get the writer all right."

Here again was just what French had been angling for.

"There's no of course about it," he declared. "There's no clue to the man." He paused, then as a sort of afterthought added: "That is, except one. But it won't help us to find the man. It'll convict him if we find him, and we must find him first by other means."

As French had hoped, Victor pricked up his ears at this. But it was with an air of elaborate unconcern that he answered. "That sounds a trifle involved," he remarked, carefully knocking the ash off his cigarette. "And what, if it's not a secret, is the clue?"

"It's not a secret to you or Mr Teer," French returned, "but don't let it go any further. The man made a blunder; a bad one for him but a good one for us. He used an old typewriter."

Victor looked anxious, but puzzled.

"It was a Number Three Corona," went on French, "and the type was worn. The script is therefore quite individual; there is only one machine in the world that could have typed it. Now look at it this way. We can scarcely believe that the writer would have been so mad as to use his own machine, therefore he'd buy one for the occasion and destroy it when used. If we had it, an advertisement in some of the trade journals would soon find the shop where it was sold. From the shop we'd soon get the description of the man who bought it. We'd also get the address of the man who had sold it to the shop. This last would certainly have something typed on it, which would enable us to prove it was the right machine. That's all straightforward; it's the sort of thing we're doing every day. If therefore we had the machine we'd not be long till we'd found XYZ, and if we had XYZ it wouldn't be long till he's hung."

There was now no question of Victor's emotion. Though he was evidently trying desperately to hide it, actual panic showed in his eyes. Teer, though he covered it better, was obviously also frightened. French was well satisfied. So far he had played his cards well. It was now, he assured himself joyously, up to Victor to do the rest.

During the remainder of the conversation French was careful to show just the same amount of interest in the subject as he had up to then. He felt that neither man must be allowed to imagine the climax of the interview had been reached and passed. So they discussed *L'Affaire Magill* until the waiter's uneasy hoverings became too pronounced to be further ignored.

It was characteristic of French, that at Plymouth he really did take a train for Princetown and visit the great convict prison. He saw that if he did not do so and if by some unlikely chance Victor or Teer discovered the fact, his entire scheme would fall through. What was worth doing...

He was careful also to let the two men know his movements. His business at the prison, he explained, would occupy him four or five hours. He feared that he would therefore be unable to catch the 6.20 p.m. from Millbay, but he hoped to travel by the sleeping car express, leaving at 12.15 a.m. Perhaps he might meet Victor or Teer on the way home?

Victor and Teer were sorry that as they were going into Cornwall he would not have that pleasure. He therefore shook hands cordially and wished his enemies *bon voyage*.

At the prison French got busy. First he rang up Chief Inspector Mitchell at the Yard, explained his plan and asked that Joss and Mallace should be shadowed and that the Great Western trains should be watched for Victor's and Teer's return to London. If any member of the quartet was seen to start for Ireland the shadowing might be dropped, but the news was to be wired to Superintendent Rainey.

Next French rang up Rainey. To him he merely explained that things were going well, that he was crossing to Belfast on the following day and would arrive at 9.35 in the evening, and that on arrival he would like an interview.

On reaching Plymouth on his return journey, French called to see his old friend, the local superintendent. It was not so long since they had met in connection with the search for Mrs Berlyn's bicycle, the discovery of which had formed so useful a clue in the Berlyn-Pyke case. From him he heard of a couple more old friends. Maxwell Cheyne and his pretty wife were still living at Dartmouth, and there was now a diminutive Maxwell, of whom the young man was even more proud than of his best sellers.

Promptly at 7.10 next morning the night mail pulled into Paddington. French, hurrying to the Yard, did what he seldom found necessary; he adopted a disguise. A few tiny lines on his face and he added twenty years to his age. A well-fitting wig and his dark locks became white. Clerical garb, tortoiseshell-rimmed spectacles, a stoop and a hesitating manner completed the transformation. When he had finished he was satisfied that it would take a sharper-eyed man than Victor to penetrate his disguise.

He had just time to catch the 8.30 a.m. from Euston. With great care he lived up to his role of an elderly clergyman. In the matter of a disguise, risks could not be taken. To hide one's identity ineffectively was worse than not hiding it at all.

In spite of his eager, though repressed excitement, French enjoyed his journey. At two o'clock they reached Holyhead and transferred to the *Scotia*. From the deck he watched the rugged Welsh coast retreat, and the gently-rounded, well-wooded Irish country grow. Shortly after five he landed at Dun Laoghaire and a few minutes later the train ran into Amiens Street Station in Dublin.

There was a short wait for the Great Northern train and French employed the time by a drive through some of the principal streets. He had not been over since the troubles and he was impressed by the air of smartness and prosperity which the city wore. It seemed cleaner than before and the new buildings made O'Connell Street a really imposing thoroughfare.

A quick run brought him to the Northern capital. At police headquarters he found Rainey and M'Clung waiting for him.

"Hullo, your reverence?" said the former, after a keen look at the clerical collar and the white hair. "Quite venerable, isn't he, M'Clung? What's usually known as a whited sepulchre. Well, you're bringing it off."

"How do you mean, sir?"

"How do I mean? Why, what I say. You've got things moving anyway. That is, if you're at the bottom of it, as I presume you are."

French looked his question.

"Just had a wire from the Yard," Rainey explained. "There's to be a gathering of the clans. Victor Magill and Teer left London this evening at 5.55 *en route* for Liverpool, Teer travelling first class and Victor third. Joss left a quarter of an hour later, in the Ulster Express for Heysham, and Mallace is in the 7.40 for Stranraer. Are you responsible?"

"I hope so," said French, rubbing his hands in high delight. "I pitched my yarn to Victor hoping to bring him across, but I never expected an exodus. Were you able sir, to give the news to Malcolm?"

"Yes, I met him – also by accident – and told the tale. He showed no special reaction. Interested of course, but nothing more."

"I'll be surprised if he knows anything about the affair. However, with luck we'll soon know."

"I hope so. Now, French, M'Clung and I are both anxious to hear your adventures, so suppose you start in and let's have the tale."

French, accepting a cigar, at once told his story. Evidently the bait had been swallowed, but he was surprised at his large catch.

"What on earth those other three men are coming over for beats me," he ended up, glancing questioningly at the others.

Rainey had been listening with close attention.

"I don't think that's so difficult," he declared. "It's the honour among thieves which doesn't exist. These precious beauties don't trust one another. They suspect a trap, and one isn't going into it without the others. They're going to see also that no one's going to get off by turning king's evidence at the others' expense."

"It might be," French admitted. "But if they suspect a trap do you think they'd come over at all?"

"Bound to. That's where I congratulate you upon your scheme. You've shown that we know so much that it's absolutely vital to them to get that machine away."

French deprecatingly admitted that this had been his aim.

"By the way," he added, "were you able to bury another Corona at the place?"

"Yes, that's been done. They'll not suspect anything till we close in. Now, French, what we've got to do is to make sure they don't still diddle us. They're a brainy crowd, and we mustn't make the mistake of underestimating them. First of all, they must be shadowed?"

"Of course, sir, and not only Victor's crowd, but Malcolm as well."

"I agree, and I'll see to it. Have you any other ideas as to what we should do?"

French was full of ideas and the meeting resolved itself into a committee of ways and means.

22

THE CAVE HILL

WHEN French reached the Chichester Street headquarters next morning, news had already come in. Victor, Teer and Joss had arrived, and all had left the city by early trains. Victor had taken the 8.25 a.m. by the Great Northern, booking to Londonderry. Teer had also booked to Londonderry, though travelling by the 9.30 a.m. on the Northern Counties line, while Joss had gone to Newcastle by the County Down train leaving at 7.30 a.m.

This information had scarcely been assimilated when a further report came in. Mallace had arrived by the Stranraer boat train, had driven across town and had taken the 10.15 a.m. train for Newry.

"They're killing time till tonight," Rainey suggested shrewdly. "They don't want to leave tracks in Belfast, so they're going to spend the day travelling elsewhere. Curse it, the glass is dropping and it's blowing up for a storm. It'll be a dirty night."

Both these prophecies seemed to French likely enough of fulfilment. He remained at headquarters, smoking impatiently and reading the reports as they came in. As the day wore slowly on Rainey's perspicacity became demonstrated. On reaching Londonderry, Victor and Teer had strolled about the city, lunching in different hotels and taking the 3.40 and the 4.00 o'clock trains to Belfast by their respective lines. Joss, at Newcastle, had climbed Slieve Donard, the highest and most easterly peak of the Mourne mountains, and was returning to Belfast by the 4.25 p.m. train, while Mallace had killed time in Newry and Warrenpoint, and was now coming back by the 4.27 train to Belfast. All these trains reached the city before seven o'clock.

"I bet you," said Rainey, when this last item came in from Newry. "I bet you they're going to act at once. You see, the Cave Hill would be as deserted at seven or eight o'clock as in the middle of the night. Besides in weather like this there'd be no one out of doors who could help it. They'll act at once and make their getaway by the boats at nine and nine-fifteen. We'd better get busy."

He began telephoning, with the result that eight men came into the office. To them he gave his instructions.

"Gray and M'Keown, get away to the Northern Counties Station and meet the 3.40 from Derry. Teer'll be on it. Take over his shadowing from Reid. Victor Magill is coming up from Derry by the GN mail. You, M'Clatchie and Brown, take him over. Joss left Newcastle at 4.15. Walker and M'Candless go and get on to him at the County Down. Ferguson and M'Nulty relieve the men who are on to Major Magill. He is still at the Shankill Road mill. Get along now, all of you. Shadow your men till they get the typewriter and be ready to close in and lift them when I give the signal. If you get no signal shadow them till they leave the country. Keep in touch with headquarters as far as possible and if you let either see you or give you the slip you needn't come back here." He turned to French. "You and M'Clung and I will watch for Mallace coming in from Newry. He hasn't seen M'Clung or me and you can keep in the background." Rainey slipped a revolver out of a drawer. "Have one?" he offered. "These men will be ugly customers. That's all, I think. If you're ready, we'll get along."

The train was due at 6.15 and they had just time to meet it. The weather had fulfilled all Rainey's evil prophecies, and now the rain was falling heavily on the glistening pavements while a squally wind howled and eddied round the corners of the buildings. The shops and offices were just disgorging their staffs and the streets were full of hurrying figures trying to balance dripping umbrellas and to keep dainty shoes out of pools. Trams packed to the steps clattered past while buses and cars sent the water flying in sheets from their spinning wheels.

"A dirty night for us, but a good one for our friends," said Rainey as their car ran into the cab rank between the main arrival platforms at the Great Northern station. "We'll stay in the car and as soon as you pick up Mallace you can get in. M'Clung will take over and keep him in view."

French was still the elderly, amiable clergyman and he fell to pacing the platform, peering benevolently at those waiting for the train. He was intensely excited as to their quest. Its success or failure would be his own. To take these four – or five – as it were in the act would clear up his case and clear it up with immense credit to himself. Though there could be no doubt as to its correctness! The very presence of the quartet was a guarantee of success. A little care now and all would be well.

At 6.20, five minutes late, the train drew slowly in. For a moment French felt at an unwonted loss as he gazed at the throng of descending travellers. Then with a throb of relief he saw Mallace. The man had followed French's own example and adopted a disguise. He also had become a clergyman and wore a dark overcoat showing the clerical collar, glasses and a soft round clerical hat. Behind the glasses French felt sure there was a pair of exceedingly keen and watchful eyes. After the first glance he was careful to turn his back till the other had passed. Then indicating the man to M'Clung with an almost invisible gesture, he moved over to the car while the sergeant took up the chase.

Mallace boarded a tram outside the station and M'Clung, dropping behind, was picked up by the car. They kept the tram in view and at Castle Junction, the City Centre, watched the quarry alight and walk to the tramway halt at the beginning of Royal Avenue. This was the point at which trams bound for the Antrim Road started, and French and Rainey exchanged satisfied glances. Once again M'Clung slipped out of the car, and mingling with the crowds waiting for trams, kept Mallace in view.

To their delight the man took an "Antrim Road – Gray's Lane" car. This was eminently satisfactory. Just a few yards beyond Gray's Lane was the end of the Sheeps' Path. M'Clung according to instructions boarded the car, going inside as Mallace mounted to the top. If Mallace alighted before reaching Gray's Lane, M'Clung was to shadow him wherever he went. If not, he, M'Clung, was to get out at the stop before the lane, walking after Mallace to the path and following him up. In the meantime Rainey and French were to drive on, and leaving the car, secrete themselves in the bushes alongside the Sheeps' Path.

This programme was duly carried out. Just before reaching the path Rainey parked the car, then watching till the road was deserted, the two men walked to the path and turned up. Away from the street lamps it was pitchy dark. There was no moon and the thick pall of clouds cut off all light from the stars. It had become a wild night. Though sheltered to some extent by the trees, the wind was even here powerful and flung the rain against them in almost solid sheets. With difficulty they pushed on, feeling their way by the dripping bushes, stumbling blindly over the rough stones of the path and slipping in the muddy earth at its sides. Some noise they could not avoid making but they were not afraid of being overheard. The hiss of the rain and the roar of the wind swallowed up every other sound.

To avoid losing him in the dark Rainey was holding on to French's wrist. He drew him close.

"We'll turn aside here," he said aloud, pushing between the bushes which lined the path.

They bent down behind the shrubs and remained motionless. They expected to have to wait about ten minutes, reckoning the difference in speed between the car and the tram. But the ten minutes passed and still they heard nothing but the noise of the storm. Crouching there in the wet and dark and with their minds on the stretch, time seemed at a standstill. Another five minutes dragged slowly by and then another. Rainey stood up suddenly.

"Curse it, we've missed him," he said sharply. "Come, French, we may go back."

As Rainey moved, French's hand closed on his arm. Both men stood tense, looking down.

Below them on the path was a glimmer of light. Slowly it approached, dancing like an up to date will-o'-the-wisp, faintly illuminating a tiny circle as it moved.

Standing rigid as pillars of stone, French and Rainey watched the flickering light draw abreast and then pass slowly on. They could hear nothing, nothing but the howling of the storm, and the solid hiss of the rain. They could see nothing, nothing but the faint splash of light on the muddy path and the scarcely visible sparkle of the drops falling through the illuminated cone. There was something eerie in the ghostly movement of that dim radiance, as if a disembodied spirit were hovering past on the road to Valhalla.

While it was yet in sight French and Rainey relaxed their stiff attitudes, and creeping back through the bushes to the path, began to follow. As they expected, the slow chase led up until the unknown was opposite the clump of rhododendrons. There it stopped and the pursuers froze into immobility. Then guessing what was about to happen, they slipped off the path on the opposite side to the clump and took cover behind its bordering laurels. With the utmost care they crept upward parallel to the path until they were opposite to the unknown. Then turning, they edged slowly forward until they were within some six feet of their victim.

Had it not been for the rain and wind they would not have ventured so near, but they thought that should the man raise his torch the swinging of the bushes would mask their movements and the noise of the storm would cover any sounds they made.

They had scarcely taken up their position when another flitting light warned them that someone else was approaching. A shadow loomed up out of the darkness and Mallace's voice called softly "That you, Teer?"

There was an acquiescent murmur and then in louder accents, "Damn this blasted weather! I'm wet through already. How long have we to wait for those other two?"

"They should be here any time. Half an hour should see the thing through."

"Got the trowel?" came Teer's voice.

"Got it here."

"A helluva place and a helluva night," Teer growled.

"I guess we'll have earned our money by the time we're through," came Mallace's voice in return. He crossed the path. "I think there's a bit more shelter under these shrubs."

French's heart missed a beat as Mallace stepped up against the bush under which he and Rainey were lying. The man stood not more than two feet away. Fortunately he had put out his torch. Teer slowly joined him. He had scarcely done so when another flickering light appeared.

It was Joss. He also cursed the weather, and shutting off his torch, took up his stand beside Mallace. By putting out his hand French could have touched him. Both he and Rainey lay scarcely daring to breathe.

"Helluva nuisance, this whole business," Teer grumbled. "If that blasted fool Magill had had the wit of a sheep he'd have seen he wasn't overlooked and we'd have been saved all this. Darned idiot, if ever there was one!"

Joss murmured some reply.

"Where's the fool got to now?" went on Teer's voice. "I suppose he's going to keep us standing here in this infernal rain till we get our deaths."

"He can't be long now," Mallace answered shortly.

"That's right," came Joss' voice. "I wish to heaven, Teer, you'd give over your endless grouse. Things are bad enough without that confounded whine going on all the time."

Teer gave a savage snort.

"A confounded whine, is it?" he answered harshly. "Curse you, Joss! Let me tell you, you're getting above yourself. Don't you forget who's boss of this outfit. I'll grouse when I want to and you'll hold your blasted tongue. See?"

"All right; all right," Joss returned irritably. "Nobody's questioning your position – and responsibility."

"What the hell do you mean by that?" Teer questioned in louder tones. "Responsibility!" He emitted a torrent of blasphemy. "You're a nice one to talk, you are, and you with murder on your soul! And easy to prove it too. Who bought a rubber tube with a closed end? Who bought shotgun cartridges? Cartridges for a man without a gun! You hold your blasted tongue or – "

"Steady on, Teer," Mallace interposed with evident relief. "Here's Magill. Now we'll get a move on."

Teer's further threats were lost in the arrival of Victor. He followed his companions' example and began by wholeheartedly cursing the weather.

"For heaven's sake, Magill, cut that and get on with the job," Teer snarled. "Where's the damned place?"

Victor subsided suddenly. "This way," he said sulkily, moving towards the clump.

"Then Malcolm's not in it," Rainey breathed, and even in his lowered voice French detected satisfaction. "You go ahead while I collect the men." He vanished instantly.

Having climbed the paling in the wake of the others, French dropped on his knees and began to crawl slowly across the grass. Out of the comparative shelter of the bushes the wind whirled down, booming in off the open mountainside above. That he was in danger French was well aware. If that flitting torch were turned in his direction a bullet would doubtless end his earthly career, and it was therefore with a lively satisfaction that at length he reached the clump. The quartet had withdrawn into its shelter, but he could see their torches flickering ahead and he pressed on after them. He was already wet, but as he crawled slowly through the dripping leaves he was soon soaked to the skin.

But he had no time to think of such trifles. The four had halted and he went on till he was within seven or eight feet of them. There he lay down under a clump of low-growing bushes, and motionless as a log, set himself to watch and listen.

"It should be about here," Victor was saying. "Naturally I didn't mark the place, so it's a bit hard to find."

For the second time that evening French's heart stood still, while bitterly he cursed himself for his rashness. All four began flashing their electric torches on the surrounding ground. He pulled his hat down over his eyes, and lowering his head so that no light could reach his face, began carefully to back away. He could not hasten lest he should attract attention, and as the search extended he realised that death was close beside him. With a sickening anxiety he watched the little circles of light advance and retreat. They flitted away, came back, veered sideways. Suddenly he gave himself up for lost. A beam flashed on the ground not a foot from his head. It began to creep slowly nearer. And then, just as the rim of the circle touched his hat there was a cry from Victor a dozen yards away.

"Here it is," he called. "We're all right."

Despite the cold, the sweat was dripping from French as the other three turned towards Victor. Dimly he could see them crowd together, gazing at the ground. He heard Teer's voice: "Well, start in and get the infernal thing opened," and digging began.

French, his panic over, began crawling nearer, but just then a hand closed on his ankle and he heard Rainey's voice.

"That the place?" he breathed. "I have seven men there besides ourselves. They're going to surround it and

298

converge to the centre and when I fire we'll close. You push in straight ahead. I'm going to the right."

French slowly wormed his way forward, then lay still. He listened to the howling of the gale and watched the faint radiance ahead, obscured at intervals by the dark silhouettes of the men as they bent over their task. This ghastly business would surely end the case! After such a give away no jury would fail to convict. French felt he should be thankful, but he was not. For some reason his nerves were still on edge. As he lay waiting Time itself seemed to be standing still. But for the four men ahead he seemed to be absolutely alone in the universe, and yet he knew that eight others, palpitating with life and energy and fierce determination, were there close beside him, hidden in the inky blackness.

He moved slightly forward to get a better view of the quartet. Victor was now digging and for five minutes he worked in silence. Then suddenly he stooped forward.

"Got it!" he said in relieved tones, and stooping down he drew a black box from the hole.

"About time," came from Teer. "Get that infernal hole filled up and we'll get away. Hell! What's that?"

A sharp crack had come from Rainey's pistol. Instantly the surrounding foliage became alive with moving figures.

"Hands up!" Rainey shouted. "You're all covered. Anyone who moves is a dead man!"

Teer gave a bellow like that of a wounded bull.

"Down with your lights, you fools!" he yelled, and in a moment inky blackness reigned.

But only for a moment. From all round electric torches converged on the four as with a shout the police officers dashed forward. Teer was fumbling desperately in his pocket and as French bounded towards him his arm flew up. A bullet whistled past French's ear. But it just missed him and instantly he closed with Teer. At first the other three members of the quartet seemed paralysed with amazement, but in a moment they also sprang to life, pulled out revolvers and began firing. But Rainey's men closed in quickly and in a couple of seconds four groups were struggling confusedly in the darkness. Round and round they crashed, reeling and stumbling over shrubs and bushes, the sobbing of their breath rising above the howl of the storm. Teer was a bigger man than French and he succeeded in getting a lefthander on French's jaw which made the latter go sick and faint. As had happened before, French saw death very near as with all his might he concentrated on keeping Teer's right hand with its automatic pistol turned away. He gripped the man's wrist with both hands and clung on for dear life. This left him undefended from the blows Teer began raining on him, and the end would have been a foregone conclusion had not M'Clung seized hold in the darkness, and enveloping the couple in his mighty arms, stopped the shower of blows. French gasped out the situation and M'Clung, at last distinguishing friend from foe, threw his weight into the balance. In a few minutes Teer was thrown, disarmed and handcuffed.

By the time French was able to stagger panting to his feet, the battle was over. All four members of the gang were secured. And at comparatively small cost. Rainey had a nasty cut over one eye, one of his men was winded and temporarily knocked out, while a couple were bleeding profusely from mouth and nose. Soon they were able to make a move for headquarters, and within an hour all four prisoners were lodged in the cells.

A short further investigation enabled French to clear up the few points which still remained doubtful. The case, when thus completed, proved to be practically as he had outlined it to the sergeants at Stranraer.

The first thing demonstrated was that the entire responsibility for the crime lay with the quartet, Malcolm Magill and Breene being absolutely innocent. Malcolm's apparent connection with it had been carefully engineered by them in the hope that he would be suspected and executed, thus bringing his £400,000 into Victor's hands. The circumstances which brought Breene under suspicion were in themselves wholly fortuitous and his predilection for Miss Magill, which was the only real justification for that suspicion, was proved to have been only another figment of Teer's facile brain.

The second discovery was that the root of the whole ghastly affair lay in Victor Magill's inordinate love of gambling. This proved to have been a much greater factor in his life than had been realised. Beginning in a small way, he had gradually increased his commitments until at last he had become irretrievably involved. Ruin stared him in the face and for a time he hovered on the brink of suicide. Then an evil chance befell him. Circumstances gave him an opportunity, as he thought, to recover himself. While in Teer's rooms one day he found an unused cheque. At the moment he had in his pocket a cheque of Teer's for a small amount together with some betting memoranda in Teer's handwriting. In a moment of desperation and madness he lost his head and forged a cheque for £3000. But he never presented it. Teer discovered the affair and in the presence of Mallace and Joss taxed him with it. From that moment Victor's last chance of happiness vanished. He soon found that he had given himself over, bound hand and foot, into the hands of a cruel and unscrupulous trio. Teer's crafty and scheming brain was just the instrument for meeting such a case. He immediately realised the advantage he had got and he worked out a plan for its utilisation. He and his friends were hard up. Victor's uncle was rolling in money. Very well; a redistribution was the idea. Old Magill was to be murdered by violence. His heir, Malcolm, was to be murdered judicially. The money, which would then come to Victor, both directly and through Malcolm, was to be shared equally among the quartet. Even Victor was to get his share. In this Teer of course only showed his wisdom and knowledge of human nature. He recognised that if Victor was pushed too far he would commit suicide and the money would be lost. All four were therefore to be bound together by equal responsibility and equal reward.

At first Victor declined absolutely to have anything to do with such a plan, declaring that he would rather go to prison. But Victor was inherently weak and in the hands of a man like Teer he was as wax. Fear and familiarity with the idea had their effect, and at last he agreed to join in. This point settled, the details were worked out by Teer. This was four months before the actual crime.

The first thing was to pay Victor's debts and to make him a substantial allowance. There must be no question of poverty to back up any breath of suspicion which might be aroused. So Victor appeared with plenty of money in hand, his explanation being that his uncle had once again come to his help.

Though Teer had completed the rough outlines of his plan before approaching Victor, there was a lot of detailed work to be done on it. This was carried out at intervals by all four concerned, every detail being rehearsed again and again before the great moment arrived. The plan was practically as guessed by French, its essentials being the tricking of Sir John into the Stranraer boat train, his murder therein, the removal of the body and its burial at Lurigan, with Victor to personate him in Ireland and throw dust in the eyes of possible investigators. French also was correct in his assumption that the legacy and the legacy alone was the goal sought. There were not and never had been any plans for the linen – silk machinery. Sir John was working in the problem, but he had not solved it. Teer had simply used his interest in the subject, firstly, as a bait to get him to Ireland, and secondly, as an explanation for Joss of his conduct in connection with Sir John.

Curiously enough, what proved the greatest difficulty to the conspirators, was what had at first sight seemed a mere trifle: the finding out on which side of the sleeping car the berths would be on the fatal night. Though in the end their choice proved to some extent a lucky shot, they had done their best to meet the difficulty. For some weeks on one pretext or another they had gone to Euston and examined the make-up of the train both on its arrival and departure. Thus they learned how the sets of carriages were dealt with. By this they were enabled to hazard a good guess as to the conditions on any given night. Unfortunately they found their guess was not always correct, but it was so, seven or eight times out of ten. To provide, however, for disappointment, they had devised an elaborate system of telegrams whereby on the pretext of Coates' sudden illness Sir John's journey and all that hinged on it could be postponed from night to night, until a coach of the right type appeared on the train.

The little additional evidence required for the trial was easily obtained. The chemist was found who supplied Joss with the trional sleeping draught, and Victor's purchase of the white wig – for an amateur theatrical performance – was traced. Mallace had bought the velvet cloaks for a similar purpose, and Teer, as airplane equipment, had had the rope ladder made.

There is little more to add. Thanks to the skill of both French and the police of Northern Ireland, murder received its just reward and justice and right were vindicated.

There was some little difficulty in deciding where the trial should take place. It was not known where the actual murder had been committed, though this was believed to have been between Dumfries and Castle Douglas. Eventually the case was tried in Belfast, a coroner's jury of Northern Ireland already having adjudicated thereon. As a result Teer and Joss paid the supreme penalty, the other two receiving sentences of penal servitude for life.

As for French, in addition to the kudos gained in yet another brilliantly successful case, he found himself the richer by a number of warm friends in Northern Ireland, together with a fresh hunting ground for exploration when the time for his next holiday should come round.

Freeman Wills Crofts

The Box Office Murders

A girl employed in the box office of a London cinema falls into the power of a mysterious trio of crooks. A helpful solicitor sends her to Scotland Yard. There she tells Inspector French the story of the Purple Sickle. Her body is found floating in Southampton Water the next day. French discovers that similar murders have taken place. After gathering evidence he learns the trio's secret and runs them to ground.

The Hog's Back Mystery

The Hog's Back is a ridge in Surrey and the setting for the disappearance of several locals. A doctor vanishes, followed by a nurse with whom he was acquainted, then a third person. Inspector French deduces murder, but there are no bodies. Eventually he is able to prove his theory and show that a fourth murder has been committed.

'As pretty a piece of work as Inspector French has done...on the level of Mr Crofts' very best; which is saying something.'

E C Bentley in the *Daily Telegraph*

OTHER TITLES BY FREEMAN WILLS CROFTS AVAILABLE DIRECT FROM HOUSE OF STRATUS

Quantity		£	$(US)	$(CAN)	€
☐	THE 12.30 FROM CROYDON	6.99	11.50	15.99	11.50
☐	THE AFFAIR AT LITTLE WOKEHAM	6.99	11.50	15.99	11.50
☐	ANTIDOTE TO VENOM	6.99	11.50	15.99	11.50
☐	ANYTHING TO DECLARE?	6.99	11.50	15.99	11.50
☐	THE BOX OFFICE MURDERS	6.99	11.50	15.99	11.50
☐	THE CASK	6.99	11.50	15.99	11.50
☐	CRIME AT GUILDFORD	6.99	11.50	15.99	11.50
☐	DEATH OF A TRAIN	6.99	11.50	15.99	11.50
☐	DEATH ON THE WAY	6.99	11.50	15.99	11.50
☐	ENEMY UNSEEN	6.99	11.50	15.99	11.50
☐	THE END OF ANDREW HARRISON	6.99	11.50	15.99	11.50
☐	FATAL VENTURE	6.99	11.50	15.99	11.50
☐	FEAR COMES TO CHALFONT	6.99	11.50	15.99	11.50
☐	FOUND FLOATING	6.99	11.50	15.99	11.50
☐	FRENCH STRIKES OIL	6.99	11.50	15.99	11.50
☐	GOLDEN ASHES	6.99	11.50	15.99	11.50
☐	THE GROOTE PARK MURDER	6.99	11.50	15.99	11.50
☐	THE HOG'S BACK MYSTERY	6.99	11.50	15.99	11.50
☐	INSPECTOR FRENCH AND THE CHEYNE MYSTERY	6.99	11.50	15.99	11.50

ALL HOUSE OF STRATUS BOOKS ARE AVAILABLE FROM GOOD BOOKSHOPS OR DIRECT FROM THE PUBLISHER:

Internet: **www.houseofstratus.com** including author interviews, reviews, features.

Email: **sales@houseofstratus.com** please quote author, title and credit card details.

OTHER TITLES BY FREEMAN WILLS CROFTS AVAILABLE DIRECT
FROM HOUSE OF STRATUS

Quantity		£	$(US)	$(CAN)	€
	INSPECTOR FRENCH AND THE STARVEL TRAGEDY	6.99	11.50	15.99	11.50
	INSPECTOR FRENCH'S GREATEST CASE	6.99	11.50	15.99	11.50
	JAMES TARRANT, ADVENTURER	6.99	11.50	15.99	11.50
	A LOSING GAME	6.99	11.50	15.99	11.50
	THE LOSS OF THE JANE VOSPER	6.99	11.50	15.99	11.50
	MAN OVERBOARD!	6.99	11.50	15.99	11.50
	MANY A SLIP	6.99	11.50	15.99	11.50
	MYSTERY IN THE CHANNEL	6.99	11.50	15.99	11.50
	MURDERERS MAKE MISTAKES	6.99	11.50	15.99	11.50
	MYSTERY OF THE SLEEPING CAR EXPRESS	6.99	11.50	15.99	11.50
	MYSTERY ON SOUTHAMPTON WATER	6.99	11.50	15.99	11.50
	THE PIT-PROP SYNDICATE	6.99	11.50	15.99	11.50
	THE PONSON CASE	6.99	11.50	15.99	11.50
	THE SEA MYSTERY	6.99	11.50	15.99	11.50
	SILENCE FOR THE MURDERER	6.99	11.50	15.99	11.50
	SUDDEN DEATH	6.99	11.50	15.99	11.50

ALL HOUSE OF STRATUS BOOKS ARE AVAILABLE FROM GOOD BOOKSHOPS OR
DIRECT FROM THE PUBLISHER:

Hotline: UK ONLY: 0800 169 1780, please quote author, title and credit card details.
INTERNATIONAL: +44 (0) 20 7494 6400, please quote author, title, and
credit card details.

Send to: **House of Stratus**
24c Old Burlington Street
London
W1X 1RL
UK

<u>Please allow following carriage costs per ORDER</u>
<u>(For goods up to free carriage limits shown)</u>

	£(Sterling)	$(US)	$(CAN)	€(Euros)
UK	1.95	3.20	4.29	3.00
Europe	2.95	4.99	6.49	5.00
North America	2.95	4.99	6.49	5.00
Rest of World	2.95	5.99	7.75	6.00
Free carriage for goods value over:	50	75	100	75

PLEASE SEND CHEQUE, POSTAL ORDER (STERLING ONLY), EUROCHEQUE, OR INTERNATIONAL MONEY ORDER (PLEASE CIRCLE METHOD OF PAYMENT YOU WISH TO USE) MAKE PAYABLE TO: STRATUS HOLDINGS plc

Order total including postage:————Please tick currency you wish to use and add total amount of order:

□ £ (Sterling)   □ $ (US)   □ $ (CAN)   □ € (EUROS)

VISA, MASTERCARD, SWITCH, AMEX, SOLO, JCB:

□□□□□□□□□□□□□□□□□□□□□□□□□□

Issue number (Switch only):

□□□

Start Date: **Expiry Date:**

□□/□□   □□/□□

Signature: _____

NAME: _____

ADDRESS: _____

_____

POSTCODE: _____

Please allow 28 days for delivery.

Prices subject to change without notice.
Please tick box if you do not wish to receive any additional information. □

House of Stratus publishes many other titles in this genre; please check our website (**www.houseofstratus.com**) for more details